Defending Honor pulled me in   ge and
kept me reading well past .   .me. Laila
Rabbinowitz is my favorite type o ..eroine. Tough,
feminine, and the best at what she does. And Preston
Whittaker? Well, there's no way around it. I do love a
misunderstood billionaire! Throw in a fake marriage
and I'm all in. The romance hit all the right notes. And
with multiple family and business rivals all vying for
the role of "Most Likely to Commit Murder," there was
no way to know for sure who the villain was until it was
revealed at precisely the right moment.

> — LYNN H. BLACKBURN, BESTSELLING,
> AWARD-WINNING AUTHOR OF THE
> DEFEND AND PROTECT SERIES

Kelly Underwood's voice is fresh and engaging. This
book hit every mark there is for Christian romantic
suspense. I'm still breathless!

> — LISA PHILLIPS, USA TODAY
> BESTSELLING AUTHOR OF LAST
> CHANCE COUNTY AND THE NEW
> BRAND OF JUSTICE SERIES

DEFENDING HONOR

AN ELITE GUARDIANS NOVEL

LYNETTE EASON
KELLY UNDERWOOD

sunrise
PUBLISHING

A NOTE FROM LYNETTE

Dear Reader,

I can't tell you how excited I am for you to get your hands on this story. Kelly Underwood is not only an amazing author, she's a fabulous person too! With a quick wit and lots of humor, she always has something funny to say that will make you laugh. Well, hang on to your socks because she's about to knock them off with some really great romantic suspense as well.

When I read Kelly's entry during the audition process, I knew that I wanted to work with her story. Then I found out it was Kelly who'd come up with the incredible premise and I was even more excited. I think you're going to LOVE Preston and Laila's story as you get to watch them fall in love while trying to stay alive--because someone sure would like to see them six feet under.

I hope you enjoy the story as much as I did. Be sure to jump on social media and let us hear your thoughts.

Enjoy the read!

Lynette

To Jackson, Emma, Harper, and Carson.
Here's proof that dreams really do come true, so dream big.

1

Laila Rabbinowitz tossed the binoculars onto the passenger seat and stifled a shudder. Jesse Cora, the man she was charged with protecting, had turned out to be a lying creep who didn't give a second thought about stepping out on his marriage.

Ten showers couldn't wash off the disgust smothering her like a blanket. But as a professional bodyguard, she didn't get paid to judge people's actions.

She just had to keep the man breathing. Once his wife got ahold of him...well, that wasn't Laila's problem.

Anabelle Cora was the one footing the bill for the protection detail. The wealthy woman's fourth husband had received suspicious text messages from an alleged stalker. When his wife had pressed him to be careful, Jesse had dismissed the danger. Worried sick, Anabelle had hired a bodyguard from the Elite Guardians Agency and simply not told him.

Covert operations weren't Laila's favorite. She'd done

enough stakeouts in her former role as a Mossad agent. Memories sprang up but were instantly dismissed. She'd long since left that life behind after moving to Columbia, South Carolina, to take a job with the Elite Guardians.

"Do *not* let him catch you following him," Anabelle had warned her after their first meeting.

"Of course not," Laila had promised. Which was why she found herself in this unpleasant situation—hiding out in her car, stalking the man she was supposed to protect from a stalker.

Jesse had told his wife he'd be working late but had instead headed to a hotel to rendezvous with a woman who appeared to be a much younger blonde wearing a little black dress and three-inch spiked heels.

Laila sighed. Why wasn't Anabelle suspicious of a husband that worked late on a Sunday evening? The woman would rather believe her husband was being stalked than admit the truth.

Babysitting the rich and elite ranked right up there with getting a root canal, but Laila had found a parking spot in front of the swanky hotel with an excellent view of the penthouse suite and waited. The hotel looked like it would cost more than her monthly rent for a one-night stay. At least they hadn't opted for some pay-by-the-hour seedy place.

Movement from the room made her reach for the binoculars. People should close their blinds. Thankfully, Jesse and his mistress didn't bother. Not that she wanted a front row seat to this show, but another peek through the binoculars confirmed her initial impression. Jesse was a money-grubbing cheat. He crossed through the room and wrapped his arms around the woman who clearly wasn't his wife.

Laila didn't want to watch any more, but she traded the

binoculars for a high-powered zoom lens and snapped a few incriminating shots. If Jesse denied his actions, well...

The philandering trophy husband was half the age of Anabelle.

Again, not your problem, Laila. Do your job and keep your opinions out of it.

Her stiff shoulders begged for a good workout. What she wouldn't give to be in the boxing ring at the gym, releasing some of her pent-up energy by sparring with anyone who dared take her on.

She'd been cramped in the car for close to three hours and just wanted to call it a day.

With the pictures as evidence, this case was closed as far as she was concerned.

She dreaded telling the sweet but misguided Anabelle that she had bigger concerns than a stalker attacking her husband.

Laila connected her Bluetooth earbuds and snagged her phone to call Olivia Savage, one of the owners of Elite Guardians. When her boss picked up, Laila didn't wait for her to utter a greeting. "Thanks for giving me the worst assignment possible. Of course, he's cheating on his wife. I'm going to stop watching before I see things I can't unsee."

Olivia laughed. "Just make sure nothing happens to our guy. I guess I have the pleasure of informing Mrs. Cora that those texts she found on her husband's phone weren't from an alleged stalker and closing this case. Without an actual threat, we can wrap things up."

"Exactly what I was thinking." A shadow in the hotel room window caught her attention.

"Hold on a sec." Laila grabbed the binoculars again and squinted. "Oh no."

A different man stormed into the room. He yelled something and pointed at Jesse.

"What is it?" Olivia asked.

"I spoke too soon." Laila scrambled out of her car. "I guess Jesse needs a bodyguard after all."

She snapped her gun into the side holder under her jacket and grabbed her phone from the cupholder. "I suspect that the other woman's husband just discovered the affair and decided to put a stop to it one way or another."

She rushed through the parking lot, the cold October air stinging her face.

"I've got to run, Olivia. I need to check on our client to make sure he doesn't get his head bashed in."

"Do you need backup?"

"I'll keep you posted." She disconnected the phone and shoved it into the back pocket of her jeans.

Jesse Cora had played with fire, and Laila had to keep him from getting burned.

She burst into the building, and a security guard rose to his feet. "Sorry," she said, "I'm in a hurry." At least she might have some backup if things got hot.

She skidded to a stop in front of the elevator and hammered the up button like it would bring the car faster while she mentally ran through the defense moves she'd be prepared to use if necessary.

Jesse would not get beat up on her watch, even if the slimeball deserved to be in traction.

Laila pushed a wayward strand of her long brown hair behind her ear to keep her hands from smashing the button again. The drone of classical music drifting through the lobby stole any remnant of patience she had left.

"Oh, forget it," she muttered and ditched the slow-to-arrive elevator in favor of the stairs.

When she hit the tenth floor, the scent of cheap liquor led

her to the room. The door hung open a crack, wide enough for her to observe the unwelcome guest facing off with her client in a heated argument.

The glint of metal in the man's hand propelled Laila through the door. She rocked the severely inebriated man with a kick to the side and ripped the weapon from his hand before he hit the ground. He went down without a fight.

She looked at the item in her hand. A spoon? Apparently, he'd grabbed the first thing he could find from the dining cart in the hallway. She tossed the flatware on the bed and patted the groaning man down. No weapons. Good.

She looked at Jesse and the other woman, who were staring, eyes wide, mouths open.

"Who...who are you?" Jesse asked.

"I'm your bodyguard. Your wife hired me to protect you from a stalker." Laila nodded her head toward the mistress. "I assume she's the stalker who's been texting you?"

Jesse rubbed his eyes. "Stalker? Texting me? What are you talking about?"

The man on the floor groaned and pushed up to his knees, attempting to stand. "He's cheating with my wife. That's what's happening. I'm going to—"

Laila pressed a hand to his shoulder. "You, stay down," she said. When he complied by stretching out on the floor, she shook her head, then pointed at Jesse. "You, come with me. I'll take you home."

The woman glared at Laila.

"It's not what you think," she said, her voice cool. "Jesse met me here because I'm only in town for a few days. He's planning a sixtieth birthday party for Anabelle. You can check me out online. I have tons of references for my event planning company, and I often meet clients all over the place. It's not unusual. My husband jumped to the wrong conclusion and followed me here."

The lies burned Laila's ears. She held up her hand for the woman to stop. "I don't need the details. What you two do is none of my business. My job is to keep Jesse out of danger."

Laila rolled her eyes when soft snores puffed from the man on the floor. She might have over-estimated the threat level a bit.

Laila looked at the attractive blonde and nodded toward the floor. "You good with this guy?" The drunk might be a light-weight, but Laila wouldn't leave the woman if there was potential for trouble.

"He'll understand when I explain this mix-up to him," the woman hissed. She glared at Laila, her face redder than her passed-out husband's. "Unlike you."

Laila shrugged and waved Jesse toward the door.

"We weren't doing anything," Jesse sputtered. "We were going to discuss party details."

"Save it for your wife." Laila paused. "I can't make you go with me, but my agency will need to get back to Anabelle about what I've witnessed. It might be better if she hears it from you."

"There was nothing to witness!" His shout bounced off her ears, and she kept her gaze steady.

"Fine," Jesse mumbled and turned toward the woman. "Celia, I'll call you later. To plan a party." His last words spat out of his mouth like bullets from a machine gun. He stared down Laila. "Just wait until Anabelle finds out what you've done."

"What I've done?" She scoffed. "I'm not the one lying to my wife and meeting up in the hotel room of some other woman."

Celia pushed forward, her nose practically touching Laila's. "You'll regret this. I won't have you trash my reputation because you can't see the truth. You're mistaken. Nothing happened."

Laila resisted the urge to put the woman on the floor next to her husband. Instead, she motioned for Jesse to go ahead of her. At first, she thought he might refuse, but then he sighed and stomped toward the elevator.

"I don't need a bodyguard," Jesse mumbled like a schoolkid caught with his hand in the cookie jar. "Why would you think I was having an affair? I love Anabelle. I can't believe this."

They rode the elevator in icy silence. At least the car had arrived this time, because Laila didn't want to prolong this adventure by even a second. When the doors opened, she marched through the lobby with Jesse in tow.

When they got to the parking lot, she turned to him. "Go home to Anabelle. You might not have needed a bodyguard to protect you from a stalker, but who's going to protect you from your wife when she finds out where you've been tonight?"

Jesse's jaw went rigid. "I'm not cheating on my wife." He muttered a few choice words at Laila and headed to his flashy car. Taillights glowed an angry red as he peeled out of the parking lot.

Laila watched him go, her disgust with the man sliding into a sadness she had no desire to explore. No sense in following him. The danger wasn't real.

Laila got back into her car and her phone vibrated. She glanced at the screen. Olivia. A swipe to the right connected the call.

"Hey," she said in greeting. "I just finished up here. Jesse is heading home and isn't in danger." She explained the situation.

"Well, that's good news. The not being in danger part, I mean. I'll have to figure out how to tell Anabelle the not-so-good news about Jesse's infidelity. But for now, I need you for a security job in the morning."

Laila suppressed a groan. Her dreams for a day off evaporated.

"I know you've caught some back-to-back assignments," Olivia said, "but this should just be a one-time thing. I'm sending you the details, but I need to arrange some personal security for a funeral tomorrow. Check your inbox and you'll understand why this is top priority."

With the phone still connected, Laila pulled up her email. A headline from the local news channel streaked across the screen. *Walt Whittaker and Son Die in Boating Accident.*

Laila frowned. "Wow. This is terrible news. The Whittakers are treated like royalty around here." They were famous, or more like infamous.

The family had become a media spectacle, fodder for tabloids and internet gossip, after Walt Whittaker's start-up tech company had hit the big league. Overnight, Whittaker Enterprises had exploded as one of the nation's leading software developers and now employed thousands of people. Walt's daughter had even starred in her own reality show, not that Laila had ever watched it. The family had more money than they knew what to do with, and every reporter loved to dish on the family's latest exploits. Scandal kept them in the spotlight.

"I got a call from the Whittakers' attorney, Sebastian Coyle," Olivia said. "He's concerned about the family's safety. He has reason to believe Walt's and his son Ethan's deaths weren't the result of an accident. The police are still investigating the scene, and I have a call in to Quinn Holcombe, since he's the detective that caught this case. Maybe he can give us an update. Walt's company is worth billions, and we know that kind of money is always a good motive for murder. Right now, the bigger issue is that the business gets left to Walt's remaining son, Preston."

Headlines from news stories flipped through Laila's mind.

Preston's antics had earned him a reputation as a playboy, always showing up to fancy parties with a different woman each time. And the women swooned over him, from his good looks to his endless flow of cash.

What a waste. Just like Jesse, Preston had paved his way in life with money and privilege, using and discarding people on the way up. But Preston had disappeared from the limelight after a lawsuit accused him of negligence at a party where a woman had died.

"Wait. I thought Preston Whittaker had dropped off the map. No one's seen him in years. I think a few media outlets even dropped rumors that he died. Are you saying Sebastian can locate Preston?" Laila remembered one twenty-four-hour news station had offered a hefty finder's fee to anyone who could help them locate Preston, but the man hadn't resurfaced. "Where has he been this whole time?"

"The family attorney has kept tabs on him, and he's very much alive. That's why we've been called in as additional protection just for the funeral. Sebastian wants someone to watch Preston's back and stick close to him for the day without being obvious about it. Because the long-lost son is coming back for the funeral. Preston Whittaker is your next assignment."

MONDAY, 10:00 A.M.

Preston Whittaker hated giving up his beloved anonymity, but his hand had been forced.

He'd been gone for almost five years. And now, his father and brother were dead. He'd contemplated staying away, but grief had sealed his decision.

He wanted to attend their funeral. *Needed* to attend.

Very few people knew of Preston's whereabouts. Five years ago, the media had run wild with news of his quick departure, and speculation had spread like wildfire, but that was probably nothing compared to the gossip-fueled frenzy his homecoming would generate. He shuddered at the thought.

For now, he'd remain as anonymous as possible. He snuck into the last row of the crowded sanctuary of his childhood church. At least he wouldn't stand out with the room packed full of people. His scruffy beard hid most of his recognizable face, but the reporters were relentless when sniffing out a story. And a double Whittaker funeral would be the biggest story of the year, until someone spotted him. The last thing he wanted to do was upstage his father and brother's funeral, so he kept his head down and hoped he could duck in and out of the service without getting into a single camera shot.

Giving up life in the spotlight had been the best decision he'd ever made. He no longer belonged here, and the sooner he hit the road and headed back to his cabin in the mountains, the better.

He sat against the pew, waiting for the spectacle to begin.

Finally, the parade started, with his mother and sister playing the roles of grand marshals. The pair entered the main doors, faces distorted in over-exaggerated masks of sorrow. They walked down the aisle to the front of the church.

Typical.

Instead of shielding themselves from public onlookers, they'd chosen to display their grief for all the world to see. Because grieving in private didn't generate nearly as much attention.

As his mother started to take her seat, she staggered a bit before catching her balance and lowering herself onto the pew. Looked like she still drowned her feelings with a bottle.

Right behind his mother, his sister-in-law, Veronica Whittaker, walked in with two young boys in tow. Preston inhaled sharply at the thought of his two nephews growing up without a father. How could Ethan be gone, leaving a wife and two kids behind? He barely recognized his ten-year-old and seven-year-old nephews. Five years now seemed like an eternity.

He bit back the swirl of emotions welling up in his chest. Despite leaving his family behind for a different life, he missed them. Especially his mother. Was someone looking after her now that his father had died? Even with their publicity-hungry antics, his heart still beat strong for the Whittakers. And now two members of his family were gone, leaving a gaping hole in his life that he wasn't sure would ever heal.

Someone bumped his shoulder, and he turned to spot his long-time family friend and attorney, Sebastian Coyle. The man had saved Preston from the repercussions of his many bad teenage decisions. Situations he now tried hard to forget.

"Good to see you, Whitt," Sebastian whispered as he slid in next to Preston in the back row.

Paranoia over the use of his childhood nickname kicked in, and Preston searched the faces of anyone within earshot. Thankfully, everyone's focus on the show at the front of the church. Sebastian had kept tabs on him during the years he'd dropped off the radar. Which was more than he could say for his family.

"Relax," Sebastian said. "No one would recognize you in that lumberjack attire. Love the beard, by the way. It gives off a rugged vibe. Not something anyone would associate with you."

Preston glanced at his plaid shirt, black jeans, and cowboy boots. While he'd embraced his casual look, he'd once been known for his three-thousand-dollar designer suits. Which outfit would the paparazzi expect him to wear now that he was back in town? And what would the media think of his transformation from rich party boy to a small-town nobody?

"I see things haven't changed much since I've been gone." Preston nodded toward his sister, Katrina Pace, giving an on-the-spot interview at the front of the church to the right of the casket. Anything to make sure she placed herself center stage. Her husband, Derek, hovered behind her, angling himself to remain in the camera frame.

"Actually, you don't know how much things have changed. Overnight."

Preston looked at his aged friend. While it seemed like time had stood still in some respects, the man's silver hairs documented the passing years.

"We need to discuss you coming back," Sebastian whispered. His eyes darted around the room, as if scanning for any signs of trouble. Was Sebastian worried that Preston's identity might get out?

Preston shook his head. "There's nothing to talk about, because it's not going to happen." He kept his voice low.

The service started, ending the conversation. For now. Preston half listened to the minister give the eulogy about the life of Walter Whittaker. Despite their differences, nothing had prepared him for the finality of never seeing his father again.

He rubbed his eyes, willing this to be nothing more than a nightmare that would vanish the moment he woke. Ethan and his dad were gone. There hadn't been enough space for the grief to register while he'd been making plans to return home, but now...it threatened to rip him to shreds. He'd never had a good relationship with either of them, but reminders of the past flipped through his mind, and he struggled to hold back the tears. No way would he fall apart—not in public, anyway.

With a few deep breaths, he regained his composure and let his gaze roam around the room. Nostalgia sparked when he spotted old friends and relatives with glistening eyes and tear-stained cheeks. A pretty brunette kept glancing his way. He didn't remember her and sent up a prayer that she didn't recognize him. She looked away, but for all he knew, she might be a reporter.

He abandoned all thoughts of the mystery woman when Veronica took the microphone.

Preston had once dated Veronica in high school, until she'd moved on to his brother. But never in his wildest imagination would he have predicted it would end this way. At a double funeral.

Grief threatened to consume him at the thought of his nephews growing up fatherless. His head pounded as he suppressed tears. Coming back had been a terrible idea. He had to get out of here. *Now.*

Preston jumped to his feet and rushed out of the sanctuary with Sebastian hot on his heels. Anger at the senseless loss fueled his feet, and he picked up speed when he hit the parking lot. How could he lose his father when he'd never had the chance to mend their broken relationship? Now it was too late. He'd waited too long.

"Wait!" Sebastian called. "Don't go."

Preston stopped and faced his friend. "I can't stay. I don't belong. My dad and Ethan are gone. There's nothing I can do to bring them back, and my presence just invites trouble." He perused the area and didn't spot a soul. At least the camera crews were busy inside getting their sound bites of the funeral.

"You have to stay," Sebastian said. "Someone has to take over the business, or your father's partner will control the entire company. The first thing Bob will do is take the company public and outsource many jobs overseas. He'll destroy everything your father worked so hard to preserve. You know your dad and Bob never agreed on the direction of the company.

You're next in line, and you're needed here. Don't you realize what this means?"

Preston knew all too well. Bob had the potential to ruin the company for his own personal gain. If jobs moved overseas, thousands of people would lose their livelihood.

His dad had started Whittaker Enterprises in his garage and turned it into one of the leading software development companies in the world. His father's biggest desire had always been to keep Whittaker Enterprises a privately held family-run company.

While the thought of Bob taking control troubled him, it didn't prick his conscience enough to make him accept the position. "There has to be someone else. There are tons of people more qualified than I am to follow in my dad's footsteps. I'm out, remember?"

Movement out of the corner of his eye triggered warning sirens in Preston's head. He noted the same woman from the church standing by the side of the building, out of earshot but definitely watching them.

Preston turned and walked through the rows of parked cars to locate his truck. Sebastian followed. "You can't outrun your past," the man said. "Or your future, for that matter."

Preston spun around to face Sebastian, but his mind refused to form words in the midst of another onslaught of emotions threatening to spill out. Why had he come here?

They stood between two parked cars, and the vehicles provided a bit of privacy. "You aren't out," Sebastian said, his voice soft. "You were never out. This is your life. You let one stupid lawsuit take away everything from you."

"I live with that regret every day. I don't expect you to understand."

"I care a great deal about what happens to you and your family." Sebastian scanned the parking area, then locked his gaze back on Preston's. "Look, I don't think your father's and brother's deaths were an accident."

Preston froze. "What are you suggesting?"

Sebastian placed a hand on Preston's shoulder. "I don't believe that the explosion on the boat was an accident. I think your life is in danger. Once word gets out that you're alive and back in Columbia, it's possible you might be the next target."

"What are you talking about? You really believe that someone wanted both Ethan and my father dead? That someone sabotaged their boat? Why?"

Sebastian shrugged. "I just have a bad feeling about this. I'll feel better once the police conclude their investigation, but your dad had called in extra security at the house a few weeks before he died. He claims that someone had followed him home one night, and there was also a break-in at the estate. Now, he's gone. It just makes me think something sinister could be going on. Not to mention that you stand to inherit a lot, Preston. And you've seen firsthand what money does to people."

Preston stared at the man who had been more of a father to him than his own. He knew he could trust Sebastian's instincts.

But murder? His head reeled at the thought.

His tarnished family legacy concealed plenty of secrets, and if all their enemies lined up, they'd circle the block. But who would act on the desire to see them dead?

He pressed his thumb and forefinger to his eyes, then dropped his hands. "I can't, Sebastian. I don't want to come back to this life. Being chased by the media, having to live up to other people's expectations. That's not me anymore. I'm sorry."

Preston walked in the direction of his truck as his mind twisted with unanswered questions. Why would he come back to Columbia after making a new life for himself? But could he sit on the sidelines and let his father's company fall apart? And what about Sebastian's crazy theory that the fire on the boat hadn't been an accident? Could it be true?

He stepped into the aisle between the rows of parked cars. A revving engine grabbed his attention. The smell of burning rubber hit his nose before his brain registered the van barreling down the lane, aimed directly at him. He pivoted to get out of the way, but the van mirrored his movements and continued to bear down on him.

"Preston, look out!" Everything around him moved as if in slow motion. Before he could run, someone tackled him and rolled him between two parked cars in one seamless motion. A rush of air whooshed past as the speeding van took off, leaving a haze of blue smoke in the air.

His body ached from its impact with the pavement. A groan escaped his lips. What just happened? Sebastian's words flashed through him like a bolt of lightning, sending shivers down his spine. *You might be the next target.*

He pushed at the weight on his chest, and when it didn't budge, he forced his eyes to focus. Two intense dark-brown eyes stared back at him for a split second before the woman rolled off him. She was on her feet before he could blink.

"Are you okay?" she asked and offered her hand to help him up.

He waved her off and stood, swiping his hands over his jeans to wipe off the bits of gravel. Sebastian rushed over, concern etched on his face. Preston stared at the stranger turned rescuer. "Who are you?"

She opened her mouth to respond, but Sebastian jumped in. "This is the woman who just saved your life. Someone just tried to run you over. To *kill* you. Now do you believe me when I say you're in danger? Your family is being targeted. What happened to your father and Ethan was no accident. You could be next."

Preston raked a hand over his head and let his gaze jump between the two. "I don't know what to believe."

The pretty brunette dusted herself off. "I'm Laila Rabbinowitz. Nice to meet you. Looks like I'm your new bodyguard."

Bodyguard? At first glance he never would have pegged this woman as a professional security guard, but maybe that was the point. Despite her petite stature, he was willing to bet she could hold her own against someone twice her size. But he needed to get out of town, not have someone trailing his every move like those paparazzi stalkers.

Preston tried to wrap his mind around the situation while Sebastian rambled. "I insisted on additional security detail for today and called the Elite Guardians Agency. It's a good thing I did. That van targeted you. Laila came to watch your back for the funeral, but you're going to need round-the-clock security. I just lost your father and Ethan. I can't lose you too."

Preston's heart warmed at how much Sebastian cared about his family, but if Preston left, there'd be no need for twenty-four-seven surveillance.

He turned to Laila. "It's nice to meet you too, but the media hasn't noticed me yet, and I'd like to keep it that way. So if you'll excuse me, I'm leaving town tonight."

"Someone tried to run you over," Laila said. "I'd say that at least one person knows you're here and isn't happy about it."

"Could have been a fluke. I wasn't paying attention when I stepped out. How do I know I was the intended target?" Even as the words left his lips, he knew his rationale sounded pathetic. That van had been laser focused on him. What if someone really had murdered his father and brother and that same person had just tried to take him out?

The church door clanged open, and Preston spotted a reporter heading to one of the parked news vans on the other side of the lot, cameraman in tow.

LYNETTE EASON & KELLY UNDERWOOD

He looked at Sebastian. "I'll stay in town long enough to sign whatever papers you need from me to forgo any share of the company. Because I'm *not* coming back."

He walked toward his truck, leaving Laila and Sebastian staring after him.

Many people had speculated that he was dead, but could his life actually be on the line after all these years?

So, the troublemaker was alive. What rock had Preston Whittaker been living under? This ruined everything. Walt's son should have been dead. What else could possibly explain his long absence? All that money wasted on private investigators to track his whereabouts only to come up empty, and he shows up five years later, still breathing.

Leave it to a Whittaker to make a spectacular entrance, even if most mourners were oblivious to the return of that spoiled playboy. Preston thought he was so slick, waltzing into his father's funeral and expecting no one would notice him.

Looked like the media darling hadn't outgrown his arrogance. Which had led to the improvised plan of taking him down in the parking lot with the stolen media van. Too bad some woman had pushed him out of the way.

Preston always had people stepping in for him, never letting his hands get dirty. Which was why he needed to go. Preston would never be the CEO.

Did he honestly believe he could swoop in and take Walt's place?

Apparently.

Sorry, Preston, but the position belongs to someone better and smarter.

Time to call in some reinforcements. The phone rang twice, then a gravelly voice answered. "What?"

"I need a favor."

"Another?"

"Shut up and listen. Lots of people assume Preston Whittaker is dead. Your job is to make that a reality."

2

MONDAY, 1:00 P.M.

"Let's just say I didn't score a winning first impression with Preston Whittaker."

Laila sat at the conference table in the Elite Guardians office while her coworkers filtered in for their Monday afternoon staff meeting.

Christina Sherman, fellow bodyguard, tried to stifle a laugh but failed. "Tell us again how you tackled *the* Preston Whittaker?"

Laila shrugged. "I saved his life. The incident proves he needs our protection."

Olivia put her coffee mug on the table to stake out a seat and shook her head. "That's one way to do it. Take the man down like a linebacker."

"It doesn't matter. Preston wants nothing to do with having us around. He bolted out of that parking lot and plans to disappear again."

"I just got off the phone with Sebastian Coyle, the Whittaker family's attorney," Olivia said. "Despite Preston's claims that he's not going to stick around, danger seems to have tracked him down. Sebastian is very concerned and wants to hire us to be Preston's personal bodyguard, but Preston's not on board. Yet." Olivia shrugged. "Maybe Laila could guard him, but not let on that he's being guarded? She seems to have a knack for that."

"Don't remind me." Laila groaned at the flashback from last night at the hotel.

Lizzie Tremaine took a seat at the table. She beamed brighter than the engagement ring on her finger. "So, is he as attractive in person as he appears in the tabloids?"

"Oh, please." Laila had accepted that her colleagues liked to tease her about her perpetually single status. The team's good-natured ribbing came as naturally to them as breathing, and Laila was one of the last unattached women left in the group. "He looks different now with a beard. The old Preston never would have shown up to a funeral wearing jeans and a flannel shirt. Not to mention the shaggy hair. He snuck into the back row with a casual appearance that didn't scream *look at me*. Not the man's usual style at all. I doubt anyone recognized him unless they knew to be on the lookout." Which was how she'd spotted him at the funeral. "But a rich elitist isn't my type."

"You actually have a type? Tell us more." Christina didn't miss a beat.

Since getting engaged, Christina had attempted and failed to set Laila up a few times with some of her fiancé's friends. Payback for Laila's not-so-subtle encouraging of her friend when Christina had first met Grey Parker.

Laila grimaced. While she had great respect for her coworkers, her personal life wasn't up for discussion. "I'd turn down someone with a playboy reputation in a heartbeat. He's

not using his wealth or status to help anyone besides himself."
Laila paused, checking her words to make sure she wasn't
giving Christina more ammunition. "Although, I will admit to
being surprised that he hasn't jumped at the chance to inherit
his father's company. The business has to be worth billions."

"Eight billion, to be exact." Maddy Holcombe, one of the
founding bodyguards at Elite Guardians, sat next to Laila and
slid a file over.

Laila opened the folder and spotted the baby picture
Maddy had covertly stuck under a paper clip. Anything to
show off her adorable newborn. "Cute," Laila said and smiled
at Maddy.

"Cute as in Preston? Or Maddy's baby? Or both?" Christina's questions sparked laughter once again in everyone except
Laila.

She took the teasing in stride. Sure, everyone wanted her to
find love. But she was single for a reason, and she'd never in a
billion years consider someone like Preston Whittaker.

Besides, Laila had given up on love a long time ago.

Olivia cleared her throat and transitioned the team into
business mode. "So, what do we know about Preston's situation? And let's not forget that this conversation stays in this
room. If the media gets word that Preston is in town, his homecoming will turn into a three-ring circus."

Laila pulled out a photo of Preston from the file. He was
the same age as Laila at thirty, but that's where their similarities
ended. In the photo, Preston was all decked out in a designer
suit, his short brown hair no doubt photoshopped so every
strand would be in perfect position to bring out the flecks of
gold in his chestnut-brown eyes. She couldn't deny the appeal,
but the man collected scandals like an athlete amassed trophies.
Laila went out of her way to avoid that kind of drama.

"I know we were originally assigned to his protection detail at the funeral," Laila said. "But the threat seems credible. I couldn't get a license plate, but that van targeted him. Steven said the news station reported the van stolen, and officers later found the vehicle abandoned a few blocks away. They didn't recover any fingerprints except for the people who work at the station. It looks like someone stole the media rig from the parking lot during the funeral and tried to run over Preston."

"So someone either recognized him or knew he was coming to the funeral." Haley Rothwell grabbed a marker and started jotting notes on the white board.

"No one but Sebastian—and us—knew that Preston intended to attend the funeral." Laila squinted to read Haley's notes. "I guess it's possible someone spied on Sebastian and figured out the plan for Preston's return."

"Or Sebastian had something to gain from Preston's death?" Olivia asked.

Laila nodded. "The thought crossed my mind, but you vetted Sebastian, right?"

"Of course. Doesn't mean I couldn't have missed something though," Olivia said with a deep frown.

"I called Steven, and he said they didn't have any leads on the van driver yet." Haley wrote and talked at the same time. "But he gave me a few tidbits on their investigation into the boating accident that killed Walt and Ethan Whittaker."

Haley was married to Steven Rothwell, a detective with the Columbia Police Department. His partner was Quinn Holcombe, Maddy's husband. Despite the family vibe the agency pulsed, Laila's instincts tended to drive her to work alone.

Haley wrote *Accident?* on the board. "The investigators found some type of accelerant that caused the fire to burn fast. It may have been what started the fire that consumed the engine room."

"Sebastian told Preston that he suspected Walt's and Ethan's deaths were intentional. Maybe we should talk to Sebastian about it." Laila's mind spun with the implications of a double murder, not to mention the new heir to the family business. Something like that could secure a target to Preston's back if someone intended to eliminate the competition.

"In my latest conversation with Sebastian, he indicated that Walt had recently requested additional security." Olivia flipped through her notebook. "Apparently there had been a break-in at the estate that spooked Walt. But Sebastian was also certain that the boat had been thoroughly inspected before the trip. He even contacted the charter company and asked for the maintenance records. The boat was practically new. He doesn't believe faulty wiring could cause that big of an explosion."

Laila's theory gained momentum. "If someone went to great lengths to take out Walt and Ethan, Preston showing up on the scene would be seen as a threat. But who would have motive to kill both Whittakers and then try to take out Preston?"

Despite being a bodyguard, Laila's mind jumped into investigation mode, dissecting the facts and rearranging them until the puzzle pieces fit. But if they ultimately took on Preston as a client, they'd have to know what threats they were facing.

"The likely culprit is a competitor to Whittaker Enterprises," Maddy said. "I'm sure other tech firms weren't too happy when Whittaker Enterprises announced a partnership with Google to develop a new app."

Leave it to Maddy to keep up with current events. How did she find time with a new baby?

"Who's next in line to take over Walt's position if Ethan and Preston aren't in the picture?"

"According to my conversation with Sebastian, Preston's

mother and sister will keep the estate and house plus a hefty life insurance payout. But ownership of Whittaker Enterprises defaults to Walt's business partner, Bob Zimmerman." Olivia stood and wrote *Bob Zimmerman* on the board. "If Preston doesn't take the position, Bob gets a hundred percent control of the company. I'm not saying Bob is behind this, but he stands to gain a lot."

"But the one question no one has posed yet is, where has Preston been these last five years?" Christina said. "He's one of the few people to successfully drop off the grid. Private investigators supposedly couldn't find him. Are we sure he's coming back to take over his father's company? Obviously, he'd hoped to stay anonymous at the funeral."

"Five years is a long time to disappear," Haley said, sitting down next to Laila. "A lot can change in that time."

Laila crossed her arms. "Sure, after living his life off the grid, Preston can change his appearance. But remember all of his antics? The parties and scandals? The man has an ego the size of the Grand Canyon. I don't think he'll stay away, despite telling me he was leaving."

Olivia shrugged. "It's possible he's changed. Maybe he grew up, realized there was more to life than fame and money. He left after that wrongful death civil lawsuit, even though the case was dropped. Maybe he wanted a fresh start after being accused of negligent homicide."

Preston could change his clothes and style, but people never changed on the inside. At least, that was Laila's experience. The odds of that happening were microscopic. People could wear a mask and play a role, but they could never erase who they were at the core. Of course, a few of her coworkers would disagree. Like Katie Matthews, her fellow bodyguard who took turns teaching a self-defense class with Laila at the community center.

LYNETTE EASON & KELLY UNDERWOOD

Katie's strong faith in God helped her find the good in people.

Meanwhile, the only person Laila could trust was herself—definitely not a God she couldn't see.

Olivia interrupted Laila's thoughts and brought the team back to business from the side conversations that had spawned. "Preston may be in danger whether or not he moves back to Columbia. Sebastian won't hire us beyond today without Preston's consent, but I don't think it could hurt to check on him to make sure he didn't have a tail after he left the church."

Great. More babysitting the wealthy and privileged. But Laila agreed with Olivia's assessment. Preston almost getting killed in the church parking lot of his father and brother's double funeral was too coincidental to be taken lightly.

"Maybe you can talk Preston into hiring us," Olivia said to Laila. "Especially if he decides to accept the CEO position for Whittaker Enterprises."

Laila couldn't imagine the logistical nightmare that Preston's homecoming might make for his security team. "The danger increases exponentially if this turns out to be murder and Preston is the sole heir to the fortune."

Olivia nodded. "If we take the job for his personal protection, you'd have to figure out a way to stick close to him. With that many zeros after the dollar sign, we might not be able to count the number of people who'd like to see him dead. Someone's already made one attempt to erase him from the picture. And like you said, it might be someone with inside knowledge. Even a family member or friend."

"He's staying at a rental property that Sebastian owns while in town," Laila said, mapping the location out on her phone. "It's roughly thirty minutes from here. I'll ride out there and double-check the security. At least advise him of the dangers we've discussed. He needs to watch his back. And if

Sebastian is somehow involved—as odd as that sounds since he hired us—he's not safe either."

The team discussed their other open cases, and since a handful of Laila's coworkers were out on assignments, the meeting wrapped up in record time.

Laila headed to her car and hit the road. Day two of missing a good workout. Hopefully she could wrap up this issue with Preston today, especially if he was skipping town. But something sent her spy senses into overdrive when it came to the man's security, and her mind wouldn't let go of the case. Someone close to him could have been behind today's attack. Someone with intimate knowledge of the family. If he left, would the threats stop?

Her stomach churned. What if this turned into a longer assignment, or even a dangerous one? Despite Preston's protests about not staying, Sebastian wasn't backing down, and there was no way she wanted to be responsible for Preston's safety if he returned to his public throne. Granted, he'd have plenty of protection assigned to him, but if Laila got the case, she'd have to stick really close to him. Spending any time with Preston or his family would be absolute torture.

Laila turned on the radio for a distraction. No need to get wrapped up in trying to unravel a case that technically wasn't hers yet.

For now, she just needed to check on Preston and make sure he lived long enough to fall off the grid again.

MONDAY, 2:00 P.M.

Preston sat at the kitchen table in Sebastian's lakefront cabin and fanned out the paperwork. Fatigue gripped him hard, and all he could do was stare at the choices laid out before him.

Return to Columbia and take over his father's role in the company, or head back to Magellan Falls, the only place that had ever felt like home.

"I don't want to come back." His words were barely a whisper.

Sebastian set a coffee mug next to the paperwork and sat at the table. Preston stared at the man who had been more of a father to him than his own. "Is that your final decision?" Sebastian asked. "Have you considered what your departure will mean to Whittaker Enterprises? To your family?"

Leave it to Sebastian to cut to the heart of the matter.

Duke, Preston's golden retriever, lay under the table and yipped in his sleep without a care in the world. At least some things stayed constant in his life. Preston cleared his throat, shoving his emotions back where they belonged. "Thanks for letting me and Duke stay here."

"Anything for you. I've known you since you were a little boy. Which is why I want to keep you safe. I'm concerned that even if you leave town, you may still be in danger. You need round-the-clock protection no matter what you choose."

The pressure behind Preston's eyes intensified, and he rubbed his temples. His stomach churned at the thought of someone murdering his father and brother and marking Preston for death next. No one knew he was in town, and he'd kept his whereabouts secret the last five years. Yet that van had targeted him.

His hip throbbed as a reminder of hitting the hard pavement and that without Laila's intervention, he might not be sitting here right now. "It looks like someone recognized me. But if I disappear again, leave town without a trace, maybe the threat will subside."

"Or maybe you're giving a murderer exactly what he wants: the Whittaker family out of the picture. The fire on the boat was no accident. The boat Walt chartered was brand new, and I have copies of the maintenance records. Your father thought he was being followed, and it looks like he was right. Someone was after him."

"What do you want me to do, Sebastian? Take over my dad's position, which I'm clearly not qualified for? Let the media dig up every sordid story from my past and parade it around like it happened an hour ago? Have everyone bet on my failure?" Preston sucked in a deep breath to steady his voice. It would do no good to yell at Sebastian. The man had always been on Preston's side. He clutched the edge of the table to keep from ripping the papers to shreds and storming out of the room. "Why would I willingly return to this chaos? I'm not that guy anymore. The media can find their story elsewhere."

"I don't have all of the answers. I do know you're more qualified than you realize. Your father never wanted you to leave town. He always had a place for you in the company."

The burden of responsibility hung around Preston's neck like a noose. Someone needed to look after his mother and sister.

The way the business was set up, if Ethan or Preston didn't take the position, Bob Zimmerman, his father's partner, would own one hundred percent of the company.

Could Bob have been behind the boat explosion? Preston didn't even want to think that, but the man did have a lot to gain with the Whittaker men out of the picture. But could Preston fill his father's shoes?

The chair creaked as Sebastian sat back, sipping his coffee with a knowing gleam in his eye. Nothing seemed to rattle this man. And Sebastian had seen the worst of some of Preston's antics as a teenager. "Think of the good things you can do by accepting the position, Preston. This opportunity would give you the influence to change your family legacy. You aren't your father. You're better than him."

"If only the sentiment were true, Sebastian. Ethan was a carbon copy of my father, born to lead the next generation of Whittakers. All I ever did was disappoint my dad."

Two years older than Preston, Ethan had done everything right in their father's eyes, including having two sons to continue the Whittaker line. So how could Preston assume his father's position when all Preston ever did was cause problems?

The troublemaker.

That's what his dad used to call him. And the younger version of himself had decided to live up to that name by making one bad decision after another. Parties, booze—you name it, he'd done it. All documented in front of a gossip-hungry public audience.

Sebastian ran a hand through his silver hair and let out a long sigh. "I wish you could see your own potential. Sure, your dad was rough on you and Ethan, always expecting you both to fall into line and love the company as much as he did. You needed to make your own way in life, and leaving made you a better man. But it's time to stop hiding from the past. Don't let fear rob you of this opportunity."

It had taken that one awful night for Preston to look in the mirror and realize things needed to change. The madness had driven him to pack a few belongings into his car and leave everything else behind. His family. Money. Fame. He'd ditched it all for a chance to breathe again. To heal.

The day he'd left, he'd driven a few hours before stopping

in the small mountain town of Magellan Falls, SC. A weight had lifted from his shoulders when he'd walked into a local grocery store and no one had recognized him. People hadn't seemed to care who he was, so he'd stayed.

After five years, Preston had grown to love the small-town vibes. Magellan Falls had worked its way into his heart, and sadness tore through him at the thought of leaving the place that had become his home.

The nostalgia hit Preston hard. "I have a house and friends in Magellan Falls. Did I tell you that I started a company? I restore old furniture. I even go to church every Sunday."

Sebastian chuckled. "I always told you God would hunt you down. But now you have a decision to make. You can't keep running from the past. It's already caught up to you."

Preston shook his head. "This city holds too many ghosts from the past, constant reminders of my failures. I don't want to live my life under a microscope again." With the internet, moments of indiscretion now lasted forever. A quick Google search would pull up evidence of things he'd like to blot from existence. The fickle public gobbled up the next fad until the newest and hottest thing became a discarded relic, but their memories never faded.

"But maybe it's time to show the world what you're really made of."

Five years had changed him. Magellan Falls had handed him a clean slate, and he'd made the best of it. He'd have to prove that he was a different man, but how could he lose the party playboy image? Would taking the position allow him to redeem his past? Sebastian supported him. But would others find him a capable leader?

Preston pounded his fist on the table. "Why did Ethan and Dad have to die?" He rubbed his eyes, willing the dam holding back his tears not to crack.

Sebastian stood and put his arm around Preston's shoulders. "I miss Walt dearly. I can't imagine what you're going through. I'm here for you no matter what you decide, but I should leave you alone for now. You have a lot to think about. Call me if you need anything."

"Thanks for everything, Sebastian. You've always supported my family, through the good and bad."

Preston walked Sebastian to the front door of the cabin. "We'll get through this," Sebastian said as he grabbed Preston into a bear hug.

Now alone with his thoughts, the pressure mounted in Preston's chest. He picked up the paperwork and clicked the pen. Sebastian's words echoed through his ears. Maybe he *could* change his family's legacy. Make the Whittaker name stand for something besides scandals and affairs.

Preston tossed the pen on the table, stood, and grabbed a bottle of water from the refrigerator.

He needed to clear his head and think about something else. Like the woman in the parking lot. Laila, the professional bodyguard with the gorgeous eyes. He couldn't remember the last time a woman had sparked his interest like that.

Sebastian had a good point about the need for additional security, though Preston shuddered at the thought of a bodyguard traipsing around after him. It would be worse than when the paparazzi had stalked his every step. Then again, would it be so bad to spend time with a beautiful woman? Because that was exactly the image he was trying to avoid.

"I can't win, Duke." The dog perked up at the mention of his name and sat in front of Preston.

"Okay, boy. This is how it's going to work." The dog nudged him to indicate he was listening. "We're going to stick to the original plan. If we skip town tonight, maybe we can leave any danger behind."

His loyal sidekick huffed and flopped back to the floor.

"I know, buddy, I'm tired too." But it was a good plan. As long as he wasn't followed on the way out of town, he'd drop off the map for the second time. His family would move on, and he'd go back to his sanctuary in Magellan Falls, where no one knew his name. Yet.

Duke's ears perked up, followed by a low growl. Preston looked out the kitchen window that overlooked the lake and didn't see anything. But a distinct scent stung his nose.

Was that gasoline?

A bluish haze wafted through the kitchen from under the doorway that led to the garage, and he frowned. Preston touched the doorknob, and it wasn't hot. He cracked the door open, his pulse thumping. He watched orange and red flames race across the garage wall. Smoke swirled around his feet and poured into the kitchen. But the fire wasn't the biggest problem. The propane tanks Sebastian stored in his garage could blow the house sky high. Adrenaline kicked into high gear. Preston slammed the door and bolted for the living room.

"Duke! Come!" The fire alarms screeched, ratcheting up Preston's urgency to get out of the house.

The smoke thickened, making it difficult to navigate his way. But when he rounded the corner into the living room, he stopped dead in his tracks. Flames had licked up the front window curtains and engulfed the entire front wall of the house. Including the door, his last option for an escape.

Preston bit back tears that had more to do with thoughts of dying than the smoke stinging his eyes. He dropped to the ground, praying for enough breathable air to get him to the back of the house. Maybe he could get out a window.

Faint barks reached him over the crackling and popping from the inferno. "Duke!" His whole body trembled as he army-crawled down the hallway, guided by the faint sounds of his dog's cries. The intensity of the heat began to lessen the closer he got to the bedroom, but that wouldn't last long. The fire roared right behind him. A cough racked his body, the taste of ash hitting his tongue.

He scrambled into the bedroom and shut the door. Duke paced by the window. Smoke swirled in the air, but at least Preston could breathe again. He stood, wiping the sweat and soot from his forehead. Grabbing the comforter off the bed, he jammed it under the doorway to buy them some more time.

He tried to open the window, but the glass pane wouldn't budge.

This house would become his coffin if he couldn't find a way out.

3

The British voice on Laila's phone announced a left turn. Less than a mile to go and she'd reach Sebastian's cabin to check out the security.

Her mind stayed on the man who would be her client if Sebastian had his way. If Preston skipped town, would the danger subside or would it follow him?

A thick haze cast shadows on the road. The smell of burnt wood tickled her nose. Could someone be having a bonfire or maybe a controlled burn? She pulled up the map. The cabin should be on her right.

A home engulfed in flames came into view, and she slammed on the brakes. She double-checked the address again.

"Oh no. That's not good." She parked on the side of the road and ran toward the house. Heat scorched her, and she skidded to a stop.

"Preston!" She screamed over the crackle of the fire and whipped out her phone to call 911. Alarms from a fire truck blared in the distance, so she shoved her phone back in her pocket. Help was on the way.

She skirted the perimeter of the property, staying clear of the flames. "Preston!"

When she hit the backyard, the sound of barking stopped her dead in her tracks, and she looked at the burning house.

Preston's face appeared at the window across from her. He banged on the pane. "It's stuck! I can't find anything heavy enough in the room to break the glass."

Laila pulled her weapon from her holster. "Stand back!"

Preston looked at her, his eyes wide. She held up her gun. "Back away from the window. The bullet will shatter the glass."

He got the message and retreated. Once she knew she wouldn't accidentally shoot Preston, she fired a single shot. The bullet pierced the center of the pane, and the glass splintered into a thousand fragments. "Okay," she yelled.

Preston reappeared, using his elbow to knock out any remaining pieces of glass. He disappeared for a second but returned with a blanket to cover the windowsill.

Preston ducked out of view again and returned with a golden retriever. "Can you grab Duke?" he asked. He lowered the dog out the window, and Laila wrapped her arms around the dog's middle, lowering him to safety. But not before she got a paw in her face and a slobbery lick.

The sizzle of fire made Laila's heart stop. She wouldn't rest until Preston's feet were on the ground. "Preston, you're going to have to jump."

"Run, Laila. Get out of here. The propane tanks in the garage might blow. I'll be right behind you."

He threw his legs over the sill, and Laila bolted the minute his boots hit the ground.

They'd reached the woods at the edge of the property when a tremor nearly knocked her down. The house erupted into a giant fireball, and flames lit the sky like a fireworks display.

For a moment, all they could do was stare.

"I think I might need a bodyguard after all," Preston finally muttered.

She offered no reply. What could she say? Because from the looks of it, that fire hadn't been an accident.

The fire trucks screamed closer, and Preston looked at Laila. "Can we please go before the first responders and media get here? I don't want to be mobbed by a bunch of reporters. This isn't the way to announce that I'm returning to Columbia."

"Wait. You've decided? You're coming back? As in taking over your father's company?"

"I haven't made my decision, but someone doesn't want me to stay in town. If they're attacking me, they could go after my sister and mother. It's time to put a stop to this." He motioned to the skeleton of the burning house. "Plus, I have a sick feeling that I'll be a target no matter where I wind up."

"Do you need medical attention?" Laila asked. "You inhaled a ton of smoke. We should wait for the paramedics to check you out—"

"I'll get checked out, but not here. I just need to avoid having my face plastered all over the evening news."

Laila nodded but didn't like the plan. She hated leaving the scene of a crime, especially when Preston should get some medical attention. But he might be in more danger if the press mobbed the scene, so she agreed with the decision to leave. "Fine. I'll call the police from the car, and we'll make arrangements to give our statements. But don't get used to having your own way with me around."

He smirked and called to the dog. The three of them trudged through the woods that ran along the side of the house until they found her car parked on the road. The stench of smoke filled her SUV once they piled in. Laila pulled out just as the fire engines roared past.

Preston sat in the passenger seat and stared straight ahead. Sorrow and exhaustion had taken their toll on him, but he had a spark in his eyes that reflected something different. *Determination.*

Laila bit back a smile. This man wasn't going to give up without a fight. It made her job to protect him a lot easier if he wasn't inclined to give up.

"Where do you suggest we go?" Laila asked. "Do you want to go to an urgent care and get checked out?"

Preston shrugged. "I'm okay. Once I got into the bedroom, the smoke cleared a lot. Let's head to Sebastian's house. We can have an EMT meet us there if it makes you happy. And since Sebastian hired you, he'll know what to do, especially when it comes to handling the media."

Laila wanted to drive him to the nearest doctor, but she could tell he'd made up his mind. "I'm going to call the police while we drive. We at least need to inform them of our involvement in the explosion." She had Haley's husband, Detective Steven Rothwell, programmed into her phone.

Steven picked up on the first ring, and she gave him the short version of the incident.

"You left a crime scene?"

"I know, but—"

He cut her off with a lecture, and she refrained from rolling her eyes. "I know, Steven, I know, but Preston's in danger, and I didn't know if the person after him was hanging around to make sure he finished the job. My first priority is Preston's safety."

Steven fell silent. Then sighed. "All right. It's not a perfect situation, but we'll work with it."

"Will you meet us at Sebastian's house? We'll give our statement there."

"Yeah. I'll see you as soon as I can get there."

She disconnected from Steven and called Sebastian to give a heads-up about their unannounced arrival.

"They blew up my house?" His shock reverberated through the speaker.

"I'm sorry, Sebastian. There's probably not much left. What's your address? Also, can you have a medical professional head to the house? Someone needs to check Preston out after the fire."

"Preston can tell you how to get here. I'll see you soon. I have calls to make." He disconnected the call, and Laila hit the highway while Preston rattled off Sebastian's address.

"You have his information memorized?" she asked.

"I spent a lot of time at his place as a kid. He and Gloria acted more like parents to me than my own. I was good friends with his two sons all through high school, so Sebastian included me in family events."

Preston closed his eyes and rested his head on the back of the seat.

Laila tamped down the desire to pepper the man with questions. Where had he been hiding for the past five years? She had a vague notion of why he'd left from the file, but she wanted to hear his reasons for the Houdini act. The paparazzi's prized possession had managed to escape from the constant attention. She'd heard rumors that reporters had hired private detectives to search for Preston and had come up empty. Good for him.

"Thanks for rescuing me. Again." Preston opened his eyes and stared straight ahead. "I'm lucky to be alive. I guess Sebastian is right. Someone wants to kill me."

Laila stole a glance at Preston. Dark circles, a mixture of

soot and stress, cast shadows under his eyes. A devastating transformation from the picture she'd seen earlier in his file.

"It's what we do at the Elite Guardians. You need someone by your side, watching your back. Especially if you step forward and take over your dad's company."

If Preston became her client, she'd have to step up her game if she wanted to keep him alive.

Olivia was right—she'd have to stick close but be unseen. Laila had a unique advantage thanks to her undercover assignments with Mossad. She knew how to adapt and change to fit into any situation. As a result, most people didn't peg her for a bodyguard.

"What were you doing at the cabin?" Preston asked. "Did Sebastian send you? You seem to be in the right place at the right time."

Laila glanced at her map, then checked her rearview mirror to make sure they weren't being followed. "My boss sent me to do one last security check. I assumed you were heading out of town and no one would hear from you again."

"That was the plan. But then someone set that fire. With me in it. And while everything within me wants to run, I can't let a murderer get away. This just reinforces the suspicion that my dad's and brother's lives were snuffed out by some sicko. And for what? Money? Control? What could possibly motivate someone to go on a killing spree? Why my family? Why me?"

Preston looked away, pricking Laila's heart. Despite her misgivings about his reputation, the man's life had been shattered in an instant. She might not be close with her family, but at least she could pick up the phone and call them.

A wrought iron gate marked the entrance to Sebastian's property. The security at the place was over the top, but in this case, the high-tech system worked in their favor. Preston would be safe here while they figured out his next steps.

Because apparently, she'd already signed up as his body-guard in her head.

A guard inspected her ID and waved them in. Laila parked and they walked up to the front door, with Duke in tow. Preston had insisted that Sebastian wouldn't mind the smoky-smelling dog tagging along.

Before they could knock, Sebastian swung the door open and had Preston locked in an embrace. "Come in," he said and ushered both of them inside.

Laila entered into the living room, which looked like it belonged in a Hallmark Christmas movie. The spacious room had plenty of seats, with a floor-to-ceiling picture window showing off a lake view. A fireplace cut through the chill in the October air, inviting her to curl up on the plush sofa and take a nap. Not at all what she'd been expecting from the high-powered attorney to the wealthy and elite.

"Well, if it isn't Preston Whittaker," a voice called out before entering the room. A woman rushed through the room like a hurricane and wrapped her arms around Preston.

Taking in the silver hair and strong Southern accent, Laila assumed she was Sebastian's wife. Two other men, with EMT logo patches on their shirts, followed. Laila gave a thumbs-up to Sebastian, who winked.

The mother hen continued to fuss over Preston with all of her grandmotherly Southern charm. Then she spotted Laila. "Forgive my manners. I'm Gloria Coyle. And you are?"

Sebastian hijacked the conversation before Laila could speak. "This is Laila Whittaker. Preston's wife."

What?

She shot a look to Preston. His face paled and he squinted as if trying to read Sebastian's mind, which clearly the old man had lost.

"Well, I'll be," gushed Gloria as she tackled Laila with an

embrace. "Preston didn't tell us he'd gotten married. And to such a beautiful woman."

The words sparked an idea that Laila ran with. "Aren't you just the sweetest? I'm Laila." She nailed a Southern accent and slipped her arm through Preston's. Preston quirked an eyebrow at her, and she mouthed *Just go with it.*

The woman offered an assortment of beverage options with an array of snack choices. Laila took her up on the offer for a drink, and Gloria left as fast as she'd entered.

What had she just done? What had prompted her to buy into whatever crazy scheme Sebastian was selling?

But if she wanted to stick to Preston's side twenty-four seven, the plan had merit.

The second Gloria left, Preston shook out of Laila's grip. "What's wrong with you, Sebastian? Is this your idea of a joke? Now your wife thinks we're married. That's how rumors start, and the next thing you know it will be the headline story on the six o'clock news."

Sebastian gave Preston a crooked grin and shrugged. "Look, why don't you let the paramedics check you out? You can get cleaned up and then we can talk."

Preston scowled at Sebastian but complied and followed the paramedics into one of the spare bedrooms.

Laila walked to the window, scouting for any signs of trouble. Once the room cleared out, she faced Sebastian and said, "Are you crazy? Do you think this little ruse of yours will work?"

"Think of this." Sebastian motioned for Laila to take a seat next to him on the couch. "No one has seen him for five years. It's possible he settled down, got married."

Laila studied Sebastian while he talked. The man's obvious love for the Whittaker family shone in every word he spoke.

"Someone is trying to kill Preston, and whoever it is knows

him very well. If you were to pose as his wife, you'd have the perfect cover to stick by his side to protect him. I like you, Laila, and I'm trusting you with his life." Tears formed in the corner of Sebastian's eyes, and Laila looked away.

This assignment had danger written all over it. Not only was there a killer setting his sights on Preston, but she'd have to convince the world that she was married to one of the most elite and sought-after men in the world. It would be a great way for her to gain access to all aspects of Preston's life, and no one would even consider that she was a bodyguard. But this plan could also go up in flames faster than Sebastian's cabin.

Gloria returned with the promised drinks and snacks. She set a tray of food down on the coffee table and left to escort the paramedics to the front door.

Preston came back into the room, arms crossed against his chest. "The paramedics said I'm fine. But I'm not going to have you two conspiring against me." He turned to Laila. "I don't remember officially hiring you. Now you want to pretend to be my wife?" The look on Preston's face didn't mask his reaction to this plan. It mirrored her own.

"No. Not happening," Preston said. He paced the living room, wringing his hands. "I'll disappear again. And this time no one will find me. Not a killer. Not even you."

Laila stood and put a hand on his shoulder, stopping him from wearing a trench in the plush living room carpet. She softened her gaze and looked him in the eyes. Now that the shock of the potential ruse had started to wear off, they at least needed to discuss the idea. "We both know you'll do the right thing and stay. You're not going to let some thug run you out of town—not when your family's safety is at stake. My job is to protect you. And if pretending to be married will keep you safe, I think we can't rule it out."

Preston studied Laila. He'd just watched her turn into a different person right before his eyes. Like a chameleon, she changed her demeanor to fit any situation.

But was it necessary for her to assume the role of his wife? This woman had saved his life twice, but she might also be the death of him.

He turned to Sebastian. "You think this is a good idea? Letting Laila pretend to be my wife?"

Sebastian shrugged. "I just want to see you safe." The doorbell rang. "I'll let you two talk while I get the door."

Sebastian couldn't have planned the timing of that bell any better.

Laila sat at one end of the couch, and Preston purposefully chose the opposite end so she wouldn't get any ideas that he was on board with her insane scheme.

He studied the woman, with her shoulder-length brown hair and olive complexion. Would it really be that much of a hardship to spend more time with her?

Where had that thought come from?

He shook his head and rubbed his temples. Laila had been in his life less than five hours. There was no way he could pull off a fake relationship with a total stranger. He wasn't that good of an actor.

"What are you thinking?" Laila asked.

He wasn't about to tell her what was really running through his mind. Heat rushed through his cheeks, and all Preston could muster was an open-palm shrug. Or more like throwing up his hands in defeat.

How had he gotten here? Two days ago, he'd spent the morning in his workshop refinishing a kitchen table set he'd picked up from the curb on trash day. Now he had an instant wife and a killer chasing him.

He bit back a groan and conceded that Laila had a point. He'd changed his mind about returning. And despite wanting to come back on his own terms, this crazy plot twist had one thing going for it. No one would ever see her coming. Tenacity and grit pumped through this woman's veins, and he didn't doubt her commitment to the job. Despite her petite stature, Laila was a force of nature to rival a tornado.

Sebastian reentered the room with another man. "Preston, I have someone I want you to meet. This is Detective Steven Rothwell."

Preston and Laila stood to greet Steven, but the detective gave Laila a familiar head nod as if he already knew her.

"The Elite Guardians carry a special badge thanks to a mandate from the mayor," Laila said. "I'm not law enforcement, but I've worked closely with Steven on several cases. Not to mention his wife is a close friend."

"Nice to meet you, Detective," Preston said and offered him a seat.

Laila staked out a spot near the window. She never stopped watching for danger. The thought comforted him—and saddened him all at the same time.

"Please, call me Steven," the detective said. "My partner, Quinn, is at the cabin heading up the investigation into the fire. He radioed a few minutes ago indicating that this was arson. They found the accelerant used to start the fire. And someone jammed the handle on the front door, essentially trapping you in the burning building. You're being targeted, Preston."

Arson. He hadn't reached the front door because of the flames, but it wouldn't have mattered. Preston sank onto the couch before his legs gave out, his mind reeling from the news.

The confirmation that someone wanted him dead crushed him like a rockslide.

"Obviously, Sebastian was right regarding the risks facing Preston," Laila said, turning toward Steven.

Sebastian raised a shaky hand to his mouth. "This is horrible. Twice someone's tried to attack you. It has to be about the inheritance and the company. What else would cause anyone to inflict this kind of horror?"

Preston shook his head. "Nothing makes any sense, but we can't let them win. No Whittaker is safe at the moment." He clasped his hands together to stop the trembling. A tsunami of unexpressed emotions welled up inside of him, threatening to release. He hadn't had time to grieve the loss of his father and brother, and circumstances around him were changing every second. But one thing he knew with absolute clarity... He'd rather die than see his father's company fall into the wrong hands.

But if he stayed and fought for Whittaker Enterprises, he'd lose the one thing he'd grown to love over the past five years. Anonymity.

In Magellan Falls, people didn't remind him of all the mistakes he'd made. No one wanted him to dish about the details of the lawsuit. He'd tasted freedom, and the thought of losing it tore him to shreds.

Which was the right choice?

He looked at Laila. Coming back meant saving his family, but he might have a fake wife to contend with.

"The person who's targeting the family has to have inside knowledge," Laila said. "I suspect someone figured out that Preston was back in town and followed him to the lake house after the funeral. Probably the same person that tried to run him over."

Chills raced up Preston's spine. If someone had identified

him, then it was game over. News this juicy traveled faster than a SpaceX rocket, and his face would be plastered all over the six o'clock news for sure. He cleared his throat. "Have the police announced their findings with the boat fire?"

Steven nodded. "I've contacted the authorities assigned to the investigation, and you're right. An explosion in the engine room of the boat started the fire. Police are looking into what caused it to ignite."

"I'll accept the CEO position." Preston blurted this out before his brain could stop him. The abrupt statement pulled all eyes to him. This was his family. His life. He shrugged. "No one's going to scare me away, and I want to make sure my mother and sister are safe."

The tick of a grandfather clock thundered in the silent room. The memory of his father's voice echoed from the recesses of Preston's mind. *Don't worry, Preston. Ethan will be the future head of Whittaker Enterprises. You'll have plenty of other opportunities, but we both know you don't belong behind a desk.*

If he was going to do this, he was going to have to get that voice out of his head.

Steven finally spoke. "This puts a new twist on things. This is big news, and once the media sense a story, they'll pounce. I assume additional security will be requested?" Steven looked at Laila, and she nodded. "And Elite Guardians will assign you as his personal bodyguard?"

Sebastian cleared his throat. "Preston will need round-the-clock protection. Someone with access to his entire family. A person who can blend in and go unnoticed..." Sebastian's voice faded, as if he wanted Preston to finish his thought.

Preston's blood pressure spiked. "You've got to be kidding me. You really want Laila and me to pretend to be married? How could we pull that off? Who's going to believe it? My marriage would sell newspapers, so reporters would double down their efforts to put me, and Laila, on the camera. It's bad enough that I'm contemplating moving back under these circumstances, but to show up with a *fake* wife? If anyone discovered that..."

Steven shot Laila a look that said *Are you out of your mind?* Preston could only hope the guy could talk some sense into her and Sebastian.

"She'd be able to stick close to you, your family, and your coworkers," Sebastian said. "Laila could appear wherever you go without arousing suspicions. And no one's seen you in five years, so it's possible that you could have gotten married."

The last thing he'd wanted to do was come home, and now he'd have a fake wife by his side. This was all too much. Preston ran a hand through his hair. No matter how much he resisted this idea, there was one fact he couldn't ignore.

The danger was real.

He looked at Laila, and those dark-brown eyes stared back at him. Despite the fact that she was a total stranger, he went from frozen to slightly thawed on the idea. But could they fool his family and the media? He hadn't so much as had a date in the past few years, and now he'd show up with a wife? That didn't leave a lot of time to adjust to this new dynamic.

And what about Laila? She excelled at her job, and he had no doubt he'd be safer with her watching out for trouble. But could she keep up with his crazy, drama-filled life? Because as his wife, he'd be dragging her into the center ring of the media circus that awaited him.

Steven stepped out to make a call, and Sebastian excused himself, leaving Laila and Preston alone. She moved from the window to sit next to him on the sofa. "Look, I get that this will be awkward." She dropped her voice into a whisper. "We don't even know each other. But if I put your security first, this arrangement would give me the access I need to keep you protected. It's the perfect cover story."

He wondered what role she was playing right now. The bodyguard? The Southern belle? Or maybe she was preparing to be his new adoring wife. "Who are you?"

Concern flashed on her features for a split second, and then it was replaced by her composed professional mask. "What are you talking about?"

"I've never met anyone like you. You showed up the moment I needed help and tackled me like you were ten times bigger than me in that parking lot. And that Southern accent you pulled from out of nowhere? Now you want to pretend to be my wife? That's a pretty big commitment to a job. I can't tell if you're playing a role or being genuine. You'd actually go through with a fake marriage to protect me?"

Laila's face registered no reaction. His comment replayed in his head. Had he insulted her? This woman was complex times a hundred.

"This is for security purposes," she emphasized. "We don't have to get along or tell each other our deepest secrets. It's all for show. We'll be like actors in a play. But trust me, the entire time I'll be thinking about how to best protect you from whoever is trying to kill you."

Steven returned and interrupted with a question for Laila about additional security measures, but Preston couldn't focus on their words. He watched his supposed bride. He'd experienced her physical strength, but there was an intensity surrounding her that he couldn't quite place. Part of him wanted to run from this preposterous idea, but curiosity drew him in, demanding to know more about this smart and captivating woman.

On the surface, they appeared to be opposites. He towered over her petite stature with his five-foot-eleven frame. Her straight brown hair fell loosely around her shoulders, and she didn't wear a stitch of makeup, not that she needed any. Nothing about her suggested money or sophistication. Not exactly the kind of fashionable beauty his family would expect him to bring home.

But then again, a lot had changed in the past two days, let alone the last five years.

Reality forced Preston's mind to the present situation. His father and brother were dead. Someone had tried to kill him, twice. And now he'd be returning after all this time, decimating his anonymity and the peaceful life he'd created, with a fake wife in tow.

"Have you made a final decision, Preston?" Sebastian stepped into the room, interrupting Preston's scattered thoughts. "Are you really coming back home to take over the company? With Laila as your bodyguard and maybe even as your *wife*? We need an answer now, because I just got a text from the security guard. A news van is camped out in front of the house, and they're broadcasting live."

———

The news played the story on an endless loop. Speculation ran wild that Preston Whittaker had risen from the grave and was spotted at his father's funeral.

The phone on the table vibrated. A tap on the screen put the voice on speaker. "Sorry, boss. But it wasn't my fault—"

"I don't want to hear your sorry excuses. I pay you and your brother for results. How did Preston escape that fire?"

A sigh filtered through the line. "I barred the front door, but he managed to get out through a bedroom window. Some lady showed up out of nowhere and helped him."

A woman? "Who?"

"I don't know."

The plan was starting to unravel, and they needed to figure out a way to patch it back together. Once more people came to know that Preston was alive and well, he'd build a fortress around himself—one of the perks of being obscenely wealthy. "I'm paying you to do a job, and so far, you've botched it. You were supposed to be the best, but maybe I need to hire someone else."

"I'll finish the job. Just give me more time."

"We're out of time. He'll have an army of guards securing him twenty-four hours a day once the world hears that he's in town. You had your shot and blew it. He knows someone is after him, so now it will be virtually impossible to get close to him."

The voice on the other end of the line remained silent as if waiting for his marching orders.

"New plan. If we can't draw Preston out of the public eye long enough to kill him, then we take out everyone around him. Send him the message that not only is he not safe, but everyone around him isn't either. Maybe he'll pack it up and crawl back to whatever rat hole he's been hiding in. We all know that the Whittakers will take the easy way out. We need to stop him from becoming head of the company."

And once Preston left town, they'd hunt him down to make sure he never resurrected again.

4

Laila kept a brisk pace while doing a perimeter check of the estate grounds. With the press lining up outside the front gate, she wouldn't take any chances that the enemy might burst through Sebastian's fortress. Plus, she needed a break to unwind her tangled mind.

The cool breeze that whipped through her hair picked up the faint scent of pine from trees that dotted the backyard. At least Sebastian had additional security in place, because with several sprawling acres, she'd never be able to cover the entire estate.

"Sebastian has a nice place," a voice from behind her said. She looked over her shoulder and saw Steven jogging to catch up to her. She slowed her pace, and he fell into step alongside her.

"It's definitely a step up from my one-bedroom apartment," she said. Leaves crunched underfoot, and Laila looked at Steven. He hadn't tracked her down to make small talk. The man was itching to unleash his objections about this half-baked marriage plan.

She didn't have to wait long.

"Have you thought this through? You aren't really doing this, are you, Laila?" he asked. "What if the killer shifts his target to Preston's wife? Also, and I mean this with all the respect I have for you, you're not his type. How will you pull this off? You can't stand pretentious people, and I don't see you as a high society kind of woman. You'll have to become one of them, play their games."

Laila stopped and looked up at him. While he didn't know Laila as well as some of her coworkers, the man's protective instincts kicked into overdrive when it came to any of the Elite Guardians. Yet his assessment was spot-on and gave voice to the concerns nagging her thoughts.

Was she in over her head? Could she play the role of Mrs. Whittaker and convince Preston's family, not to mention the watching public, that they were in love? She had plenty of experience with undercover assignments. It wasn't like this was her first case. Pretending to be someone else had become second nature to her.

But in a split second, she'd gone from standing on the sidelines, judging the man's less-than-stellar reputation, to becoming an active participant in his world. At least until they neutralized the threat.

"Do you have any better ideas?" she asked.

"All I know is that the guy better keep his hands to himself," Steven said. "I'm not the one he'll need to fear, because wait until Haley hears the news."

He'd rightly concluded that Laila wasn't backing down, despite her own inner monologue of self-doubt. She raked a hand through her hair. "Granted, it's not the best plan, but it will allow me to closely monitor my client." She narrowed her eyes. "These attacks are an inside job. Someone close to him most likely murdered his father and brother. And Preston could be next."

Steven nodded. "Which makes this even more dangerous. The bull's-eye might shift from Preston to you."

"I know. I'll just have to be prepared for that." She shot him a tight smile. "I'm going to head back."

"I'll go with you."

Laila aimed herself toward the house, still thinking and planning, with Steven walking beside her.

The risks were endless, but once the details materialized into an action plan, she'd run full speed ahead. Until Olivia killed her for volunteering to be Preston's wife. But that's just how Laila operated. In the moment. Her adaptability made her an excellent spy. But the dark side of undercover work reared its ugly head. Genuine relationships were a lot harder to maintain when living out a variety of identities.

Which was the major reason she'd left Mossad.

Preston's question flashed through her mind. *Who are you?*

A chill swept through her, and it wasn't from the fall air. It was an innocent question that had stabbed her in the heart. Because deep down inside, her identity had fractured into a million pieces. It was why she could slip into an undercover role without effort. She'd played so many roles in her life that she'd lost sight of the real Laila a long time ago. With that thought burning a path through her brain, she vowed to unpack that baggage at a later time.

She led the way into the kitchen, where they found Olivia and Christina at the table with Gloria force-feeding them cookies.

Laila looked at Gloria, hoping that Sebastian had brought her up to speed on the fake marriage. "Don't worry," Gloria waved her hand. "Sebastian filled me in on your little ruse. But don't mind me. I'll get out of your way so you can get down to business." She gave Laila a conspiratorial wink and left the room.

Laila and Steven sat down at the table, and Laila poured some tea from the pitcher. She winced when the sticky sweetness hit her. How would she perfect the role of a Southern debutante if she couldn't handle a little tea with her sugar? She pushed her glass to the side. "Did anyone fill you in on the plan so far?"

Olivia stared at her before pummeling her with questions. "This was your idea? To pretend to marry Preston Whittaker? In front of all those cameras? Can you pull this off?"

"I think so."

Olivia studied her. "I'll admit that the concept has some merit, and I can see why you would think it might be Preston's best chance at survival. But putting yourself in the public eye is a risky move."

"I can handle things as long as Preston's on board. He'll have to sell this to his family."

Preston walked into the room as if on cue. "I don't like any of this, but I've decided to take over my father's position in the company. Sebastian will make the announcement tonight. No sense in hiding anymore. They know I'm here."

Laila tucked her hair behind her ears. Her stomach did a backflip, and her tongue might as well have been made of lead. Not at all her usual reaction to stressful situations. But she'd volunteered herself to be Preston's wife for the sake of his security. Was he up for the challenge? Was she? "So he'll tell everyone that you and I are—" She couldn't bring herself to vocalize the word. Maybe she had some reservations about this plan after all.

"I think the word you're stumbling over is *married*," Preston said. "But no. He's leaving that part out until my family hears it from me. I'm confident my sister will live tweet the news that her dead brother has returned with a wife, so everyone else will find out every juicy detail soon enough. Besides, Sebastian and I agreed to offer an exclusive interview to one reporter, and I guess that's where I can share the news about my...our marriage."

"Great. That's great," Laila said with a forced smile.

Preston looked at her and ran a hand through his hair. "It's just...I don't know you. At all. I met you this morning when you tackled me. This is all so weird."

Laila shrugged. "The less we say to the press, the better. And remember, your family hasn't seen you in five years. A lot can change."

"I guess."

Olivia and Christina stood. "We need to discuss security measures with Sebastian," Olivia said. "He's hired an outside firm that will be here later this evening with some reinforcements. In the meantime, you two should talk. This is a pretty big decision." Steven followed them out of the room.

"She's not fully on board with this," Laila murmured. "Did you see the look on her face?"

"I saw it." Preston sat across from her, propping his elbows on the table.

She stared at her soon-to-be husband, a man she'd met this morning. She summoned her inner confidence, and her normal nerves of steel returned. How hard could it be to pretend to be the wife of an heir to a billion-dollar fortune? The absurdity of that thought made her lips pucker.

Her past assignments flickered through her thoughts like a movie reel, but she squelched them. This wouldn't be the toughest assignment she'd ever had.

But it certainly would be the most awkward.

"We should talk this over," Laila said. "Get to know each other. Make it believable."

"Okay."

"Where have you been living for the past five years?"

"Magellan Falls."

Couldn't he be more forthcoming than two-word answers? "What have you been doing?"

"Making furniture."

"That's it? Making furniture is all you've got?"

He shrugged. "I live a small-town life. Work. Go to church. Keep to myself. Sorry if I'm no longer Mr. Excitement. If you're looking for a scandal, go read my sister's blog. I've got nothing for you."

She tried not to roll her eyes. Day one of their fake marriage and they were already heading for divorce.

"Are you always this stubborn?"

"Yes."

"I'm going to need more information if I'm to pull off being your wife. Trust me, you don't want me improvising on the spot."

"Fair enough." He held up his hands in mock surrender. "But maybe I should ask you the questions." He shot her a wink and her pulse spiked.

Up close to the infamous Preston Whittaker, Laila began to understand the hype. Even with his current backwoods style, his dark hair still fell perfectly into place like he was walking into a photo shoot for the cover of an outdoor magazine. But the last thing she wanted was to have this man pry into her private life. How could she create a convincing pretend relationship and not let things get personal between them? Her role as a bodyguard meant occasionally digging into people's lives and habits, but never the reverse.

The last time she'd let her emotions go unchecked on a

mission, a colleague had lost his life. She'd never make that mistake again.

"Where are you from?" he asked. "I mean, your Southern accent is flawless, but there's no way you're a Southern gal." He got up, took her iced tea glass to the sink, and poured it out. He returned with a bottle of water from the refrigerator.

"Oh, thank you." She took a swig from the bottle. "I was born in Tel Aviv, Israel."

"But you don't have an Israeli accent."

"My mother is American, my father Israeli. I spent time in both countries after they divorced." Laila let loose her natural Middle Eastern tone. "But in my line of work I've managed to ditch the accent. Is this better for you?"

Preston nodded. "It's nice. You should talk like that more often."

"I'm sure that would impress your family." What would the Whittakers think of Preston's foreign wife?

"Trust me, nothing impresses them."

Ah, finally. A clue about his home life. Now they were getting somewhere.

She switched back to her nondescript American accent. "I assume they won't be overjoyed to hear that you have a wife. Not when money is potentially on the line."

Preston shrugged. "They all squabble about everything. I've never been good enough for them, so I'm sure they will view anyone I bring home as some sort of pariah. They'd expect me to be with a drop-dead gorgeous woman, so you fit that role perfectly. But you might have to dumb it down a bit. They won't expect someone so smart. And definitely not a woman with the fighting skills of a ninja."

Heat rushed through Laila's face, and she coughed to cover it. This man was a notorious charmer with a legendary playboy reputation. She refused to get sucked into his world, even if she had to endure it for a little while. "I'm pretty sure I'd never be mistaken for a ninja, but I have a black belt in both karate and Krav Maga. What gave it away?"

"You tackled me a like a linebacker, remember? You've got some serious power. What did you do before becoming a bodyguard?"

The conversation had just taken a sharp turn in the wrong direction. Laila never talked about her past with anyone. "I worked for an intelligence division with the Israeli government."

"Like a spy?"

"You watch too many movies. It's much more boring than that."

Preston smiled, probably for the first time since she'd met him. "You'd be surprised how much I like boring."

Silence filled the space between them. She studied the man in front of her, questions pinging rapid-fire around her head. But she decided to give voice to the one thing she'd been dying to know since they'd first met. "Why did you leave and drop off the map without a trace? You gave up your family, money, and fame. Why?"

Another awkward pause. He dropped his gaze. "I assumed you had some thick file on me with my life story laid out for you in black and white."

Laila huffed. "I figured you wouldn't tell me the truth." She softened her tone. "You disappeared without a trace right after that lawsuit, even though you were acquitted. But your abrupt departure just made you look guilty. You never gave your side of the story. You just walked away from your life."

Preston ran his hands through his hair. He leaned in, close enough that she could pick up his woodsy scent. His chestnut-brown eyes bored into hers. "Do you think I'm guilty?" he asked, his voice a whisper.

LYNETTE EASON & KELLY UNDERWOOD

She matched his movements, leaning in across the table. "I really don't know. My job is to protect you. I just was curious to hear your side of the story."

"If I told you why, would you believe me?"

She paused. "I don't know."

He sat back in his chair. "At least you're honest. Let's just say that it's hard to change your life when no one will forget your past, and leave it at that."

The man sitting across from her looked different from the Preston of the past. The scruffy beard and flannel shirt wouldn't hide his ego once the cameras were pointed in his direction again. Because she didn't buy this humble, small-town Boy Scout persona—not when it came to fame and money. Had he really shed his bad-boy image for some alternate life?

Her thoughts flashed back to a recent conversation with Haley. *People can't change on their own. Only God can change people's hearts,* her friend had said.

Had Preston really found a way to quit his life, start over and become someone different? Her past experiences raised red warning flags that the man in front of her was likely just another con artist, pretending to be someone he wasn't.

Christina stepped into the kitchen. "Can I borrow you for a second, Laila?"

Perfect timing. She'd met her quota for clumsy small talk with the man she was about to marry. She gave a mental facepalm. How could they pull off a fake marriage when she couldn't make it to the end of a conversation without wanting to run away?

She and Christina walked outside onto the wraparound porch overlooking the backyard. "I didn't need anything," Christina said. "I've just never seen you look that uncomfortable."

"Oh, thank you." Laila had so few friends. An invisible wall guarded her heart, enforcing a perimeter that no one would dare cross, which never made it easy for people to get up close and personal with her. But she and Christina had tag-teamed on many assignments, and after work the two enjoyed getting together for boxing matches at the local gym. "I'll admit, I wonder if I'm in over my head with this one. I never allow myself to become personally involved with a client, but what's more personal than being married? I'll have to cross lines I've never crossed before on the job. But the biggest issue is whether I can trust him. He's got that legendary reputation that makes him a wild card. I've got some big blind spots going into this mission—and I don't do blind spots well."

"This is a tough assignment, but I know you. And if I were Preston, I'd want someone like you by my side. Especially if the danger escalates."

"Olivia sent you to talk me out of this, didn't she?"

Christina let out a low laugh. "Yes. Is there any chance of that?"

Laila shook her head. "I kind of went along with the idea after Sebastian not so subtly suggested it. And as weird and out of my comfort zone as it will be"—*so* far out of her comfort zone—"I'm not backing out now. I've got a job to do, and I think Preston's in real danger."

"Well, you've got your team behind you. We'll work with Steven from the outside to keep you safe while he and Quinn hunt for the killer. Olivia put out an alert for extra staff. She's bringing in Charlie Lee to help you. He'll go undercover as your driver and run down leads if you find anything. And Juliette Montgomery is a new recruit Olivia just hired. She's agreed to pose as an intern at Whittaker Enterprises. You'll have people you can trust watching your back."

"Thanks," Laila said. "That's a relief. I appreciate all of the support, but I'm surprised Lizzie is letting Charlie out of her sight." Once Charlie and Lizzie had finally admitted their love for each other, they were engaged in record time.

Christina shrugged. "He's probably so overloaded with wedding planning details that he'll relish the break."

Duke, Preston's dog, trotted up to them after a romp through the backyard. Laila bent down to pet the dog and Christina snorted. "How are those allergies holding up?"

Laila laughed. "Right. My dog allergy. It comes and goes." Laila may have faked a sneeze or two to get out of an assignment destined for Christina. But she'd never admit it.

They walked back toward the kitchen, Laila mapping out her next few days in her head. She had a lot to accomplish in a short time span if she was going to pull off this new role.

As if reading her mind, Christina said, "Before I forget, I stopped by your place to pack you some clothes and things you might need. It looks like you're not going anywhere until tomorrow. Sebastian has enough rooms for you to stay the night."

"I didn't realize when I left my house today that I wouldn't be returning. But here I am, about to let everyone think I'm Preston Whittaker's wife."

A mischievous grin spread across Christina's face. "It could be worse. He's still gorgeous, even with that backwoods vibe he's got going on."

Laila couldn't suppress a giggle. She'd never admit this to Christina, but up close, Preston's looks definitely lived up to the hype. She rolled her eyes and nudged Christina toward the door. "Leave it to you to find the silver lining. Anyway, we'd better get inside. Sebastian is about to hold a press conference from his lawn."

Laila took in her last breath of freedom before she stepped into a world of chaos.

TUESDAY, 11:00 A.M.

The next morning, Preston slipped into the back seat of the Suburban, and Duke hopped in after him. The cavalry had arrived like Sebastian had promised late last night. Just in time for the press conference that had confirmed to the world Preston was alive.

He relished the momentary silence, giving him a chance to steel his nerves. In a few minutes, he'd be heading to the Whittaker mansion to reunite with his family after his five-year absence. With a wife in tow. He was still having trouble wrapping his brain around it, but had decided, begrudgingly, it wasn't a bad idea. In fact, it was downright brilliant.

That didn't mean he hadn't spent most of the night avoiding Laila, wanting a few precious moments to drink in one last sip of freedom. Because from this point on, everything would change. In the solitude, away from all the prepping and planning for his return, he ticked off his to-do list.

Face his mother and sister.

Show himself to the media after living life off the grid.

Prove he has the skills necessary to run his dad's company.

Become a convincing husband.

Stay alive.

Make sure no one gets hurt trying to protect him.

Sadness played a melancholy song across his soul. The past he'd once escaped threatened to drag him under again.

Laila interrupted his thoughts when she climbed into the back seat next to him and Duke.

In spite of the stress of the situation, she'd held herself together well. Nothing seemed to faze the woman. Except maybe for the part where he'd called her *drop-dead gorgeous* and she'd blushed.

A glint of light caught his eye. "Where did you get a wedding ring?"

She flashed her hand so he could inspect the large cluster of diamonds. It consumed her slender finger. "Sebastian told Gloria that we aren't actually married. I'm pretty sure he didn't want to be caught lying to his wife." She wiggled her fingers, sending fragments of light dancing across the roof of the SUV. "But she insisted that I needed a ring for it to look official. It's big and sparkly, so I guess it will work."

"I hadn't thought about rings. I guess it makes sense."

"Here," Laila said and dropped a ring into his palm. "This one's courtesy of Sebastian."

Preston slid the ring on and stared at it. He didn't need the visual reminder of what was at stake. He was bringing a wife home to meet his family. What if his mother fell in love with Laila? Once the truth came out, they'd be labeled as fraudsters.

Sadly, he'd wasted so much of his life lying to those closest to him that this latest con wouldn't be much of a stretch. Only immediate family had known he was still alive, but the fact that he'd severed contact with the outside world for five years would carry some hurt, especially with his mother. Then again, if it would help find the person responsible for the deaths of his father and brother, it was worth it.

"We requested two additional identical vehicles," Laila explained. "One of the cars will go first and draw away the media parked outside the gate. The second car will follow us for backup. Also, I'd like you to meet Charlie. He'll pose as our driver, but he works with the Elite Guardians, so he'll be someone else on the inside with us."

"It's nice to meet you, Preston, aside from all this drama." Charlie glanced at Preston through the rear-view mirror.

"I'm sorry to drag you into all of this, but I'm glad you're here." Preston had gone to bed last night rather than listen to the security plan discussions. The thought of needing this much protection had made him sick to his stomach.

Besides, Laila and her team were professionals. Initially, she'd seemed a bit apprehensive about the whole fake marriage idea, but today the woman had shown up infused with confidence and already in character. She'd replaced her tough-as-nails bodyguard persona for a casual look that hinted at elegance. With her simple light-blue dress and her hair gathering in waves across her shoulders, she'd be joining his mother's bridge club in no time.

Drop-dead gorgeous might have been an understatement.

The reporters followed the bait car, and the volume of spectators at the exit had dwindled. The tinted window shielded them from view. Duke plopped his head on Laila's leg and promptly passed out while she stroked his fur. It sure hadn't taken the dog long to warm up to her. And he was starting to see why.

The city whipped by, and Preston tried to make peace with his homecoming.

"Looks like we've ditched most of the paparazzi," Laila said.

He shrugged. "I'm sure they'll line up outside of the estate, waiting for our arrival." *Our arrival.* Meaning he had a plus-one to consider. "Sorry I wasn't talkative last night, but I guess we should figure out a story. I mean, how did we meet? I can't exactly tell people you tackled me in the church parking lot."

"When making up a cover story, just remember to keep it simple. Don't stray too far from the truth. We met at church."

"Cover story? I take it you've done this before? Invented a whole new identity and pretended to be someone different?"

Laila flinched. "I've had a few undercover assignments. You get used to it."

"But it sounds a lot like lying. That's the part I struggle

with. It's not real. My entire life I've been deceptive, and just when I want to change and be truthful, be a different person, I have to lie. What do I do when the truth comes out and I've proven them right all along? How do I explain that?"

"I'd ask you to explain that whole statement, but we don't have time at the moment. Right now, just remember this is about keeping you and your family safe. You're protecting those you love. Someone tried to kill you, Preston. This person likely killed your father and brother. That's why we're doing this."

"You make it sound almost noble. Heroic."

"It is. Undercover work isn't about a lie. It's about a means to an end. Bringing the bad guys down. If playing a role will do that, then I'm all in."

His head throbbed with tension that started in his toes and radiated throughout his body.

The stress of the past few days tightened its grip the closer they got to the estate. Could they pull this off? Would anyone believe he was a happily married man? He wasn't sure he was that good of an actor, but he'd have to do his best, because Laila was right. Her words simply reinforced what he already knew. Protecting his family and staying alive were the priorities. "I still don't know anything about you. Or us. How long have we been together?"

"Just over a year. Married for six months. If we're newly-weds, it's forgivable if we don't know everything about each other."

"How did I propose?"

"You took me on a picnic at the beach. Got down on one knee. Nothing flashy."

"Down on a knee? With all that sand? That doesn't sound like my style at all." He flashed his cheesiest grin.

She rolled her eyes. "So how would you propose?"

"I've never thought about proposing to anyone, but it definitely would involve a helicopter."

"That's absurd."

"Fine," Preston grumbled in mock despair. "Have it your way. We'll roll with the down-on-one-knee-in-the-dirt cliché. But how about you? What do you do for a living? I can't say bodyguard. Or ninja."

Laila laughed. At least he'd pulled a reaction out of her that had broken through her all-about-business demeanor.

"Do you even know what a ninja is?" she asked.

"A crime-fighting turtle, last time I checked."

Another giggle escaped her mouth. He could get used to the sound of her laughter.

"Who knew Preston Whittaker has such a goofy side?" she said. "I'll alert the six o'clock news."

"There's a lot you don't know about me." And he hadn't scratched the surface of discovering what made this woman tick. She flashed him one of her hundred-watt smiles, and he wondered if it was real or just her character taking over.

"Well, I'm definitely not a ninja. We'll tell everyone that I'm an interior designer. That way I can check out the place while researching the history and the architecture of the estate."

Preston stared at his "wife." The woman in front of him was a complete mystery. Complex didn't even begin to describe her, and he had to sell their relationship as if he really were in love.

They rounded the corner and turned onto his childhood street. The scene at the Whittaker estate resembled an outdoor concert. People camped out in lawn chairs as if waiting for a parade. Cameras and reporters dotted the road leading to the house. Police barricades held the crowds back.

Flashes ricocheted through the SUV like bolts of lightning.

When the driver pulled up to the gate, the crowd pushed forward. Security attempted to keep onlookers away from the vehicle, but the paparazzi shouted rapid-fire questions. Someone tapped on the window while others pressed in for a chance to glimpse inside.

"Preston, you should get down." Laila nodded toward the car floor. "You're too exposed and anyone could take a shot. I can't see around this mob."

"Are you always this bossy?" he grumbled.

"Yes."

Great. She was bossy while he was stubborn. What a fantastic way to kick off a fake relationship. "Who's going to shoot me with this much security and police around? I'll be fine."

Preston watched the scene unfold around the car. The police moved the crowds away from the car. Throngs of people were still pressing against the vehicle. He recognized a few of the reporters, like the ones that had trailed him around town in his former life. He'd gotten to know a few of them and had occasionally granted exclusive interviews to the reporters that weren't over the top in their pursuit of a headline story.

A shot cracked through the air.

Piercing screams ripped through the SUV. The crowd scattered. Blood speckled the car window, and a reporter clutched his shoulder and dropped to the ground.

Preston hit the floor at the same moment Laila threw herself on top of him. His arms and legs trembled. Had that bullet been meant for him?

"Charlie, get us out of here!" Laila shouted over the chaos outside the vehicle.

The SUV lurched forward. "Wha— What happened?" Preston asked from his blocked vantage point with Laila on top of him. He stared into brown eyes that mirrored his own horror and confusion.

"Someone took a shot. I didn't see the shooter," Charlie yelled from the front seat. "But that had to have been a sniper, someone with long-range skills."

Laila peered out the window, and Charlie continued to maneuver the car toward the estate.

The clank of the metal gate signaled they'd reached the house and were free from the crowd. Not that Preston felt any safer. Had he brought trouble to his mother's doorstep by simply showing up?

"Do you think the shooter was aiming for Preston?" Laila asked Charlie.

"I don't know. I saw the reporter clutch his shoulder before falling."

"That reporter. The one who was shot. I...I think I remember him," Preston said. "Colton Larkin. A local journalist."

What if Colton had taken the bullet that'd had Preston's name on it? Preston raised a shaky hand and covered his mouth. "Is Colton dead?" he asked Laila.

She had moved back to the seat but stayed low with her ear pressed to her phone. Preston's heartbeat whooshed so loud in his ears that he couldn't make out her end of the conversation. He attempted to move to the seat, but Laila waved for him to stay down. Visions of the blood-spattered reporter tore through his mind. *Please, God, let the man live.*

Laila dropped her phone into her purse. "Looks like the journalist will make it," she said. "I just talked to Steven, and the paramedics were close by because of the crowds. The man was shot clean through the shoulder, and they're tending to him now. The police are looking for the shooter."

Preston sucked in a deep breath. "I can't live with anyone dying on my account."

Laila extended a hand, and he moved from the floor to the seat. "I'm not going to let that happen."

"We're not going to let that happen," Charlie called from the front seat.

"Thanks for navigating us through that scene." Preston shuddered. What kind of trouble had he brought to his family's doorstep?

Charlie nodded and headed up the driveway toward the garage. "I wouldn't put it past the paparazzi to send out an army of drones to snap pictures," Preston said. "At least the landscaping blocks the view from the street."

"Don't worry," Laila replied, always one step ahead of him. "When the travel plans were being drawn up, I insisted that we have cover to avoid any aerial intrusion. We're pulling directly into the garage."

Nothing like being a prisoner in your own home.

Charlie pulled into the five-car garage, parked, and opened the back-seat door. Preston got out and willed his legs to cooperate. He'd have time later to process this ordeal in private. Right now, his family needed him to be strong.

He extended his hand to Laila to help her. She looked at him and smiled. "Smooth moves, Preston," she said, her voice soft.

She took his hand and held it. Her grip was solid, but could she feel the adrenaline coursing through his body? Between the reporter getting gunned down and the impending family meeting, his nerves raced. But no turning back now. They were officially a couple from this point forward.

Preston led her up through the garage. At the door to the house, they were greeted by a smiling face. He let go of Laila's hand to give the man a hug. "Julian. I can't believe it's you." He gave the estate manager a slap on the shoulder.

Julian had been a permanent fixture of the place, and it was a relief to find that some things had stayed the same. But familiarity gave way to a reality check at the sight of the man's almost-all-white hair and the fine lines around his eyes. Five years had weathered his old friend.

"Preston." Julian returned the hug. "So glad to have you back. We've missed you around here."

"I wish I had returned on better terms. Please keep an eye out for the police. They'll be arriving shortly."

"I heard a few details from security," Julian said, his voice somber. "The media presence upset your mother. The doctor prescribed something for stress."

Leave it to Julian to care for his mother after all these years, while warning Preston as to the state he might find her in. Drugged and blissfully unaware. Just one more thing that had stayed the same.

"Julian, this is my wife, Laila." Julian blinked at the news but masked his shock like a pro. The man had learned to suppress his reactions after working for the Whittakers since Preston was five years old.

"I hadn't been told of your marriage. Congratulations to you both. So lovely to meet you, Laila."

Julian ushered them inside through the door that led to the entry hall of the house. Five years away had erased some of the memories of growing up in an 11,000-square-foot mansion. He'd forgotten the cavernous feel of the foyer with its vaulted ceilings and grand staircase gracing both sides of the room.

"Wow," Laila whispered. "Just...wow."

Julian looked over his shoulder and kicked off his spiel about the estate, delight lighting his face as he spoke. "The Whittaker estate was built in 1927, and the family has kept it up over the years. The house has ten bedrooms, a conservatory, and a library. I'd love to show you around after you have lunch on the lanai with Preston's sister and mother."

"I'd love a tour, Julian," Laila said, spinning around for a three-sixty view of the ornate architecture.

Despite sheltering him from the cold outside, the house did nothing to warm Preston. To him, it was just a big house. Most of his fond memories as a child were tied to Sebastian's place.

They headed to the back of the house, and before they reached the lanai a sharp voice greeted them.

"There's no way you're taking over the company. Over my dead body."

Yep. No matter how much time had passed, some things were still very predictable.

5

TUESDAY, 1:00 P.M.

Laila watched a tall brunette stomp toward Preston like a bull stalking a matador. Warning bells ricocheted in Laila's head, and her protective instincts flared. Based on the woman's designer dress, pristine makeup, and flawless hair, she assumed this was Preston's sister, Katrina Pace.

"You can't seriously expect that you're the best person to run the company?" Katrina spat. "You left us." She poked her perfectly manicured finger in Preston's chest.

Laila wanted to knock some sense into the woman, but Preston beat her to it with his words. "A man was just shot outside our house. Get your priorities straight."

A woman rose from the couch and enveloped Preston into a weak hug. She then turned and wrapped her arms around Laila in a half-hearted limp embrace, as if she were too fragile for contact.

"Welcome, darling. I'm Sophia, Preston's mother. So glad you could make it. Preston never introduces us to his girlfriends, so this is a real treat." She nearly spilled her drink on Laila—a glass that contained alcohol from the smell of it.

Concern over Sophia gave Laila pause. If she took medicine to deal with stress, should she be drinking?

Poor Preston. Some homecoming.

It had been five years since Katrina had seen Preston, and yet the woman had verbally assaulted him. And his mom was blitzed. From what little Laila knew of Preston's father, no one ever described Walt as warm or kind, and it was apparent that his legacy lingered in the remnants of his family. There would be no welcome home reception for her client.

A chill settled into Laila's bones, and it had nothing to do with the draft flowing through the large rooms of the estate.

This was Preston's life. Or former life. *Cold* and *lonely* were the best words she could think of to describe it.

"Come, sit down." Sophia waved Laila toward the couch. Whatever the doctor had prescribed had done the trick, because the matriarch of the family was in her happy place. Sophia downed her drink in three gulps. A butler placed a new drink in her hand before she sat down.

Preston clarified the girlfriend comment. "Mom, a lot has changed since I left. Laila is my wife."

Silence followed Preston's announcement. Mrs. Whittaker's eyes filled with tears, while Katrina's glare intensified. No one spoke, until Laila couldn't take it anymore. She crossed the room and sat next to Sophia on the love seat. "It's a pleasure to meet all of you. I wish it were under better circumstances."

Katrina huffed, tossing her mane around her shoulder. "You got married and didn't tell anyone?" She directed the question at Preston but stared Laila down like she was sizing up her competition. And she wasn't finished. "So typical. You cut us out of your life, and we're supposed to welcome you and your wife with open arms now that you've returned?"

Laila refused to be baited by a reality-star wannabe. But instead of anger taking over, another emotion rose to the surface. A foreign feeling that resembled pity.

Since Katrina posted everything she did online, Laila had been able to do plenty of research on Preston's sister before they'd arrived. The woman had built her life out of her celebrity status and then had to work double time to keep up appearances. From her provocative low-cut dress to her Botox-injected lips, the twenty-three-year-old spent time and money destroying her natural beauty to stay perpetually youthful. And for what? So the world would extend her fifteen minutes of fame?

Laila glanced at Preston, who ignored his sister's outburst and sat down next to Laila, taking her hand. He could have lived his life just like this, and yet somehow, he'd traded high society drama for a simpler life.

Her admiration for Preston increased. He'd walked away from a clearly toxic environment to become a better man. Most people would have been so enamored by money and power, like his sister, that they'd have clung to the superficial stuff. But not Preston. He'd traded money for the chance at a fresh start and seemed to be better for it.

When no one responded to her dramatic flare-up, Katrina flipped her hair behind her shoulder and sniffed. "Whatever. Preston, you haven't been here. Derek's been working tirelessly for Daddy since you ditched us. He should be the new CEO. He's worked for it. You haven't."

As if Katrina's rant was a rehearsed speech, Derek ambled into the room on cue. The man looked like a mannequin from a high-end department store—stiff, hollow, and a hundred percent plastic. His navy-blue suit and matching skinny tie screamed money. Even his painted-on smile matched his effort to look the part of a corporate big shot. He had at least five years on Katrina.

The room defrosted a bit when Derek introduced himself to Laila before dropping into a chair across from her and placing his drink on the coffee table.

"Now, Katrina, play nice," Derek said. "Preston's been home for less than an hour. Let's give the man a chance. We don't know where he's been or what he's been up to."

Laila sized up her new "brother-in-law." What did Derek have to gain if Preston wasn't back in town? The man had the sincerity of a used car salesman, and she had a feeling the guy wouldn't think twice about stabbing Preston in the back to get his grubby hands on a promotion.

Katrina huffed to retake the center of attention. "You did so much to help Daddy, and now he's gone. And what did Preston do? Where's he been? This is so unfair. Too bad the rumors weren't true. Why couldn't you have stayed dead, Preston?"

Preston flinched and started to say something, then pressed his lips together in a hard line. Laila could tell the effort cost him. A lot. She almost bit her own tongue in two to stay silent.

Katrina turned to Preston. "You won't last a second in Daddy's job," she spat. "All Derek needs to do is wait until you mess up. Maybe the board will offer him the position once he's there to pick up the pieces after you tank the company."

Laila sucked in a breath and moved to stand up, but Preston tightened his grip on her hand and she stilled. Wow. No wonder Preston had left home.

Welcome to the world of the rich and self-absorbed.

The family lived their public lives in front of a camera while their private lives crumbled around them. Laila hadn't spoken to her brother in a few months, but there wasn't a raging bitterness and animosity between them like what was playing out in front of her. At least Mrs. Whittaker showed a layer of empathy for Preston underneath her inebriated state.

Laila seized the opportunity to score some brownie points with Sophia while tuning out Katrina's high-pitched whine. "Thanks for hosting us. I love what you've done with this house. Who's your decorator?"

"Oh, I did most of the design myself. My favorite pieces are the Berringer rocking chairs. They're handmade and unique. Quite pricey, but I just had to have them." An exquisite pair of hand-carved rockers faced the large picture window that over-looked the garden.

Sophia droned on about architecture and color schemes, all of which held little interest for Laila. But she nodded and smiled in all the right places. "Wow, I can't wait to check out the rest of the house," Laila said. Katrina rolled her eyes, and Laila imagined going head-to-head with her in the boxing ring. She bit her lip on the smile that thought produced.

A doorbell chimed, and a minute later, Julian stepped into the room to announce that the police needed to question Laila and Preston. The tension in Laila's shoulders unwound a bit. She'd been counting the seconds until this get-together would end.

Sophia paled, waving a limp hand until it rested on her forehead. "How awful. I can't take it."

Concern washed over Preston's face. Sophia might not be mother of the year, but clearly Preston's love ran deep for her.

Laila had firsthand experience with dealing with an alco-holic mother, so she understood the conflict he battled. After her parents' divorce, she was left to pick up the shattered pieces of her family. She flashed back to the aftermath of her mother's drinking binges and immediately stuffed the grief into the mental lockbox she'd created for those memories.

Preston knelt in front of Sophia and put a hand over hers.

"Why don't you go upstairs and rest. Laila and I will deal with things, get settled in, then be ready for the dinner tonight."

Sophia stood with the aid of a maid, who appeared from out of nowhere. What would it be like to have invisible people jump out of the shadows and take care of one's every need? Laila would never know and wasn't sorry for the fact.

Preston took Laila's hand and helped her up from the couch. Sophia turned to her. "I'm so glad Preston has you in his life. He needs someone who will look out for him. He's been alone far too long." She flashed what appeared to be an authentic smile and ambled toward a private elevator, staff in tow.

Preston walked Laila through the main atrium, never letting go of her hand even though no one was watching them. Sophia's fairly lucid comment replayed in Laila's mind. Once the truth came out, Sophia might need some stronger stress pills.

The place was a maze of hallways and wings that extended out from the center room that looked more like a hotel lobby than a home. She'd studied the layout of the house, but to see it in person, she might need to use the GPS on her phone to navigate her way.

"Do you think your mother and sister bought our act?" Laila asked, very aware of her hand tucked inside Preston's even though there wasn't a soul in sight.

"I don't think they suspect that we're lying to them. My mom seems to relate to you, but Katrina thinks everyone is hiding something. She's always sniffing out gossip to sell to the highest bidder." He sighed. "My sister isn't a bad person. Don't let first impressions taint your view of her. She just prioritizes fame and money over acting like a normal human being sometimes. Underneath the layers of makeup and hairspray is a kind heart."

Laila gave a sideways glance at Preston as they walked to the library. Even with the train wreck they'd just witnessed, not to mention Katrina's vicious outbursts, Preston looked past their craziness and saw the best in his family.

Preston offered her a thirty second tour of the various rooms as they walked. The haunting beauty of the structure contrasted with the contemporary decor. The stark white walls and marble floors screamed modern, hiding the rustic and earthy bones of the original architecture.

"I looked at the floor plan before we came and noted the existence of a few secret passages that seem to lead behind this main area. That's going to make security a challenge."

"I'm sure you memorized the entire layout." Preston grinned. "I'll have to show you a few of them. The waitstaff use them during parties because, of course, we Whittakers can't have our servants seen." He mocked a snobby accent, and she stifled a laugh. "It's all part of the estate's history. It was built in the '20s, but we've done a lot of work to keep it up."

If she closed her eyes, Laila could envision flappers dancing the night away in the original splendor of the place, reminiscent of *The Great Gatsby*.

They walked into the library, where Quinn Holcombe and Steven Rothwell waited. Built-in bookshelves graced the walls, filled with everything from the classics to contemporary novels. Several chairs overlooked the expansive grounds of the estate. Laila wouldn't leave Preston's side on this assignment, but the room beckoned her to lock herself away for a few hours and lose herself in a good book.

"Nice digs you've got here, Mrs. Whittaker," Quinn said, not masking his sarcasm.

Laila shot him a look that said he'd better watch himself. "What's happening outside?"

"We found the spot where the sniper took the shot," Steven

said. "Of course, he was long gone, but we're looking for someone with skills."

"Was the killer randomly shooting people, or was that bullet meant for me?" Preston asked.

Quinn snorted. "You don't hire a sniper for a random attack. Our unknown suspect planned this, and I'd say that Larkin was the intended target. If he'd been aiming for you, you'd be dead."

Preston paced the room, not venturing near the big picture window. "I've met Colton a few times. He was a reporter who used to follow me around, but he was nice about it. I got to know him and occasionally granted him interviews or photo ops. Why would he be the target? It doesn't make any sense." He stopped moving, rubbed his chin, and frowned. "Unless the killer is sending a message. Sebastian had offered an exclusive interview with me to one reporter and had picked Colton. I think he'd even reached out to coordinate. I wonder if this is another warning. That no one's safe around me."

Laila's mind spun to untangle a spiderweb of clues but came up empty. Why shoot a reporter? And who might be the next target?

Because if her first impressions of the situation were correct, who could be a bigger target than Preston Whittaker's wife?

Once the officers had taken statements, Preston showed Laila the rest of the house since Julian was occupied. He pushed the images of the shooting from his mind.

Exhaustion had taken its toll on him, and Laila looked like she'd been hit by a truck. Her pale face and tired eyes proved that this woman wasn't unstoppable after all. Even the best superheroes needed to rest and recharge before saving the world again.

He stopped at the room they would share. *Let the awkwardness begin.* Because that's what married couples did. They shared a bedroom. "My mother gave us the guest suite. At least it's separate from the rest of the family." He breathed a sigh of relief that they weren't stuck in his old bedroom. Not that he hadn't snuck girls into that room in the past, but he didn't need the flood of memories from his childhood taunting him. What he wouldn't give for his mountain cabin back in Magellan Falls.

He opened the door and Laila stepped in. "It's only two o'clock, and my mom will want pre-dinner drinks at five," Preston said. "She's invited a few people over, but at least we can rest for a bit. Maybe you can catch a nap."

Laila said nothing and surveyed the room, probably looking for possible security breaches. At least the suite had ample space for them to stay out of each other's way if it came down to that.

The king-sized bed created a focal point for the room, but a sitting area off to the side might keep the peace between them, because he could sleep on the full-size sofa.

Preston sighed. "We have to share a room, or the rumor of our divorce will be headline news before they announce that I'm married. And us in separate bedrooms would tip off my sister in a heartbeat that something isn't right in the relationship. I can sleep on the sofa, and you can have the bed." He paused and let Laila process. "And just so you are aware, I'll keep my hands to myself at all times. I've seen you in action, and I don't want to lose a hand when you whip out a samurai sword in self-defense. I know better."

Laila shook her head. "I prefer Chinese throwing stars, but

whatever," she muttered. But he scored a hint of a smile from her.

The walk-in closet was bigger than his bedroom back home in Magellan Falls. His mom must have asked the staff to buy clothes for him, because the closet held a variety of outfits, and he hadn't packed that much. "I can request the maid to do some shopping for you. Did you bring something to wear for dinner tonight?"

"Right. I guess dinner is a formal event." Laila opened her small suitcase and riffled through a few things. "Christina packed for me, and it looks like she threw in a dress. I should be good."

Laila carved her usual path to the window to peer out the blinds, never dropping her guard for a second. Looking over her shoulder, she said, "You take the bed. I'm not going to sleep much with a killer on the loose. I can't be sleeping on the job while protecting you."

"So you're just going to fall over from exhaustion? Brilliant plan." Preston tossed a blanket and pillow from the bed onto the couch.

Laila retrieved her suitcase and stuck it on the other side of the sofa. "You're not sleeping on the couch. Tomorrow is your first day of work. You'll need to stay sharp. Can't have you looking so...so..."

"What do I look like? Just say it."

"Homeless."

Laughter erupted from the depths of him, and he let it roll. It felt good. No, it felt *great*. When was the last time he'd laughed like that? He couldn't remember. "That's one way to put it. I live in the woods. This is how I dress now. I kind of like it."

Laila sat on the blanket with her, arms crossed. "I'm not moving. You take the bed."

"What are we, twelve? We can be adults and compromise. We'll take turns."

"I've got a job to do, remember? You take the bed. I'll be fine."

Preston moved her bag and sank down next to her. "Are you ever off the job?"

"My *job* is to keep you alive. Do you want me going off the clock?"

He needed to make an effort to get to know this impossible woman. After all, they were stuck together. But she was a complex labyrinth, filled with quicksand and land mines. And he had a feeling she wasn't letting anyone near her heart. Not that he wanted to be.

And at the same time, that only made him want to try harder.

"So how do you do it?" he asked. "I mean the undercover work. You're a pro. But how do you keep yourself separate from it? I know what it's like to live life on a stage, but what you do has got to take a toll."

Silence hung between them for a moment. Would she even answer? Maybe he should have started with something more innocuous and asked her what toppings she liked on her pizza.

"I can't talk about my undercover days," she finally said. "But it makes it hard to have a normal life, one with friends or a family. I haven't done undercover work in a while, so we'll see how well our little act goes."

"I take it you're not married. If so, I'm sure your husband would like to kill me right about now."

Laila flashed a brilliant smile, and his heart skipped a beat. What was that about?

"Not married. Not dating anyone. I'm fine on my own."

"I can't imagine you on a first date. You're intimidating.

What man would stand a chance? Has any man lived long enough for a second date?"

Something flashed through Laila's eyes that looked a lot like sorrow. He'd definitely struck a nerve. Caused her pain. "I'm sorry, I was just joking—and obviously, it was a bad one."

"It's okay. If we're going to be married, I have to get used to someone being in my personal space. Let's just say I was engaged once, and it ended badly."

"Oh, I'm sorry. I didn't mean to pour salt on an old wound. But you can look up any of my ex-girlfriends with a quick Google search if it makes you feel any better. You obviously know my track record." Heat crept up his neck, and he wanted to look away. But he kept his eyes fixed on hers. "But I've changed now."

He could tell from her reaction that she wasn't sure whether to believe him or not. At least she hadn't laughed out loud. "It's true," he said. "I'm not the party guy anymore. I left that life in the dust. Just so you know, I haven't even been on a date since I left."

For some reason, he desperately wanted Laila to overlook his past and realize that he hated the man he used to be.

"Now, that I don't believe," she said. "You're Preston Whittaker. What are the tabloids going to print now?"

"Um, tomorrow they'll think I'm married."

She laughed. A short, low sound that drew him like a magnet. "Right," she said. "Well, I guess it will be a shock to the world when this is over and you can announce that you're back on the market."

He scrubbed a hand over his face and sighed. "I hate lying to everyone. That's the part I can't get over. The old Preston lied about everything. But how are people ever going to believe I've changed when they learn I've been lying since day one of my return?"

"Everyone's got their own secrets. People rarely tell the truth. Your lie is no different than the next guy's. And this diversion is helping to save your life. Isn't that justification for what we're doing?"

"I'm not sure my pastor friend would agree with you."

She blinked. "I forgot you were a churchgoer now."

"I told you I've changed my ways. That's why it's so hard for me to return. I feel like I'm about to lose myself again when I'm just figuring out who I am."

"Who are you?"

Preston paused. She'd turned the tables on him with that question.

How could he explain all that he'd learned over the past five years? He'd spent time and effort trying to redeem his past, make up for his numerous mistakes. It hadn't been until he'd let God fight his battles for him that Preston had felt like he could move forward with his own life. A life that wasn't scripted by everyone else.

But would Laila even believe him? For some reason, what she thought of him was important.

"I'm just a guy trying to do the right thing for once in his life." He shrugged, needing to divert the conversation away from himself. "Look, I don't want to give all of my secrets away at once." Especially since her story was a closed book, a mystery he couldn't wait to unravel.

He got up and went to the closet to find something to wear to dinner later. "You take a nap—in the bed, please—and I'll hit the shower. Apparently, I need to wash off this homeless look." And shake the anxiety pulsing through him.

Because how were they ever going to make it through dinner as a married couple?

"Shooting that reporter right in front of him ought to do the trick. Preston should be packing his bags as we speak."

"I pay you for results, not opinions. But that isn't going to scare Preston off. It's not enough."

Preston had moved himself into the estate. Coward. He'd hide behind iron gates and a security team that rivaled the President's.

"We need to hit him where it will hurt. If we can't kill him, we need to get to anyone he's associated with."

The list of targets formed without any effort.

His mother.

Sebastian.

The mystery woman.

Whoever she was, he'd moved her into the estate. But her identity wouldn't remain hidden forever.

"Tonight, at the dinner party. You'll go after the woman. I'll take care of Sebastian."

They'd take out everyone that Preston loved. If they couldn't get to him, they'd send him a message.

Welcome home, Preston. Too bad you're not welcome here.

6

TUESDAY, 4:40 P.M.

After her big speech about not sleeping on the job, Laila woke up from a two-hour nap.

The luxurious bed had tempted her and won. She stretched out on the satin sheets and checked her phone.

She bolted from the bed, adrenaline pumping. Good thing she was low maintenance, because she had twenty minutes to get ready.

Preston had left a note on the nightstand that he'd run to the kitchen for a snack. She debated following him but needed to get ready for dinner.

Her one-bedroom apartment could fit in the palatial bathroom. She jumped in the shower and washed her hair with a premium brand shampoo that probably cost ten times as much as the generic version that graced her shelves at home. But she had to admit, it smelled divine. Lingering in the hot stream of water would make her late, so she'd have to savor the rainfall shower head with fifteen different settings later.

While drying her hair and dabbing on makeup, she replayed the conversation from earlier with Preston. The one where he'd gotten under her skin by bringing up her relationship status.

Memories surfaced that she'd locked away, never letting them see the light of day. Why had she told Preston about her failed engagement? Her past would stay buried, and she'd be careful to not let her guard down again.

She threw on the dress Christina had packed for her and pushed the images from the past out of her mind. Time to get her head in the game. She had a job to do.

So maybe there was something to the hundred-dollars-an-ounce shampoo, because she caught her reflection in the mirror, and her long dark-brown strands fell perfectly into place. Preston had better notice her ability to get ready in under fifteen minutes—a feat most women couldn't pull off.

When she opened the bathroom door to the bedroom, a man she didn't recognize sat on the couch. Instinct drove Laila's hand to her sidearm with an automatic reflex only for her to realize that she didn't have her gun on her. Yet.

The stranger turned and she did a double take of the beardless man. "Preston?" He'd even cut his hair, now neat and trimmed versus wild and scraggly. His jeans and boots had been traded for a tailor-made suit.

"Does this ensemble meet your strict non-homeless dress code standard?" he asked.

Her mind scrambled to put together words to form a sentence. The man looked like he'd stepped off the cover of *GQ* magazine. She'd seen his image in the media a million times, but up close, she realized he lived up to every word of the hype.

And he hadn't taken his eyes off her in the sleek black dress either.

Normally Laila didn't wear anything so fancy—or so short.

What had Christina been thinking? But the silky material definitely made her feel like a rich wife.

Heat rose in her cheeks, and she moved to the door to avoid his gaze. "You look good. Just as everyone would expect for your first night back in the Whittaker mansion."

He rose to join her, and they walked to the atrium for drinks before dinner. Not that Laila would touch alcohol while protecting Preston.

Preston leaned in. "I'll introduce you to everyone," he whispered. "Later, you need to fill me in if anything sets off your inner spy detector."

Laila gave him a light jab in the ribs.

She recognized a few faces as they entered the atrium, from unpleasant ones like Katrina and Derek to some new people Laila hadn't met.

An older woman around the age of Preston's mother approached and wrapped her arms around Preston. Tears brimmed her swollen eyes. "Oh, Preston, isn't it all so dreadful what's happened?"

He extricated himself from her grasp and introduced her to Laila. "This is Margot Harrington, my father's right-hand woman. She is...or rather was, my dad's administrative assistant. Margot, this is my wife, Laila."

Margot's jaw dropped for a fraction of a second. "I—I hadn't heard about you getting married. But then again, after you disappeared, we weren't sure what had happened to you. I guess I should say, welcome to the family, Laila."

"Nice to meet you," Laila said.

"How is Seth doing?" Preston asked. "I heard he recently graduated from Harvard." He turned to Laila. "Seth is Margot's son."

Margot took a sip of her drink. "He finished grad school with a business degree. You should stop by and see him. He worked for your father, but I guess he works for you now." Her voice choked with emotion, but was her countenance for show or was the grief real?

The woman composed herself. "I hope you'll keep me on your staff. I work with the other executives, of course, but since I managed your father's schedule, you can step in and not miss a beat."

"Of course. I'd love to have you as my assistant. It will be a load off my mind to have you on my side to help me transition."

"Good. That's a relief." She hugged him one more time before excusing herself to refresh her drink.

Laila leaned in, putting her hand on Preston's arm. "Do you trust her?" Laila whispered in his ear, making it look like an intimate gesture. They were supposed to be married, after all.

"I don't trust anyone here, but Seth and I were childhood friends. He's a few years younger than I am. Seth followed me around a lot when I was in high school, so I let him tag along. His dad was never in the picture. Margot is another fixture at the Whittaker estate, and she definitely kept my dad organized."

Laila surveyed the area. Katrina and Derek stood in the corner, whispering and sending a quick glance toward Laila and Preston every so often. Sophia was engaged in conversation with Sebastian and Gloria, and from her body language, the woman had indulged in multiple cocktails since they'd last seen her.

An older man met her gaze, his dark eyes boring into Laila. He had a hawk-like appearance, with a pointy beak of a nose and a thin face. Then the man spotted Preston and his scowl softened. "Welcome back, son," the man said, slapping Preston on the back. "So good to see you, even under these terrible circumstances. I'm so sorry for your loss."

"Thank you, Bob. I'd like you to meet my wife. Laila, this is

Bob Zimmerman. The man who started the company with my dad." Preston's introduction landed with another shock-and-awe moment.

"I'm pleased to meet you," Bob said. "I'm Preston's new partner from the look of things."

Before she could reply, Bob turned to Preston, cutting her out of the conversation. She'd love a chance to show this guy her ninja skills, as Preston put it.

"I assume you'll be at the board meeting tomorrow?"

"I'll be there. Afterward, I'd like to schedule a press conference and officially announce my new role."

Bob's forced smile didn't reach his eyes. "Great. But let's keep your antics out of the media, because now you have to think about the company's reputation. You need to watch yourself, because the board won't tolerate any missteps."

Laila wanted to drop-kick the man for talking to Preston like he was a twelve-year-old. While she wasn't sure how much of Preston's good-guy routine she believed, he didn't need anyone muddying the waters on day one.

She snaked a hand around Preston's arm. "He's going to be better than his father at running the company. You just watch." She dragged Preston away from the sour man, suppressing her satisfaction at seeing his jaw swing open before he could snap it shut.

"Um, what was that?"

"He was getting on my nerves. Setting you up to fail without giving you a chance to even prove yourself. Maybe he'd do anything to get Whittaker Enterprises for himself."

"But it's one thing to be competitive. It's another thing to murder all of your competitors."

A petite blonde woman in a slinky red dress set her sights on Preston and approached. She draped him in a hug that seemed a little too familiar. *An old girlfriend maybe?*

Preston grabbed Laila's hand. "Laila, let me introduce you to my sister-in-law, Veronica. Ethan's wife."

"You've probably seen my two boys running the hallways of the estate. We live in the east wing." She turned to Preston. "Mom told me you'd gotten married. I'm so happy you've found someone." Veronica didn't seem distraught for just having lost her husband—or maybe it was just one too many cocktails making her seem ambivalent.

The two chatted about old times. Preston made every effort to include Laila in the conversation, but she didn't belong. These two obviously had a history, but she made a mental note to ask Preston about Veronica and added the sister-in-law to the ever-growing suspect list. Life insurance payouts often served as great motives for murder.

A loud crash halted all conversations. Glass shattered, and someone screamed. Laila stepped in front of Preston, protective instincts humming.

"Sebastian!" Gloria's horrified cry echoed in the sudden silence.

Preston pushed through the crowd while Laila followed.

Sebastian lay on the floor, surrounded by Gloria, Sophia, and other guests.

Preston rushed to his side. Laila checked to make sure someone had called 911 and then wrapped her arms around Gloria to keep the woman from falling apart.

"What happened?" Laila whispered.

"He...he said he felt faint and his chest hurt." Gloria sucked in a breath. "Then he grabbed his arm and just collapsed. He had a heart attack a few years ago and has been on medication ever since. Maybe the stress of everything brought on another heart attack." Gloria's tears tracked through her makeup to drip off her chin.

Could Preston have been right? Was the killer going after

people close to him to get his attention? Sebastian was a father figure to Preston, and now the man lay unconscious on the floor.

A neighbor of the Whittakers who happened to be a doctor arrived to assess the situation. Laila breathed a sigh of relief that someone was close by and could help.

Stepping away from the onlookers, she texted Steven and Charlie. Her instincts screamed that this wasn't a heart attack.

The paramedics arrived, and Julian ushered a few party guests into the dining room to give Sebastian and the medics some space.

"I should go with him," Preston said, never taking his eyes off Sebastian.

Laila moved close, wrapped her arm around his shoulders, and whispered. "Gloria's with him. I think you should stay here. Don't put yourself in danger."

"Me? Or the people I'm with?"

She sighed. "I wasn't going to put it that way, but we can't rule out the possibility that this was foul play. But until we know for sure, let's just watch your back."

He raked a hand over his newly shaved cheek. "Yeah." He spun on his heel and headed for the dining room.

The paramedics wheeled Sebastian out the front door with Gloria in tow. The other party guests had followed Preston into the dining room. While they were occupied, Laila asked the bartender for a napkin and an empty glass.

She noted that Sebastian's glass had shattered when he fell. Could this have been foul play? Laila picked up a few of the pieces with the napkin and stuck them in the empty glass. One piece still had some liquid cradled in the groove of the fragment. She did her best to keep it intact.

Charlie and Steven appeared from behind a wall. "I need

to get a house with secret passages," Charlie said. "Rich people get all the cool stuff."

"I'm sure your fiancée would love that." She shook her head. "Here." She grabbed another linen napkin and wrapped it around the glass, then handed it to Steven. "I don't think this was an accident."

"He had a history of heart issues, but I'm not ruling anything out," Steven said. "I'll send this to the lab and have my guys sweep the area for any evidence."

Laila headed to the dining room and took a seat at the table next to Preston, scanning the faces around her for any clues that might give away a traitor. Because if Sebastian had been poisoned, someone in this room was behind it.

Preston's pulse jackhammered a steady pounding rhythm in his head. Sebastian had been targeted. There was no doubt in his mind. Someone was going after anyone close to him.

After dinner, the throbbing headache made the perfect excuse to call it an early night. A few guests lingered, but the party had dwindled after Sebastian's collapse.

Preston had kept an eye on Laila the entire evening, which wasn't a hard task. Her killer black dress and spiky heels drove his imagination wild as he tried to guess where she'd stashed her weapon under the form-fitting attire.

As for playing the role of wife, her performance deserved an Academy Award. Her constant touches to his arm and her adoring glances had made it all seem so real.

But while she'd made a convincing wife, the bodyguard in her had never stopped looking for suspects or danger. Stealth and beauty intertwined to create an intriguing combination. He could spend the rest of his life trying to understand this woman and probably never scratch the surface—unless she let him. But he wouldn't get the chance. Once they caught the killer, their sham relationship would be over faster than it had started.

As they walked toward the bedroom, he couldn't shake Sebastian and Colton from his mind. His throat tightened and his lungs begged for some fresh air. If he couldn't get back to his reclusive cabin, at least he could get out of the house. "Can we take a walk outside?" he whispered to Laila. "I need air. I'm feeling trapped in this house."

Laila's eyes widened. "Someone with a long-range rifle shot a reporter today. I don't think we should be outside."

She had a point.

"What about the backyard garden? It's got tall shrubbery strategically placed to block out a telephoto lens. Can we at least sit on the patio? We'll keep the lights off and stick close to the building. I miss my mountain air. This house reminds me of a crypt."

Laila conceded and called Charlie to check out the area. After the shooting of the reporter, Preston had requested that Charlie move into the garage apartment to give his undercover chauffeur an excuse to have access to the grounds at all times.

Once they had the all clear, Preston asked Julian to grab their coats. A chill had crept into the October evening once the sun had gone down. "I want to show you something." With an automatic reflex, Preston grabbed Laila's hand. Part of him figured it kept up the ruse, the other part simply wanted an excuse to hold her hand. Somehow, her presence had steadied him during the tragedies of the day.

"Where are we going?"

"Check this out." He pulled Laila behind the stairwell in the atrium. She followed without question. "Watch." He placed his hand on the wall and, with a little push, slid the panel to the right. "You mentioned the secret passageways. Well, here's one of them."

Her eyes squinted and she tilted her head. "How can I keep you safe if people swoop in and out of rooms through hidden tunnels?"

"Only a few people know these exist, other than through rumors. And there's no access to the guest suite, so we should be safe enough."

The small, dark passageway ran parallel to several rooms and ended with a doorway that led to the lanai. Antique candelabras retrofitted with modern lightbulbs provided enough light for them to see but added to the overall creepiness of the area. Laila's eyes told Preston she wasn't impressed with the less-than-stellar security hidden entrances would provide.

"It's not that bad," Preston said. "There are just a few rooms that have a second entrance. Like this sitting room. The kitchen is on the other side of this hallway, making it convenient for the staff to get from one place to another."

He pulled a latch on the wall, and the bookcase in the room swung inward. He showed Laila how to slip in and out of the room virtually undetected. "Don't worry. The library we were in earlier is one of the rooms that has total privacy. That's why I picked it when the police arrived."

Preston swung the bookcase open again, and they were walking through the corridor when voices stopped them in their tracks. Laila put her finger to her lips, and he nodded. Leave it to the spy to want to eavesdrop.

"Look, once Preston makes a mockery of himself, the position will be yours."

Preston mouthed *Bob* for Laila to identify the speaker.

"And you're sure he'll fail?" *Derek.*

"I'm a hundred percent positive he won't make it a week.

He'll be up to his old antics in no time. Let's just say I've got the board supporting me on this one."

The men's conversation shifted to the stock market, and Laila nudged Preston to continue on. Preston's stomach soured from the conversation, but he pressed on toward the door that led to the lanai where they could access the garden.

"We don't have to go far," Preston said. "Just enough for some fresh air." He stopped at the half wall dividing the patio from the garden.

Laila glared at him. "Just stick close to the house. I don't want you out in the open."

Preston rolled his eyes but complied, leaning back against the brick exterior wall.

His mind replayed the overheard conversation. Was Bob such a bully that he'd sabotage Preston's first day at work? And what about that promise to Derek? Had Derek been conspiring behind his father's back to gain a higher position in the company? Both men would put profits before people, something Preston's father would never have done.

He looked at Laila, her hair rippling in the gentle breeze. She'd been quiet since dinner. "What's on your mind?" He hoped she'd refute Bob's claims and tell him he was the right man for the job.

She filled him in on her suspicions about Sebastian being poisoned, confirming his own fears. More victims at his expense.

They stood in silence for a few moments. Laila looked at him, concern flooding her eyes. "You never told me your side of the story about why you left."

"You presumed me guilty just like the rest of the world." He shrugged, the fight leaving him. While he didn't want to rehash his past mistakes with Laila, maybe he should offer her something other than a superficial response. Would she understand?

"Sorry. It's none of my business," she said. "But I want to hear your perspective on the events. I can make assumptions or find speculations on the internet, but would rather hear it from you. Would you tell me?"

The moon illuminated the shrubbery, casting flickering shadows across the landscape. But this matched his mood perfectly when dredging up buried memories. Haunted by the ghosts of his past, he hid from conversations that made him want to run and never stop.

His resolve melted when he looked into Laila's dark-brown eyes. For a split second, he wondered if he could trust her. "You're my wife, so I guess there aren't many off-limit topics."

He sighed at the look on her face. She'd never accept some surface-level response. Something about the way she glanced at him gave his confidence a boost. "The lawsuit was dismissed, but that doesn't make me innocent. Plus, we all know my family paid her family off in our traditional hush-hush fashion."

Images from the past flooded his mind. "You've seen my family. The Whittakers are every bit as shallow and selfish as the media portrays, and I was just like them." He paused, taking a deep breath. He'd never told his version of the story, and it was harder than he'd imagined voicing his deepest pain. "I had stopped at a party that night with a girl that I'd been seeing. The scene was lame, so I took off without finding my date to take her home. I abandoned her, and she overdosed on drugs in the bathroom. If I had been responsible and taken care of her, she'd be alive."

"Oh my. I'm so sorry. That's a heavy burden to carry."

"Very." He shook his head.

"Although, in my experience, if she was using drugs,

chances are she'd have overdosed at some other point anyway. You can't take responsibility for someone else's choices."

"Well, her family thought I was to blame, so they brought a civil suit. They claimed I supplied her drugs and left her to die. For what it's worth, I didn't do drugs. Alcohol was my vice. But the burden I carry isn't what happened but more who I was back then. I only cared about myself. I abandoned her at the party, and when someone told me that Chelsea Berringer had died—" He paused, forming his next words. Would she think less of him if she discovered the whole truth? Maybe, but he forged on. "I didn't recognize the name. I'd gone out with her, had even slept with her, and I didn't even know her name."

He'd never admitted that to anyone and half expected Laila to flinch or storm off in a whirlwind of disgust. But she remained still. "You disappeared out of guilt and for a chance at a fresh start," she murmured. "Where people wouldn't know your name. Where your past didn't have a choke hold on you."

For a moment, he couldn't speak. She'd seen into his head... his heart...so clearly.

"I couldn't shake the image of Chelsea dying alone in some bathroom, scared and drugged out of her mind. I just kept replaying the events of my life on a never-ending loop. The parties, the endless flow of alcohol, the women. I hated myself and wanted to quit my life. Stop being the media darling that sold newspapers for every outlandish thing I did. Because at that moment in time, I realized that if Chelsea had died, it was very possible I'd be next."

He'd bared more of his soul than he'd intended. A hole ached in his heart that never seemed to heal. No matter how much time separated him from those events, the wound throbbed like it had happened yesterday.

"I left with no money, no fame, no Whittaker moniker strangling me to death. Walked away with nothing, not even my name. My father had groomed my brother to take over the company. No one expected me to amount to anything, so why stick around? I had nothing, and what I found on the other side of this façade was freedom. The ability to make my own choices and be my own man."

"They aren't right about you," she said. "Bob and Derek are wrong. You can do this. They may get in your way, but you've faced bigger obstacles than a couple of rich guys trying to leech every dime out of your family."

He looked into Laila's eyes and saw no condemnation. She didn't judge him based on the sum total of all his bad choices, like everyone else had.

She saw something in him that others had overlooked his whole life.

Laila broke eye contact to scan the yard for any signs of trouble. She turned back to him. "Thank you for telling me the truth."

Preston shuffled his feet, warmth chasing away the chilly night air. "After living the way I did for so long, I don't want to lie to anyone."

A gust of wind took Laila's scarf, and she bent over to pick it up. A whoosh sounded next to Preston's ear, and the plaster on the wall behind them exploded. Right in the spot Laila had just stood.

"Sniper!" Laila yelled, and they both hit the ground.

7

TUESDAY, 9:00 P.M.

"Do you have eyes on the shooter?" Laila yelled to Charlie through the phone just as Preston rose and raced in the direction of the shooter. "Preston! Get back here!"

Was the man out of his mind? Why was he running toward the shooter? Her eyes scanned the horizon for any sign of trouble as she got up and raced after him.

"What were you thinking?" Laila gasped for breath as she caught up with Preston by the wrought iron fence that lined the edge of the property. At least no other shots had been fired, but they were out in the open and exposed.

"I just can't stand doing nothing." Preston ran a shaky hand through his hair. "This has to end. You could have been killed. I won't let anyone else die because of me."

Charlie sprinted toward them. "I didn't see anyone. Security did a sweep of this area not more than twenty minutes ago. Everything was quiet. I've already called Quinn and Steven to let them know."

Preston's face paled. "That shot was meant for Laila."

Charlie nodded. "It wasn't from a long distance, and I suspect the shooter had access to the grounds."

Laila looked at Charlie. "If you check out the rest of the area, I'll get Preston back inside."

They walked toward the house, Laila examining every tree branch rustling from the wind as if someone might jump out and attack them. "What were you thinking? A sniper could've picked you off when you crossed the garden. You should have stayed close to the house."

"I can't stand feeling so helpless. I'm sick of hiding."

Laila tamped down her irritation. She had one job, to protect Preston. And she'd failed.

They never should have gone outside. But what would happen tomorrow, when he went to work while the whole world clamored to see him?

Julian had escorted Quinn and Steven into the library. The two hadn't left the last crime scene, and now they had a new one to contain.

"Can't you stay out of trouble for five minutes?" Quinn asked Laila when she entered the library.

She wasn't in the mood for Quinn's sarcasm. "Sebastian's fainting reeks of foul play, but that bullet was aimed at me." Her chest tightened. Her own safety was one thing, but had she made a mistake by letting Preston outside? He could have easily been the intended target.

Steven sighed and looked up from his notebook. "It looks like the killer is sending a message to Preston. We'll know more tomorrow when the toxicology report comes back from the remnants of Sebastian's drink." He turned to Laila and Preston. "Are you two going to be okay?"

Preston shook his head, stress written in the fine lines of his face. "How did someone get into the estate? Security was tight."

Ideas buzzed through Laila's brain. "Someone from the party might have been the shooter, or at least let the gunman in."

Steven nodded. "We're planning on questioning the party guests first thing in the morning."

Katrina and Derek lingered in the atrium as Preston and Laila escorted the detectives to the front door—probably trying to glean any juicy details to blast out over the internet. Had Katrina been livestreaming the police presence in her home? The woman had no shame. The hardened expression on Quinn's face was enough to send Katrina scampering away with her camera phone.

Would Preston's sister be so vain that she'd let a sniper in just so she'd have some drama for her social media? Laila mentally moved Katrina up the suspect list. The woman had it in for her brother, but just how far would she go?

Laila itched to check the perimeter with Charlie, but knew she'd better not let Preston out of her sight.

As she followed him to the bedroom, exhaustion nipped at her heels, but she pushed on, prepping herself mentally for a sleepless night. No one was getting to her client on her watch. Not again.

They reached the bedroom, but Preston blocked the door. "Laila, it's not your fault."

"What are you talking about?" She looked around to check for eavesdroppers and confirmed they were alone in the hallway.

"The shooter. Someone got close to me while you were on duty. And I've got a feeling you blame yourself."

"You don't know me." The retort was out of her mouth before she could clamp it shut.

His face shuttered and his jaw tightened. "You're right. I don't." His voice was calm. Emotionless. "But I do know you'll be up all night drawing new security plans. Take the night off. Let Quinn and Steven handle this. Charlie won't be sleeping. With two sniper attacks in one day, your adrenaline is going to crash. Despite appearances, you're not a superhero. And even if you were, heroes need rest. This has to be affecting you."

Was Preston giving her orders now?

Fatigue clouded her judgment, because she wanted to storm off and help Charlie look for a killer. But she conceded that Preston had a point when she saw Katrina coming down the hallway and remembered that she had a role to play. It would be tabloid fodder for Laila to be spotted running around the property with the chauffeur.

Katrina gave a nod and walked past them. Preston opened the bedroom door, and Laila braced herself for a fight about the sleeping arrangements. Except she hadn't expected Preston's dog to be passed out asleep on the couch. The mutt barely opened an eye when they approached.

"We're both adults." Preston shrugged. "We can compromise. And the bed is really big."

Where was he going with this? If he dared suggest they share, she'd put him on the floor.

He picked up Duke and carried him across the bedroom. "Whoever gets the bed takes Duke. This way, we both lose. That dog stinks."

The golden retriever snorted in agreement, turned in a circle, and was snoring before Laila could blink.

"Take the bed," he said. "Let me at least do one noble thing, since you keep coming to my rescue."

She didn't want to concede, but exhaustion made it hard to argue with his plan. "Fine," she muttered. "But he better keep those giant paws to himself." She headed to the bathroom to get out of the dress and into some yoga pants and a T-shirt.

"I make no guarantees that you won't wake up with a paw in the face."

Once changed, she crawled into bed and created a wall of pillows to ensure Duke stayed on his side. She looked at Preston, who was stretched out on the long sofa, and turned off the light on the nightstand.

But her mind refused to power down. "I forgot to ask you, what's going on with your sister-in-law? She doesn't seem that broken up over losing her husband."

His sigh hung in the darkness. "I don't think she loved my brother. She just saw the dollar signs. We dated briefly in high school, but she left me when she realized that Ethan was the one being groomed for my dad's position."

"Do you trust her?"

"Not at all. I mean, she'll take care of her boys, but she's as catty as Katrina. She wants the attention and fame as much as any of the Whittakers. In a way, she did me a favor when she ditched me for Ethan. But I'll admit that her rejection stung for a long time."

Silence followed his statement. What would it be like to live in a world surrounded by so many deceptive people?

Preston's faint voice drifted from across the room. "Do you trust me?"

Did he want the truth? What did he expect her to say? "No." The word escaped her lips before she had a chance to overanalyze the response.

"Is there anyone you do trust?"

She didn't like where these questions were headed. "No."

Silence indicated the conversation was over, and Laila let out a breath. But Preston lobbed one more bombshell of a question her way.

"Who broke your confidence so bad that you can't trust anyone?"

Laila stopped herself from jumping out of bed. The wound in her heart ripped open and had her patting her chest to check for shrapnel.

She'd learned the hard way that trusting in people would only let her down. Love always came with conditions. She shoved back the memories into the recesses of her mind and cleared her throat. "Why are you asking?"

"You don't trust easily, and I just wondered why."

"Do you want to understand what would make me trust you? Here it is. Don't lie to me."

"Okay. I won't."

"Just like that? Come on. I get that you've supposedly *remade* yourself, but everyone lies. You. My father. My former fiancé. It doesn't matter how much anyone cares about me, they're all habitual liars at the end of the day."

Acid rose in her throat. She ground her teeth to keep from yelling at Preston. His attempts to get to know her cut far too deep. If only she could jump into a boxing ring and go a few rounds to clear her head. She didn't want to dredge up these memories, not with Preston or anyone. Their fake relationship would end the second the police picked up the murderers. So why were they talking about this? She had one toe on the boundary line between small talk and oversharing.

Solomon's lies had led to her team being ambushed on a mission. Her father's affair had drilled into her head at an early age that everyone kept secrets.

"I'm sorry the people close to you did you wrong, but I'm not them. I won't lie to you." Preston paused, his words soaking into her. "You might not like what I have to say, but at least it will be the truth."

This conversation needed to end. Laila had walled off her

heart a long time ago. And the last person on earth she'd let in would be Preston.

"Goodnight, Preston."

"Goodnight, *wifey*."

Relieved that he'd changed the subject, she couldn't stifle a smile. "I'm rolling my eyes in the dark at you, in case you can't tell."

"Oh, I can sense it."

WEDNESDAY, 6:15 A.M.

The first day jitters drove Preston from the couch. But despite waking early, he found Laila was up, dressed, and had a cup of piping hot coffee waiting for him. Did this woman ever take a break?

They found Charlie and got on the road. Their undercover driver expertly navigated through the downtown traffic on the way to Whittaker Enterprises. Laila tagged along to the office under the guise of redecorating Preston's office. At least she could keep an eye on things while he was in meetings all day. Gossip had a way of providing credible information, so Laila planned to schmooze the staff while looking out for signs of trouble.

"Tell me why we couldn't take a helicopter to the office?" Preston asked Laila. The only response was an eye roll.

"Unbelievable," Laila murmured. "Check out the crowds outside." Cameras, vans with antennas, and people hoping to catch their first glimpse of Preston now that he was back from the grave lined the sides of the road in front of the building.

They pulled in through the parking garage while police and the company security team blocked the entrance. But telephoto lenses would capture every move once they crossed through the lobby.

His entourage filed into the elevator and rode it to the top floor.

The office buzzed with excitement the minute the doors parted. Margot greeted him and gave a rundown of his schedule while they walked. He shook hands and hugged a few old friends. There were new employees in the group that he'd not met before.

"Seth," Preston said and gave Margot's son a slap on the shoulder. "Great to see you."

"I'm so excited to be working with you." They were about four years apart in age, and Preston had always considered Seth as a little brother. The two had spent a lot of time hanging out at the Whittaker mansion as kids while Preston's dad and Margot had worked late into the evenings. Preston had a soft spot for the kid and looked out for him.

He couldn't ask for a better assistant than Margot. Loyal to a fault, she'd poured her life and energy into helping his father make the company into a global operation.

His whole body tensed. This was it. He walked down the hall and stopped in front of Ethan's office door. Despite his death, Ethan would cast a wide shadow over the place.

One door down was their father's office.

His office.

Old wounds ripped open when he entered the space his dad had spent so much time in. How could he sit in his dad's chair as if it were no big deal?

He closed his eyes when he caught a faint whiff of his father's cologne. Memories surfaced and he could imagine his dad sitting in the plush leather chair, a pen in one hand and a cup of black Columbian roast in the other. The man had always kept a notepad handy and had written down everything.

The stale aroma of coffee and cigar smoke tore Preston's heart open. "I—I can't do this."

Laila stood in the doorway, saying nothing.

Tears threatened to spill, but he stuffed his emotions down where they belonged—buried where they'd never see the light of day.

At least he'd learned something from his dad.

Laila scoped out the office space. "I need to measure the curtains," she said, shutting the door. "Those are the first things to go." She took out a device that looked like a transistor radio and swept the blinds and area around the desk. The machine lit up like a Christmas tree when she got near the corner of the desk.

"Looks like someone gave you a welcome gift." A plant with a sign stuck in the dirt that read *Welcome Home* sat on the edge of the desk.

Preston grabbed the card that went with the gift and Laila cringed. "Oops. I forgot about—"

"I'll take the plant home so we can enjoy it later." She cut him off before he could say *fingerprints*. They'd agreed to say nothing of the investigation, and he'd nearly blown it.

Too late to do anything about it, he held the envelope by the corners and opened the note card, signed by the executive staff. He showed Laila.

Laila peeled back the foil wrapper on the plant. Grabbing a notepad from the desk, she wrote *This plant has a bug.*

Laila sealed up the foil. "I'll have our driver take this to the car so we remember to bring it home with us. This will look so good on the lanai. Your mother will love it."

She took the plant and put it in the hallway, reclosing the door so they could talk in private.

Preston sank into the chair across from his father's place and visualized his father at the helm. "Ethan and I used to play in here when my dad brought us to work. But I knew I'd never be in the *big chair*. It was always reserved for my brother. I can't be the legendary Walt Whittaker or even take Ethan's place. This is all wrong. My dad made it clear that this position would be Ethan's. I'm just not qualified."

Laila walked over and put a hand on his shoulder. "You're right."

He cringed at her words. Did she really think he wasn't capable?

But more importantly, why did it matter to him what she thought?

"You aren't your dad. And you're definitely not Ethan. So stop trying to live in their shadows. Leave your own mark on Whittaker Enterprises. Do things your own way. Imagine the legacy this company could leave for not only your family but also the families that depend on this business for their livelihood."

She moved to sit on the edge of the desk, leaving his shoulder tingling from the absence of her touch. "You deserve to be here, Preston. Don't sell yourself short. You're not the same man that left five years ago. Let them see this side of you. This is your opportunity to take the company in a new direction."

Her job was to protect him, not to be his counselor. But when he looked into her eyes, he understood she wasn't just feeding him a line. It was the truth. "That's what Sebastian said. Now I have to add mind reader to your list of superhero abilities."

She smiled, and it wasn't a pity smile. Her face lit up, making her irresistibly attractive. "I believe in you, Preston."

His pulse spiked. He'd agreed to never lie to her, but was she being one hundred percent honest with him? Or was this just another part of her job? Did her duties include comforting the falling-apart-on-the-inside client on his first big day back in town? Because those five words reached into his dungeon of unexpressed emotions and sparked a pinprick of light.

He soaked up her words, and a glimmer of a new attitude took shape. One that resembled courage.

He stood. "I need to head to the board meeting and set up for my presentation. Will you be okay while I'm gone? I can't exactly have my wife follow me into meetings."

The security plan had Preston covered at all times. Juliette Montgomery, a new bodyguard with Elite Guardians, would pose as Preston's new personal assistant. He'd made sure Juliette was included in the meeting to take notes.

Laila nodded and smiled. "I've got more redecorating to do."

"Then I'm going to go prep for my first meeting." He'd laid out a few ideas for the company's future. But what would the board think? If they had a lack of confidence in his abilities, they could have him removed from the position.

Laila grabbed the plant from the hallway as she left the office to find Charlie. Preston forced one foot in front of the other to propel himself toward the conference room. Fear threatened to replace the resolve he'd just mustered. How were his father's peers going to react to his arrival? The next few hours could shape his entire future. That was why he wanted to be early and have a few minutes to prepare.

He stopped dead in his tracks at the sight of his sister marching into the room before he got there. Sweat trickled down his back, his nerves already ramped up for the meeting.

What was Katrina doing here?

He made a beeline for the conference room. Katrina's presence signaled trouble.

A woman he assumed was Juliette met him outside of the

conference room, her eyebrows arched high under the bangs of her blonde pixie haircut. "Is everything okay?" she asked.

"Stay outside for now. Maybe it's nothing, but let me see what's going on with my sister."

Juliette nodded but her eyes betrayed that she wasn't happy with the plan.

He opened the door and froze.

All seven board members sat around the rectangular table. Preston checked his watch. The meeting didn't start for another forty-five minutes.

Silence made the situation all the more uncomfortable. Preston cleared his throat. "I thought the meeting started at ten."

No one spoke. Preston surveyed the room. Joe Skiles, the vice president of operations, motioned for Preston to sit. Not at the head of the table but off to the side, reminiscent of being ushered to the kids' table at family gatherings. They squeezed in a chair for him next to Joe.

Bob Zimmerman stood at the head as if he were the one in charge. It didn't take a Harvard business degree to interpret the statement the chair placements made.

Preston surveyed the room. He'd grown up with these men gathered around the table. These were his father's peers, the ones that had helped start the company. But Preston bit his tongue when he noted Derek Pace sitting directly across from him. Katrina sat in a row of seats against the wall. Neither belonged at this meeting.

No one made eye contact with Preston. He didn't need a crystal ball to predict the outcome of this secret gathering.

They wanted him out.

So, Preston Whittaker had made it to the first day of his new job. An incoming text lit the screen.

We did what you asked. Went after that attorney and the girl. Waiting further instructions.

Adrenaline pulsed. If they'd done what had been *asked*, Preston's wife would be dead.

Preston was the one thing that stood in the way of success. The plan should have worked. Walt's son should have high-tailed it back to whatever hillbilly town he'd spent the past five years holed up in.

The man was a wretched coward who always fled at the first sign of trouble. Why dig his heels in now, with his life on the line? Not to mention the lives of those around him. Should've known targeting those closest to Preston wouldn't yield the desired result, because he only cared about himself.

The anger triggered a raging headache. This spoiled, rich playboy wouldn't take what rightfully belonged to someone else. Like he'd done all of his life. Steal opportunities from others. Squander his privilege and power only to be heralded by the media like he was some type of god.

No, Preston Whittaker had to be stopped.

I'll text you when he's on the move. Time for Plan B. You know what to do. This time, the troublemaker dies.

8

Laila met Charlie in the parking garage and wordlessly handed off the bugged plant. He'd get it into Steven's hands for analysis. If they got lucky, they'd find a fingerprint on the label or the listening device.

Charlie peeled the device off the pot and put it in a Faraday sleeve that would keep it from transmitting. "Steven said they have a tech team that can remove the bug and destroy it so the person on the other end thinks the device is on the fritz. At least this way they won't know we're on to them." He put the plant in the back of the car to take back to the house.

"I do have some news," Charlie said. "I talked with Steven. He's still waiting on the lab tests from the remnants of Sebastian's drink that you recovered. However, there was a fingerprint on one of the glass remnants."

Laila gasped. "Whose?"

"Preston's sister, Katrina. Steven just called me. He met up with her this morning before she left the estate, and she said she was the one that brought him and Gloria drinks when they arrived. She didn't see anyone tamper with them. She got the drinks straight from the bartender. Steven's questioning the waitstaff next."

Could Katrina be their prime suspect? Seemed like she'd do anything to get her husband that promotion.

"Thanks for the update, Charlie. I'm going to snoop around the office and see what I can dig up."

With Preston in a meeting, she now had some freedom to move around the office and chat with a few staff members. She didn't trust the vipers in the boardroom not to pull something when Preston was out of her purview. But her cover would be blown if she inserted herself into the meeting, so she'd have to rely on Juliette to be her eyes and ears.

She rounded the corner and almost collided with her fellow Elite Guardian pacing outside the conference room. Juliette's polished look nailed the part as Preston's assistant, from her tailored business suit to her stylish short blonde hair. "Did they kick you out that fast?" Laila asked.

The seriousness of Juliette's face said it all. "They never let me in. It was an ambush. They called an earlier meeting. Without Preston." She filled Laila in on Katrina's unannounced guest appearance.

Laila's vision blurred and her blood pressure spiked. If these people messed with her client, she'd take them down one by one.

Her heart went out to Preston. After their talk, she'd hoped he would have the courage to stand up and fight for his position. But this would be a big setback if they'd already ganged up against him.

Margot waved at Laila and rushed over. "Do you have some

time to go over Preston's schedule? If he wants to keep some of his father's commitments, I'll need to know. Otherwise, I'll have to cancel a few things and offer apologies. I'm sure they'll understand, given the circumstances."

Laila hesitated, not wanting to leave in case Preston needed something. She nodded to Juliette and trailed Margot to the woman's office. There wasn't much either of them could do to help Preston other than just remain alert.

This was one battle he'd need to fight on his own.

The bright walls and modern furniture of Margot's office contrasted with the old and stodgy space Preston had moved into. Even if Laila wasn't an interior designer, someone needed to remake that space.

Margot offered Laila a seat in front of the desk. The older woman clicked on her keyboard and spun the monitor so Laila could view the calendar. "Let's see. This weekend is a birthday party for a longtime family friend. Do you think Preston would be willing to attend as a gesture to his father? It would mean the world to his mother if Preston made an appearance."

Laila grabbed her notepad from her purse and jotted down the date. This Friday night. "I can ask him, but it might be too soon for Preston to socialize. He's quite broken up about the boating accident."

Margot's face fell. "I understand. It's been a difficult adjustment for all of us."

"Do you know what happened? Did they hit something that caused the boat fire?" Laila assumed that nothing escaped Margot's radar when it came to office gossip.

"I'm not sure. The police haven't said anything. I just can't believe Ethan was on board. Because Bob initially had me charter the boat for him, I assumed Bob and Walt had been the ones in the accident. But apparently Bob hadn't felt well and decided to stay home. So Ethan went instead." A tear rolled down the woman's cheek, and she swiped it with the back of her hand.

Jackpot. Laila's spy senses tingled with this bit of information. Bob had chartered the boat for Walt and then hadn't gone on the trip. Could he have set the whole thing in motion to get rid of the Whittakers?

Laila jotted a few more notes regarding upcoming appointments. "Well, I guess I need to go take some curtain measurements." As she stood, Margot grabbed her hand.

"I'm so glad Preston found someone like you. It's a relief to see that he's settled down. Sadly, no one expected much from Preston when he was growing up, and now he has someone like you to help tame him. Hopefully you can keep him in line, or at least keep him away from other women."

Laila frowned. Did Margot think her words were helpful? How had Preston grown up with so many people set on his failure? The desire to defend her pretend husband came from out of nowhere and overwhelmed her. Margot's comments were completely out of line, and Laila wasn't one to back down from a fight.

She snatched her hand back from the two-faced assistant and plastered on a fake smile. "I wouldn't bet against Preston if I were you." Her words came out like a threat, despite peppering them with some insincere Southern charm.

She spun on her heels and left the woman's office.

The buzz around the office had died down from earlier, and Laila headed back to Preston's office. She shook off Margot's comments. Why couldn't people give Preston the benefit of the doubt that he could run this company?

Something had shifted in her mind. She no longer saw Preston as the rich playboy with the scandalous past. Now her instincts drove her to defend the man's character. As a wife, it would be expected that she'd stand by her man, but as a body-guard, her only responsibility in the relationship was to keep him alive. However, overnight, something had changed. She didn't have to fake her belief in him.

She rounded the doorway to his office and stopped short. Preston stood looking out the window. "I heard the meeting didn't turn out so well," she said.

But when the man turned around, it wasn't her client.

"Oh, sorry. I thought you were Preston."

"I'm the one who's sorry. I didn't mean to intrude. I was just leaving some project documents for Preston to review, and I stopped for a second to admire the view. I'm Seth, by the way."

How had she mistaken Seth for Preston? They bore a slight resemblance. Seth did look a bit like a younger Preston. But apparently the few hours she'd slept last night hadn't done her justice. The bigger question was, what was the young man doing in Preston's office, alone? Was there a new suspect to add to her list?

"Hi, Seth. Please make yourself at home. I know Preston thinks very highly of you."

The young man blushed. "I always looked up to him when we were kids. He even saved me from a bully once. I'm so happy to be working for him, despite the tragic circumstances."

Loud voices from down the hall interrupted their conversation.

Preston stormed into his office and slammed the door, fury radiating off him in waves.

"What happened?" Laila said, afraid to even ask.

"They want me to step down voluntarily. Assumed I'd take a bunch of money and run. Bob and Derek want to take over the company and buy me out." He ran his hand through his hair, his face flushed. "Maybe they're right. It certainly would make my life easier. I can get out of town and pick up where I left off without all the drama hanging over my head." His eyes conveyed a surrender that tore at Laila's heartstrings. But before she could interject, Seth spoke up.

"It's not my place to say anything, but please don't go. I've grown up admiring you, and I didn't like the direction Ethan and your father were taking with the company. We need a fresh perspective. Someone who will make the hard and unpopular choices to create a better future. Please don't give up on the people who believe in you."

Preston gaped at Seth. "I—I don't know what to say. Thank you. I just can't keep fighting for this position with Bob and that snake of a brother-in-law sabotaging me at every turn."

Seth nodded and looked uncomfortable. "Whatever you decide, I'm on your side. But I'll leave you two to talk." Despite his youth, Seth had integrity written all over him. He excused himself to go get some work done, and Laila moved him down the suspect list.

When the door clicked shut, Preston sank into the guest chair and put his head in his hands. "You should have seen them, Laila. The room was like a den of lions out for my blood. I didn't have a single ally. They slid a piece of paper in front of me, as if some figure with a bunch of zeros in it would make me take the deal and run. The board doesn't think I can do this. And I'm beginning to agree with them."

The memory of Bob dropping a pen in front of him ignited a fire in the pit of Preston's stomach.

This is a good thing, the old man had chided. *You'll be free to pursue your own passions knowing that Derek will look after your family. You can disappear again to chase the life you really want.*

Preston slammed his fist on the desk. "With one signature, I could be done with the drama." He picked up a pen and spun in through his fingers. "Why should I stay, Laila? I'd leave defeated, but I'd be out forever. I was happy in Magellan Falls."

Seth's and Sebastian's words seeped into the darkest parts of his soul. There were a few people who supported him, even if his enemies outnumbered his true friends. He peered up at Laila, who stood sentinel by his side.

He'd expected her to be appalled that he was even toying with the idea of quitting. But instead, her look shone with something else. *Admiration?*

Laila sank into the chair next to him and covered his clenched fist with her hand. Jolts of electricity sparked through him at her touch.

"Who are you?" she asked, her voice soft. "You said you'd tell me later. Because based on the answer to that question, something tells me you might not want to give up on this opportunity."

"I'm just a guy who wants to make a difference in this world. To use my sphere of influence for good and to help others." *To make amends for past wrongs.* He'd never admit that to Laila, but she'd probably picked up on it after he'd confessed his struggles with Chelsea's death.

"You see the potential in the people you care about, but somehow you miss your own."

Memories of his childhood flooded his mind. "If only my dad could see me now. I'm not that troublemaker kid anymore, hiding in Ethan's shadow." It's what his father had seen when he'd looked at his two sons. One would take over the company; the other would be lucky to stay out of jail. And for a long time, Preston had thought even God saw him as nothing more than a troublemaker who deserved the guilt and shame that plagued him.

Laila listened, saying nothing, and somehow her silence soothed him.

He pulled two pieces of paper out of his suit coat pocket and tossed them onto the desk. "I wrote some notes for my vision for Whittaker Enterprises on the back of an old furniture order form." He shook his head. "But what's the point? No one believes in me."

Laila picked up his old order form and held it in her hand without reading it. "Tell me about your vision for the company."

He shrugged. "I want to work for a company that cares for its employees as well as serves the community that buys its products. Whittaker Enterprises has thousands of employees, and I want to improve our image. Too many times the Whittaker name has stood for corporate greed. We have the means and resources to take care of people and still make money. I intend to start a foundation within Whittaker Enterprises that supports and raises money for local charities and employees in need."

He smoothed out the crinkles of the other piece of paper on the desk. "But this document would absolve me of all responsibility. Allow me to go back to Magellan Falls, keep my furniture business, and live in blessed anonymity."

One choice was safe and protected his own interests, but the other would change the course of his life permanently. Was the reward worth the risk?

He looked up and voiced the biggest concern that held him hostage. "What if I fail?"

Why was he confiding in her? The bodyguard was only doing her job.

Yet, even in their short amount of time together, she

seemed to understand him in ways no one else ever had. It was weird. And...what? Cool? Freeing? Scary?

All of the above.

"If you fall down," she said, "you get back up again with double the fierceness to succeed the next time."

He laughed. "I don't think anyone could be as fierce as you."

She grinned, a hint of a blush coloring her cheeks. As if the compliment had startled her, she stood and walked to the window. "When I first met you, I assumed we had nothing in common." She turned and leaned against the wall, her assessing gaze commanding his attention. "I pegged you as this spoiled rich kid with Peter Pan syndrome—the boy who refused to grow up. Meanwhile, I became an adult at the age of twelve, dealing with my shattered family after my parents' divorce."

Her gorgeous dark-brown eyes sent his stomach into somer-saults, but a surge of joy sparked because this secretive and alluring woman was finally opening up to him.

She tilted her head, her gaze pensive. "We both grew up with fathers that placed winning over love. I just worked hard to never lose, while you decided to not even try." Her words had that faint hint of a Middle Eastern lilt, and he relished the sliver of familiarity that had sparked between them.

"It's time to stop running from your past, Preston. You've grown up and are a different man now. Stand and fight. Quit trying to become your father and be yourself. Because you *can* transform the image of this company from one that's filled with scandals and sensationalized media stories to one that's known for caring about its people and the community. Think about the potential to change lives. You owe it to yourself and others to see this through."

He'd never known any woman to speak her mind like Laila.

She never sugarcoated the truth, and right now he didn't need someone to coddle him.

Her speech lit a fire in his heart, but the flame was also tinged with anger. Bob would destroy everything Preston's dad had worked so hard to build, and many employees could lose their jobs if Bob moved the operations overseas. Preston had reinvented himself once when he left. But now he had the power to recreate not only his own image but that of the company.

"Maybe the best way you could honor your father's legacy is to change it," Laila whispered.

Those words were like a healing balm for his soul. He stood and grabbed both papers.

Laila flashed him one of her thousand-watt smiles. "Go show them who's boss."

He made a beeline for the conference room, tore the contract in two as he entered the room, and shoved half of it across the table to Bob. The other half he tossed in front of Derek.

"I have a list of ideas I want to review with the board. I'd like to discuss ways we can change the image of Whittaker Enterprises."

All eyes watched Preston lay out his plan for the future. A few board members leaned in, asking questions and taking notes. Minus Bob and Derek, who scowled.

"Let's set up a press conference later today and announce that I'm accepting my new role." A few people around the table nodded their approval. Preston's gaze landed on Bob. "And you can get out of my chair."

Bob shoved back and left the room without a word.

The meeting adjourned, and Preston's stomach untangled some of its knots.

He'd just stood up to his father's peers and announced his

intention to run the company. Tension released from his shoulders. He'd taken a flying leap off the point of no return, and the thrill of victory had replaced the fear of failure.

But how long would this moment of triumph last with so many sharks circling in the water?

9

Laila hovered outside the conference area, partly for Preston's protection but also to eavesdrop. She'd turned her back as Bob stormed out of the room, and he'd never noticed her through the red film of rage no doubt clouding his vision.

A smile crept across her face as she watched Preston own the room. Her fake husband used his gift of persuasion to sell his ideas. The charisma and charm that had gotten him into trouble in the past now convinced others to see his vision for the company.

Once the details of the impromptu press conference had been hammered out with Margot, Laila and Preston headed back to the estate for lunch and to get ready for the event later in the day.

If she closed her eyes, she could envision Preston taking the helm of Whittaker Enterprises. The man was born for the job, even if it had taken him a while to get there.

Preston's sister-in-law had asked to see him in order to

discuss settling some of Ethan's affairs. Veronica had been secretive about the issue and requested to meet Preston alone. Laila hated the idea of Preston being out of her sight, but if they were at the estate, she'd at least be able to remain close by in case of trouble. She perched herself on the edge of Sophia's overpriced rocking chairs on the lanai and waited for Preston.

The floor-to-ceiling picture window overlooking the gardens made this her second favorite spot in the house. The library still claimed first place.

Sophia entered the room, her tailored pantsuit seeming more fitting for a photo shoot than a day sitting on the lanai. Her hair and makeup were flawless, and Laila noted the woman didn't have a drink in her hand for once.

Sophia slid into the rocker next to Laila. "These rockers are my favorite pieces of furniture," she said. "I spend a lot of time admiring the beautiful garden."

Veronica's two boys played in the garden, chasing each other and rolling around in the dirt. Laila couldn't help but smile at their antics.

"Are you and Preston thinking about having children?" Sophia asked. Apparently, tact wasn't in her social skillset.

Laila turned to Sophia and smiled. "We've only been married six months, so there's still plenty of time."

Even if a family of her own just wasn't on the agenda for her life, it didn't mean that she didn't occasionally think about the whole marriage and kids deal. But now Preston's mother was talking about, maybe even planning, a future that wouldn't come to fruition. Because this wasn't real.

Sophia launched rapid-fire questions at Laila. "How long are you and Preston planning to live at the estate? How many kids do you want to have? Are you attending events with the family, like the birthday party this weekend?"

"I spoke with Margot earlier about attending the party. I'll see if Preston's up for it." Laila dodged the other personal questions, but Sophia pressed on.

"I'm so glad Preston has you in his life. You complete each other. Just like my Walt and me." She wiped her eyes with the back of her hand. "I can't wait to see what the future holds for you two. Preston's going to do great things with the company, especially with you by his side."

For a split second, sadness rippled through Laila. She'd been on her own for so long she'd forgotten what it was like to have family, even one as over-the-top dramatic as the Whittakers. Sophia's love for Preston warmed Laila, and she started to see the woman in a new light. Underneath the expensive façade, Sophia's love for her son ran deep.

Laila lowered her gaze, not wanting to meet Sophia's eyes. Overnight, Laila had gone from *I* to *we*. In a way, Sophia reminded her of her own mother. Caring and loving yet tormented by her addiction to alcohol. But Laila knew better than to get attached. Her time at the estate had an expiration date, and she'd be back to her regular life in the blink of an eye.

She remembered Preston's hesitation about undercover work, asking Laila how she dealt with having to lie. Yes, she was playing a role to protect her client, but watching Sophia rock in the chair made her rethink this whole operation.

Charlie stepped into the lanai, giving Laila an out from the conversation. "Sophia, I need to review some plans for the meeting later today with our driver."

"Nonsense, I'll leave you two to plan. I have things to do anyway." Sophia stood and left the room.

Laila checked her watch. They had another hour before they needed to leave for the afternoon press conference. Charlie slipped into the rocking chair next to her. "You actually let your man out of your sight? I'm shocked."

"He's in the library, which has no access from the secret

passageway." She spoke freely, having swept for bugs, but kept her voice low. "And Preston has my cell on speed dial." Even though Veronica had requested the private meeting, he'd told Laila that he didn't want to air all his family's dirty laundry in front of her. So she'd relented. The man was entitled to some privacy, despite Laila's reservations. "This area is clean. Can you fill me in on the device from the plant?"

"The bug has been squashed, and Steven's team is trying to trace it, but it will take time." Charlie sat back in the rocker, admiring the view. "But what's interesting is that Bob Zimmerman's fingerprints were all over the plant. Bob ratcheted up to the top spot on the police's suspect list, and they've brought him in for questioning."

Bob looked guiltier with every passing second. Laila filled Charlie in on the conversation with Margot about how Bob had rented the boat and backed out at the last minute.

"But at least we received some good news," Laila added. "Sebastian is going to pull through. Gloria called earlier with an update."

Charlie leaned in closer, keeping his voice low. "Speaking of Sebastian, it looks like you were right. Steven got a report from the lab. They found traces of methamphetamines in the drink remnants you recovered. Someone spiked his drink with something to speed up his heart. And with his pre-existing conditions, that could have been fatal. The police will be questioning anyone who attended the party, but especially Katrina, since she gave Sebastian the glass." Charlie handed her a flash drive. "I also called in a few favors and had someone dig into Preston's finances during the missing years. Interesting stuff. You might want to take a look later when you have some privacy."

She shoved the drive into her dress pants pocket and heard a door slam hard. Charlie took that as his cue to leave, and

Preston entered the room, his face beet red. He dropped into the rocking chair Charlie had just occupied a moment before.

"That bad?" Laila asked.

He sighed, clenching his hands into fists. "I don't want any of this," he said through gritted teeth. "Not anymore. When this killer is caught, I plan to find my own place. I need somewhere to escape the insanity." He looked around the room to make sure they were alone. "And speaking of family drama, it seems my classless brother left Veronica penniless. He put all his assets and life insurance contracts into a trust for his boys. She gets a meager stipend per month. His sons get the rest when they turn twenty-five."

Laila's jaw nearly hit the floor. "That's insane. What did she want you to do?"

"What else? Help her get money. But if Ethan set it up this way, I'm not sure what she thinks I can do."

Could Veronica have killed her husband thinking she'd receive a nice chunk of change from the life insurance payout? But why then go after Preston? Everywhere Laila turned, she found more shady characters to add to her suspect list. She'd at least have to tell Steven and Quinn about the possibility so they could do a background check.

Derek and Katrina entered the lanai. Speaking of shady characters...those two were nothing but trouble.

Katrina let out an exasperated sigh and glared at Preston. "I can't believe you. Why can't you just go away? We were fine without you. And now the police are questioning me. They think I tried to poison Sebastian."

Disgust distorted Katrina's features, and she continued her rant. "There's also no way you're married. You'd never settle down with one woman." She gave a dismissive wave of her hand toward Laila. "I had someone try to find your marriage certificate. Guess what? There isn't one."

Laila stood and faced off with Katrina. Her patience level had hit zero for tolerating the selfish diva. "Are you saying my marriage is a sham? We had a destination wedding in a different state. Of course there's no record in South Carolina."

Preston stood and snaked his arm around Laila's waist. "Since you didn't win with your boardroom antics today," he said, "you now have to pick on my wife? That's low even for you, Kat."

The woman's nostrils flared like a wild horse. "I mean, I've never even seen you kiss."

Instincts kicked in before Laila's brain could catch up. She reached up and looped her arm around Preston's neck and pulled him into a kiss.

This was supposed to be an act. Supposed to mean nothing. But suddenly, just like that, her heart stopped beating. The taste of his lips melted her mind into a blurry haze. He ran his hands through her hair, and her mind screamed to pull back. But her body protested, because this man could kiss.

She was in trouble.

When she let go of Preston, she forced herself not to gape at him. After all, she wasn't supposed to act like this was their first kiss. But...wow. Her lips tingled, rebelliously wanting more.

Katrina's huff brought Laila's head down from the clouds. "That doesn't prove anything. You two are hiding something. And I'm going to make sure the world hears about it. Face it, Preston. It's only a matter of time before you mess things up, like you always do."

The diva stormed off, Derek trailing her like a puppy dog.

Laila looked at Preston. "I'm so sorry, I just acted and I—"

He put his finger on her lips. "It's no big deal. I get it. We just needed to stall my sister."

Her heart rate returned to a normal rhythm, but the kiss, while fake, had unearthed something she'd kept buried inside.

She was starting to trust Preston.

No, they weren't a real couple. But an invisible connection bonded them unlike anything she'd ever experienced.

She blinked away the red warning flags flashing in her mind. The last time she'd trusted someone, things had turned deadly and her world had been shattered. She'd vowed to never trust the wrong person again.

But as much as her past whispered lies in her ear, she believed in Preston. He wasn't going to betray her the way her former fiancé had. Didn't Preston deserve a chance to prove his honor before she judged him like everyone else did?

He turned to leave the room, and she grabbed his arm. "I've changed my mind. The answer is yes."

Preston stopped, confusion flickering across his face. "What was the question?"

"You asked me last night if I trust you. I said no. Now I'm saying yes. I do trust you."

She did trust him?

Maybe she shouldn't. Because Preston had lied to her.

Twice.

That kiss had definitely been a very big deal.

And, unfortunately, he'd omitted a few things about his meeting with Veronica.

Of course she'd chosen this moment to decide to trust him. Great. Before he could say anything, she nodded toward the door, and they headed to the car so Charlie could drive them to the press conference.

Once Preston was buckled in and they were headed down

the road, his mind sped faster than the moving vehicle. The memory of their kiss sent Preston's pulse pounding. He hadn't had time to process the implications of the kiss or the sultry, intriguing, and dangerous woman behind those lips.

If it weren't for their arrangement, he would have sworn that they were a couple.

But did Laila have feelings for him, or was this just part of her act? He'd blown off the kiss to give them both an out. But it'd felt oh so real.

He circled back to the conversation with Veronica. And the details he'd kept under his hat.

It was true that Veronica had drama going on with the insurance paperwork. Ethan had gone behind her back and cut her out of the estate. But the meeting with her had been nothing more than an elaborate trap, and he'd stumbled right into it.

His former-girlfriend-turned-sister-in-law had made a pass at him.

He looked out the car window, his mind replaying the encounter with Veronica on an endless loop in his mind. How had he not seen it coming?

He hadn't wanted Laila to be a part of the conversation with Veronica and agreed to his sister-in-law's request to meet alone in the library. She'd taken the couch and he'd deliberately sat in a chair across from her, his arms crossed.

"Preston, Ethan left me with nothing," she'd said, tears brimming her eyes. "He set up a trust for the boys, and I get a small allowance for their care. It's like he never loved me at all."

What had his brother been thinking? He uncrossed his arms and leaned forward. "Veronica, I had no idea. He never told me he changed his will. I'm so sorry. But what can I do? Maybe you can get a lawyer and contest it."

His heart thawed slightly toward Veronica. After all, she'd lost her husband and didn't deserve this.

She sniffed. "I miss him so much. Even after stabbing me in the back like this. He was such a good father. I just wish he were still here." The tears now streamed down her cheeks.

Not thinking, he moved to the couch and let her sob on his shoulder. "I miss him too. But Mom and I will help you, no matter what. We're still family, and we'll get through this."

"Thanks, Preston. I knew you'd be there for me. You always were, even when I was so awful to you." She turned her head, leaned into him, and her mouth caught his. The kiss lasted a fraction of a second, but long enough for him to jump up, heat blooming across his face.

"What are you doing? I'm married."

And he didn't know where the indignation came from, because he wasn't married, really. But Veronica didn't know that.

And somehow, he *felt* married.

Veronica shook her head. "Seriously, Preston. That woman isn't even your type. When did you become so boring?"

Preston had bolted from the room.

"Are you okay?" Laila asked, bringing him back to the present as they sat in the car.

He had to get his head in the game if he wanted to be sharp for the press conference. But what would Laila think when she found out about Veronica's shenanigans?

He looked at Laila and mustered a smile. "I'm fine. Just thinking about my conversation with Veronica. I'll fill you in on the details later."

Preston had vowed to be truthful with Laila, but he'd rather shield her from this kind of ugliness. Scandals were synonymous with the Whittaker name.

His chest tightened. He hadn't done anything wrong, but

even though he and Laila weren't actually married, he felt like a cheater. Plus, he knew Veronica's intentional actions were a weapon aimed straight at Laila's heart.

Or maybe it was the other way around. Once Laila caught wind of Veronica's impropriety, she'd bury his sister-in-law alive.

Charlie merged onto the highway, and Preston stared at the flashes of scenery.

Laila trusted him, but that trust was fragile. She'd had issues in the past with men who'd lied to her, and he refused to treat her the same way. He hadn't had time to tell her before they left. And then there was that kiss she'd laid on him. If he closed his eyes, he could still feel the softness of her lips on his. His inner voice kept reminding him that she'd just been doing her job, but that kiss was now permanently etched into his brain.

The screeching tires hit his ears before the crunch of metal vibrated through the car.

Everything around Preston faded into slow motion, like he was having an out-of-body experience. A sharp bang drowned out the sound of someone's scream. The airbags deployed, but not before Preston had gotten a split-second look at the other driver. Was he delirious or had that man been wearing a ski mask? More squealing tires indicated their attacker was retreating.

Preston's head continued to spin even after the car skidded to a stop. The smell of burnt rubber mixed with gasoline exhaust burned his nose, but it brought him back to his senses and he looked around. His side of the car had borne most of the impact, which had pushed him closer to Laila's side. At least the side air bags had kept him from getting crushed. Pain tore through his shoulder from where the seat belt had tightened during the impact.

He finally put together that a large SUV had rammed straight into the side of their vehicle, pushing them off the road.

"Laila! Charlie!" he called out and was met with groans and murmurs. Music to his ears, because at least they'd all survived the crash.

He turned to Laila, ignoring the stab of pain in his neck. He reached for her but stopped short when he spotted the trickle of blood seeping under her hand that was pressed to her forehead.

"I...I'm alive. I hit my head on the window."

"You're bleeding," he said and took off his seat belt to scoot closer to inspect her wound. He shrugged out of his jacket and pressed it against her forehead. She winced and his heart shattered. More pain had been inflicted on others because of his attacker.

"It's just a scratch," she said with a weak smile.

"Charlie, are you hanging in there?" he called to the front seat.

"That airbag nailed me, but I'll be okay." Charlie paused. "Or at least I was until I watched that SUV turn around. Guys, I don't think this is over."

Preston looked out the window over Laila's shoulder. A guardrail separated them from the steep embankment that led to the river below.

An engine revved. "Looks like he's coming back for round two," Charlie warned.

"Not good," Preston said. "There's nowhere left for us to go." He braced his arms around Laila just as the SUV hit.

Metal scraped and groaned, the impact of the attacking SUV throwing Preston and Laila against the passenger door.

The rail creaked and groaned, bowing under the heavy weight of the vehicle. Death surrounded them on all sides. Either the madman with the weaponized SUV would crush them or the thin barrier would give way and they'd plunge into the icy water. Preston muttered, "God, where are You? Can You get us out of this mess please?"

And then a crack ricocheted through the car.

The bullet-proof glass on the back window spiderwebbed. "They're shooting at us!" Preston yelled. Because being run off the road wasn't enough, someone wanted to be a hundred percent sure they didn't walk away from this. There had to be at least two people working together in this well-coordinated assault.

"Put your seat belt on and pray harder!" Laila cried over the cacophony of the crunching metal and the roar of an engine. "The rail is giving way. We're going into the river. Which might be better than being shot at."

He'd thought nothing could ever rattle Laila, but the terror flickering in her eyes tanked any hope he had of making it out of this alive.

Preston grabbed the seat belt and strapped in. With one more push from the SUV, the guardrail disintegrated into fragments. Their car rolled down the embankment and slid nose first into the river. They hovered on the surface of the rushing water, but the strong current pulled the front of the car under.

"Laila! Charlie!" Preston shouted over the sound of the rushing water. "Are you okay?"

"Yes," came a groan from Laila. "Hold on." A ripping sound competed with the flowing water. Laila appeared in front of him. "I keep an emergency car escape tool in my purse."

Of course she did.

The car gurgled and pitched forward, the front diving deeper. Laila used the seat belt cutter to free Preston.

"Charlie?" No answer. Laila reached into the front seat, checked Charlie's pulse, and gave a thumbs-up. "He's out cold but has a steady pulse. Let's get him and us out of here."

"We don't have much time," Preston said when water

started to puddle on the front seat, seeping through a crack in the windshield.

His clothes soaked up the icy water, but the venom flowing through his veins made him impervious to the cold. These men could not get away with destroying the lives of everyone around him. He'd make them pay, but first he had to get Laila and Charlie out of this car or they'd all drown. "We need to find something to bust out the back window." It was the only portion of the car that wasn't submerged.

The vehicle pitched, sinking at a faster rate. Preston braced himself against the back of the driver's seat, gravity pulling him down. Laila tried to revive Charlie, but the man was still unconscious.

She passed Preston the car escape tool. "Use this to crack open the back window. The tool has a hammer on it, and the bullet should've weakened the glass."

This woman took the motto *be prepared* to a whole new level.

The pool of water in the front seat grew, covering Charlie's legs. "I'll have to pass Charlie up to you so you can get him through the window."

"No way am I leaving you behind. Watch out, this glass is going to fly down." He struck the window with the spring-loaded hammer. It shattered with the second hit, covering them with small shards. When he looked through the window, he saw the sky.

But that wouldn't last for long with their rate of descent. The river sucked them farther down into a watery grave. He didn't have time to argue with Laila. Charlie needed help. He dropped the tool so he could grab him.

"I'll lift Charlie and you can pull him up and out. You'll have to swim with him. I'll be right behind you."

They moved Charlie to the back seat, but at that moment,

the daylight became blurry as water poured in from the open window. The river had reached the edge of the back window and splashed down on them with the waves. Time was up.

Preston climbed out the back window, his movement causing more water to pour in from the opening. Reaching back, he grabbed the limp Charlie by the armpits while Laila lifted him up. The water had risen and covered the back seat.

Once free of the watery coffin, he shoved off the trunk of the car and powered his way through the current, towing Charlie.

Movement under his arm signaled that Charlie was reviving.

Thank You, God. The icy water must have shocked Charlie, because he began treading water on his own. Preston raked a hand down his face and spun, looking for Laila.

She didn't surface. "Where is she? She was right behind us." Preston did a three-sixty in the water, but there was no sign of Laila. No! Something wasn't right.

"She's in trouble, Charlie. I don't see her. I'm going under to see if I can find her. That car was seconds from filling with water. Maybe she's trapped."

"I'm right behind you," Charlie said.

Preston dove, trying to find her. At least the river water was clear, but they'd drifted with the current. He pointed to a trail of bubbles. They both came to the surface for more air. "We have to go after her. I'm not letting her drown."

"Let's go," Charlie said. Preston filled his lungs with air and dove again, Charlie on his heels.

10

Laila knew there was a reason she hated dressing up. She'd just never expected her cause of death would be her overpriced sandals.

When she had lifted Charlie to safety, the strap of her intricate sandal had caught under the brake pedal. She'd attempted to untie the shoe, but her fingers had been too numb from the cold to maneuver the buckle and free herself. As hard as she'd tried, the shoe strap wouldn't budge. She couldn't even get her foot to slip out of the shoe.

Water reached her neck. She willed herself to remain calm and sucked in a deep breath. There was no guarantee that the next time she surfaced the water wouldn't be over her head.

Plunging under the freezing water, she gave her all to untangle the shoe. But nothing worked. Reaching for the top, only her nose and mouth skimmed the surface of the water. One last breath, and she'd be completely submerged.

Her lungs started to burn. How long could she survive on

one breath of air? She spotted Preston's escape hatch through the watery shadows and refused to quit.

Internal warning bells told her that she was near the end. Spots danced in front of her eyes, and she blinked to clear her vision.

Wait! The cutter tool! Where was it? She felt around the front seat and floor until her fingers curled around the metal object.

Jackpot.

She hacked at the strip of fabric that stood in the way of her escape. She willed her hands to work.

With one last swipe of the cutter, the shoe released, but fogginess settled into her brain, and she fought to stay conscious.

The rapid beat of her pulse hammered in her ears and ticked off the seconds left in her life. The car drifted downward, and she could no longer see the surface out the back window.

The burning in her lungs subsided. Her body and mind succumbed to the frigid water, and she felt nothing. Numbness took over her arms and legs, turning them to jelly. She thought she'd been swimming up only to discover that she was free-floating in the back seat of the car.

The surface hung out of reach like a dream. She'd never make it. The fight drained from her body. A sense of peace called to her. Her eyelids became heavy, as if waiting for the proverbial moment her life would flash before her eyes.

But the images never came. She looked into the great abyss, and loneliness stared back at her. Repercussions of a life spent keeping people at a distance.

What had she expected? She'd shunned intimate relationships and forged her own path without any help. An unexpected sadness washed over her. Her whole life had been spent taking care of everyone around her, being the strong one while others fell apart.

But now, dying alone seemed like such a waste of her life.

An image flickered faintly in the distance, as if beckoning her to have one last dying thought.

Preston.

How odd that she'd think of him at a time like this. She barely knew the guy. Heat rushed through her, probably from the lack of oxygen, or maybe from the memory of that kiss. Had her heart thawed ever so slightly toward the man? Even if it was pretend, being with him for the past few days had chipped away some of her self-imposed isolation. Something inside of her wanted more of that connection to him. Because as the image faded to black, all she wanted was one more opportunity to kiss him for real.

At least she could die knowing that she'd done her job. Preston Whittaker lived.

Preston prayed that he'd find Laila alive.

A shiver raced down his spine at the image of finding Laila's lifeless body trapped in the car.

The shattered back window loomed in front of him once more. He pushed into the interior of the car and fought a wave of nausea. Was he too late?

Laila's long brown hair floated around her in the stillness of the submerged vehicle, her eyes closed and her skin translucent.

Lungs burning, he wrapped an arm around Laila's waist and pushed her through the window to Charlie. The two propped her up between them as they swam to the top.

Laila stirred, and Preston's adrenaline soared at the movement. She was going to make it.

All three of them crashed through the surface.

Laila expelled a gallon of river water from her lungs, but her sputtered gasp was music to his ears. If he'd been a few seconds later...

Preston kept a tight arm around Laila as they drifted with the current. He wasn't letting go of her until their feet were firmly planted on solid ground. Laila's chattering teeth echoed in his ears, but there was no mistaking the sound of a boat engine slicing through the water. Charlie waved and yelled for help as a small fishing boat pulled closer.

"Man, are we glad to see you," Charlie said.

"Let's get you out of the water." The fisherman cut the motor and drifted close to them. He had to be in his eighties, but he secured a strong arm around Laila and pulled her into the boat. Then he helped Preston and Charlie aboard.

They managed to fit four people on a three-person boat without capsizing it. Laila collapsed on the bottom in a puddle of soggy clothes. The fisherman handed Preston some blankets, and he wrapped Laila in the layers of warmth.

Preston crashed onto the first row of bench seats next to Laila, the smell of bait making him want to throw up the river water he'd ingested on this misadventure. She looked up at him, her hair plastered around her face, blankets vibrating from her shivers.

"Wow. What happened to you guys? I saw your car go over the bridge," the boat captain said. "I'm Bud, by the way. I guess I was in the right place at the right time."

"Thanks for the rescue, Bud," Charlie said, water trickling down his face from his hair. "We got ourselves into a bit of trouble." He groaned and looked at Preston. "I'm not sure how I'll tell my fiancée that we almost drowned after being rammed off the road by a homicidal maniac."

"Add escaping a shooter to the list too." Preston shuddered from the cold and the thought of a second person involved in the attack.

"If you two are done with the chitchat," Laila said, her teeth chattering and her breath coming in gasps, "we need to get out of here." She pointed to the shoreline where news crews had started setting up, their telephoto lenses trained on the boat.

"Oh, don't worry about them," said Captain Bud, waving a hand as if to dismiss the onlookers. "I've got a private dock a few miles up ahead. I can get you there and have an ambulance waiting for you." He made a call on his radio. Charlie borrowed the man's cell phone and called Quinn.

Laila moved to the seat next to Preston, the blanket wrapped tightly around her. A hand emerged from under the covers and grabbed his. Somehow the ice thawed from his veins at the warmth of her frozen touch. "Looks like I owe you one for saving my life," she said. "And Charlie's."

"As if you haven't saved my life. Twice now, if I'm not mistaken."

"So then it's two to one. I'm still in the lead."

He laughed at the return of her spunk. The boat sloshed through the river and pulled into a marina, where they were greeted by Quinn and Steven. As promised, Bud had an ambulance waiting for them at the end of the dock.

Paramedics checked out all three of them while Quinn took their statements.

A blur rushed past Preston, and a woman flung herself into Charlie's arms. After introducing Lizzie to Preston, Charlie clung to his fiancée like he'd never let go. Christina walked down the ramp toward the dock, a bag of dry clothes for all of them in hand. The paramedics were kind enough to let them change in the ambulance bay after clearing them to return home with the promise that they would all rest.

A chill settled in Preston's bones, and it wasn't from his swim in the river. He had no intention of resting until these madmen were caught. Memories of Laila's lifeless body would haunt him forever. Preston had power and money on his side, but what good were all of the resources in the world if he couldn't protect the people closest to him?

They thanked Bud for rescuing them, and the old fisherman headed back out on the river while the fish were still biting. Steven offered Laila and Preston a ride back to the mansion. Charlie would take the night off to recover, but Preston knew Lizzie wasn't letting the man out of her sight.

Preston's attire of baggy sweatpants and a police charity 5k T-shirt reminded him of his Magellan Falls days. Comfort over style. But now he was toasty in the back of the police car with Laila by his side.

Once they arrived at the estate, Preston's mother nearly knocked them both over with a hug. Not her usual countenance, but tears streamed down her cheeks. "You two could have died."

The stress of the day plus the loss of the past week hit Preston like an avalanche. His mother could have lost another son today. He wrapped his arms around her and fought to hold back the tears.

Settling her on a decorative bench in the foyer, he knelt in front of her, covering her hands in his. "It's going to be okay, Mom. Everything will turn out just fine. You'll see. I'm here for you."

Laila sat on the other side and wrapped her arms around his mother, letting her cry. He could tell by the look in his mother's eyes that she'd taken something to help her deal with the stress, but his soul tore in two at the sight of her tears. If this bad guy had wanted to destroy the Whittakers, well, mission accomplished.

"I don't want to lose you like I lost Ethan," she whispered through sobs.

Preston noted she didn't mention his dad, but he had a feeling she'd lost him long before his death. There'd never been a rumor of divorce, but they'd slept in separate wings of the house for years, rarely seeing each other.

Preston stood. "Look, we could all use some food and a good night's sleep. I'd love a hot shower and maybe my own pants. Not sure where the ones I have on came from, although I'm grateful for them."

Julian stepped from the shadows. "Come now, Mrs. Whittaker. Why don't you lie down for a bit?" He ushered Preston's mom away.

Katrina rounded the corner, her eyes glassy with unshed tears. "I—I'm glad you're okay. I can't believe someone tried to run you off the road like that. We could have lost you. I don't want you to die like Ethan."

Preston opened his arms wide. "Come here, Kat." He wrapped his arms around his sister. Nostalgia knocked him over. He remembered a time when they were younger, and Katrina had been scared by a thunderstorm. She'd needed her big brother then and now.

He vowed to put a stop to this madness. For the safety of his family, this needed to end now. Before he lost everyone he cared about, including Laila.

———

The television gave a play-by-play of Preston Whittaker's near-death ordeal. Cell phone videos showed Preston's sedan sliding over the embankment while an SUV sped from the scene.

Other angles caught the car bobbing down the river. One recording showed Preston and his wife being pulled from the water by a fishing boat.

Why wouldn't the man just die?

They'd taken a big risk with the assault in broad daylight. Hiring the two brothers might have been the biggest mistake of this operation. How had they completely missed their mark? They'd run them off the road, shot at them, and sent their car down the river, and yet Preston and his wife had walked away without a scratch.

Amateurs. So much for their supposed military training experience.

An incoming text pinged the phone on the coffee table.

What's the plan?

Of course those two didn't have the foggiest idea what to do next.

We wait until he lets his guard down and strike again.

Only this time, they'd better not miss, or they'd find themselves next on the hit list.

11

Laila soaked in the hot water from the bath, letting it seep into her muscles, washing away the aches from the day. Now if only she could unwind her mind. She should be checking on Preston, but her dip in the river had left her on empty.

The splash of the water from the tap brought back memories of the car filling up with water while she fought with her shoe. The killer—make that killers—were in her head, and she rarely got rattled. But her near-death experience had changed her perspective. These men were relentless to have come after them in broad daylight. That took guts.

Or desperation.

And yet, when all hope had been lost, her thoughts had lingered on Preston. If she were honest with herself, she didn't want to go through the rest of her life alone, unable to have close friends. And maybe after this was all over, she and Preston could be just that. Friends.

Or more.

147

The logical part of her brain chided the uninvited thought. No way would she fall for a billionaire playboy. She chalked it up to her oxygen-deprived mind playing tricks on her.

Although, he'd shed that bad-boy persona and claimed he hadn't dated anyone since he left town five years ago. Didn't he deserve the benefit of the doubt and a second chance at redeeming his less-than-savory reputation?

The Preston she knew had saved her life. He cared about his family when they seemed incapable of showing love back. The man had stood up to his father's peers and taken over the company, vowing to change the mission of the organization.

He really had changed.

And the thought of that *fake* kiss still sent sparks of joy racing through her.

She heard an unfamiliar chime, so she got out of the tub, wrapped herself in a plush towel, and grabbed the burner phone from the bathroom vanity. Her real phone was fish food.

A text from Charlie, with a possible lead.

Forcing her mind to focus on her job, Laila threw on some jeans and a T-shirt in record time and headed into the bedroom. Preston had coffee and sandwiches waiting for her.

"I have some good news," she announced with a giddy smile that she couldn't contain.

"Finally. We need to catch a break and find some closure to all of this."

"According to Charlie, traffic cameras caught the license plate of the SUV that ran us off the road." She sank onto the couch next to Preston. "It leads to a rental car place, but they're closed for the night. The police are trying to wake up the owners, but it might not be until tomorrow that we find out who rented the vehicle that attacked us."

"Definitely good news."

Laila sipped her coffee. "I don't think I thanked you properly for saving me earlier today. You risked your own life to come back for me. I—I almost didn't make it."

Preston shrugged. "You've put your life on the line multiple times for me. There's no way I was going to leave you behind. We're a team."

A team. She liked the sound of that, but what happened once the killers were caught and things returned to normal? She'd go back to her empty apartment, filling up her schedule with new assignments to distract her from the loneliness that reared its ugly head on occasions.

Preston stared at her to the point she thought she might blush. His intense gaze communicated that he sensed the spark that was growing into flames between them.

She stood. "I should get outside and help security sweep the perimeter before calling it a night. Charlie will be back in the morning, but I'd feel better if I checked things out tonight."

Preston grabbed her hand, sending a jolt of electricity through her. "You need to rest. Remember, the paramedics made us promise. I called earlier and hired additional security. We've got plenty of reinforcements."

She sank back down, but he didn't let go of her hand.

They sat on the couch, hand in hand, this time not in front of an audience. They didn't have to pretend to be a couple in the solitude of the guest bedroom.

Common sense prevailed, and she pulled her hand free. How had she let things get so personal on the job? No way would she compromise his safety by clouding her judgment. "I can't do this, Preston. It's one thing to pretend for the sake of your safety, but this isn't real between us."

"Because of what happened to end your last relationship?" He frowned, crease lines pulling in the corners of his eyes. "I don't even know the story, but I'm not that guy. I wouldn't do anything to hurt you like the pain I see etched across your face whenever you think about him. I'm not expecting anything from you, Laila." He reached for her hand again and squeezed. "But I think we both struggle with leaving the past behind."

His touch unlocked the places in her heart that she never let see the light of day. The look in his chestnut eyes wasn't demanding, and in them she found a sense of peace. After almost dying, it seemed like holding back was no longer the safest option, because Preston understood loss and betrayal. If Preston could share about his struggles with getting over Chelsea's death, she could reciprocate.

She sighed, relishing the warmth of her hand in his. "I was engaged to a colleague. We'd been dating for about six months when he surprised me with a proposal. Little did I know that Solomon had some dark secrets. We were spies, and I can't believe I didn't pick up on anything. He had a lot of people fooled."

Laila's mind screamed for her to run, leave—anything to avoid talking about the pain Solomon had inflicted on her. A headache flared at the memories of her ex-fiancé, but when Preston shot her a small smile, it grounded her. "Solomon was a double agent, selling secrets to Israeli enemies."

Preston let out a small gasp but didn't say anything. Laila continued. "We were on an undercover assignment together with a team of agents, and he was our handler. He fed me false data, and I based decisions on his intel, never sensing anything was wrong. We were ambushed, and Solomon was nowhere to be found. We were captured by our enemies in a place we weren't supposed to be, and they'd known we were coming. Twice I've stared death in the face. Today was the second time."

"That's unbelievable," Preston said. He inched closer, their legs touching. "How did you make it out?"

"Reinforcements were sent in to break us out of the

compound where they kept us. But a close friend on my team had been shot before we could get out. He didn't make it. One of the other men on the team carried his body back when we made our escape."

Laila bit back tears, but one streamed down her cheek.

Preston brushed it away with the back of his hand. "I can't imagine how awful that experience was. Being captured like a prisoner, knowing your fiancé was the one who sold you out."

"Solomon was eventually caught, and he's now in prison where he belongs. But the sting of betrayal seems to only get worse with time. I can't shake the memories. He'd been using me the whole time. He wasn't interested in me, just wanted what he could gain from our relationship. In hindsight, I should have seen the signs. But I trusted him. I never thought it was possible that he'd sell me out the way he did."

How could she trust Preston not to do the same thing? Trust meant giving the other person too much power.

Preston let go of her hand and pulled her to him. She melted against his chest, as if it were the most natural thing in the world.

"Sorry," she sniffed. "I think almost dying today has reminded me of the last time I faced my own mortality. I'll sleep it off and be better tomorrow."

He pulled back and looked at her. "That's just it. You're fighting battles that aren't even yours. You're so busy putting up walls and keeping people out that you're too tired to fight for the things you want. The things that matter."

A chill crept up her spine. His words cut her to the core. How did he know her so well when they'd only met a few days ago?

"I got to the point in my life where I couldn't fight any longer," Preston said. "When I found myself at the end of my rope, I reached for God. And I know it sounds like a cliché, but there wasn't anything else I could do. No matter how hard I tried, I couldn't escape the grief and shame of my past. I had to lay down all of my man-made weapons, because the harder I fought, the more defeated I became. I mean, I kept showing up to the fight with weapons that didn't work."

"Like showing up to a knife fight with a spoon?" Laila said with a low chuckle.

"Um, sure. I guess that works. I can't fight the past that haunts me if the only weapon in my hand is a spoon. Meanwhile, God has the whole arsenal of heaven waiting in the wings to fight on my behalf. But I have to let go of my useless weapons and step out of the way."

His hand brushed her cheek. "Maybe it's time you put down the spoon. And maybe those Chinese throwing stars too. And let God, and other people, help you. You can't do everything on your own. You can only fight on behalf of others for so long."

There he was, tossing out the God card again.

She'd bounced between church and temple off and on through her childhood, but neither parent had ever fully committed to their religion. It was more to check a box than an actual way to live. At least, not in the way Preston was talking about. And he seemed to have made the most out of his second chance at life.

Could that apply to her too?

The idea of letting anyone else have control in her life made her stomach twist in knots. If she couldn't trust people that she could see right in front of her, how would she ever trust a God she couldn't see? If she didn't have weapons, wasn't that the equivalent of quitting?

What would it be like to allow someone to get close to her without feeling like she had to be the strong one, holding all the pieces together?

The intensity in Preston's eyes increased. Her heart jack-hammered in her chest. *The* Preston Whittaker was about to kiss her. For real this time.

And while she desperately wanted him to, she still had a job to do. And that came first.

He leaned in and she stopped breathing. She closed her eyes, anticipating his lips on hers. But instead of a *for real* kiss, he pressed his lips to her forehead and let them linger there for a second. "I think rest might be good. I'll take the couch again, and I'll even take Duke this time."

"Duke would be fine if he didn't snore so loud," Laila said, lightening the mood between them. But on the inside, she ignored her skyrocketing pulse. Stifling a sigh, she turned away from Preston so he wouldn't notice the steady rise of red creeping up her neck. Her head knew the kiss would be a big mistake, but passion had short-circuited her brain, and all she could think about was how badly she wanted to kiss him.

She stood up and moved to the window, partly to do her nightly check of the area, and partly to step away from the man's magnetic pull.

Fatigue had hit her hard. Her body had been through the wringer today. She got ready for bed and double-checked her gun on the nightstand. She texted Olivia an update and crawled under the quilted comforter. Warmth chased out the chill that still lingered from earlier.

Duke jumped up next to her and pressed his back into hers. Her eyes closed and she couldn't fight slumber any longer. She turned out the light and heard a faint whisper from across the room.

"G'night, *Wifey.*"

"Goodnight, *Preston*," she muttered before sleep took her under.

THURSDAY, 6:00 A.M.

A knock at the door woke Preston from a deep sleep. He jumped up, stashing blankets and pillows on the floor beside the couch. Whoever was at the door couldn't think he'd been relegated to the couch after some fight with Laila. But before he could shove the morning grogginess from his head, Laila had her gun in one hand and her phone in the other.

"Who is it?" She rubbed the sleep from her eyes, looking as disoriented as he felt after a solid night's slumber.

Crashing on the couch hadn't been so bad, thanks to his mother's impeccable taste in furniture. Plush with lots of space to stretch out, it hadn't been a hardship to give up the bed for Laila to feel comfortable with their sleeping arrangements.

"It's me," Charlie whispered.

Laila cracked the door open wide enough for Charlie to slip in. "I tried to call, only got voicemail," he said. Charlie gazed around the room, giving Preston an almost imperceivable nod when he saw the evidence of Preston's makeshift bed. Of course her coworkers would be curious about that.

Laila flung her phone on the bed. "I hate this new phone. I must've accidentally put it on do not disturb."

Preston stretched and looked out the picture window overlooking the backyard garden. The breaking dawn light highlighted the early morning mist as it filtered through the trees. All looked calm and serene, but after yesterday's events, Preston looked at every flickering shadow for signs of danger.

Charlie sized up the two of them. "How are you two doing after our dip in the river?"

Preston moved the collar of his T-shirt to show a sizable black-blue-and-yellow mark growing across his chest. "Seat belt caught me. I'm sore, but it could be a lot worse. At least I slept well last night."

Laila nodded. "I'm fine too." But the bruise peeking out from her hairline said otherwise.

Preston squinted at Charlie. "Did you find anything out about the car rental? I'm assuming you have news."

"That's why I came up. The police want to meet you at eight a.m. They've got some information and want to discuss it with you and Margot. It looks like the car was rented by someone at Whittaker Enterprises. Steven didn't give many details, but he said your father's credit card was used to secure it."

"That makes no sense. It must be someone with access to the corporate account. I can call Margot. She'll know who arranged for a rental yesterday."

Charlie shook his head. "Let Steven handle it. We'll meet him at the office. I'll get the car ready. They've already sent a replacement after yesterday. But I think it's time to ask Margot a few questions. She seems to manage a lot of people's schedules, so hopefully that will give the police some new leads."

They got ready, grabbed some breakfast and coffee to go, and headed to the car.

Once they arrived at Whittaker Enterprises, Preston made a beeline for Margot's office, but Steven had beaten them there. Laila waited outside the office door, but Preston barged right in. Nothing was going to stop him from getting some answers.

"Glad you're here, Preston." Steven sank into a chair in front of the desk, and Preston took the other. "You might be able to help. I want to find out who has access to the corporate credit cards. Specifically, a card with your father's name on it." He passed a sheet of paper to Margot. "This is the rental agreement. Someone at Whittaker Enterprises rented a car yesterday and used Walt Whittaker's credit card."

Margot paled. "I—I rented a car yesterday. I just charged it to whatever card they had on file, so it must have been Walt's card. They know me. I arrange cars for the executives quite often."

"You rented an SUV yesterday?" Preston jumped in. "The same car that ran us off the road on the way to the press conference?"

Her hand flew to her mouth. "What? Another accident?"

"We're fine, Margot. Who did you rent the car for?"

"Bob. His car was in for repairs. I called the rental place, and they delivered one for him early that morning."

Steven and Preston exchanged a look. "Looks like we need to talk with Bob," Steven said.

They left Margot and marched toward Bob's office. Laila waited outside, and Juliette arrived to keep her company, but Preston knew they'd figure out a way to eavesdrop.

Bob raised his head when they entered. Steven introduced himself, and Bob stiffened. He ushered them to take seats. "What's happened now? It seems like as soon as Preston arrived in town, trouble started. I hope you have a good excuse for not showing up at your own press conference. I had to cover for you. Just like old times."

"Did you not watch the news?" Preston's fingers curled into a fist. "We were attacked yesterday on the way to the press conference."

Bob didn't react.

"Seems like you've a lot to gain if Preston's out of the way," Steven said.

"I don't like your tone, Officer. We've got a business to run here. Can't have our CEO off gallivanting around town, shirking his responsibilities—"

Preston cut him off. "Did you not hear me? We were almost

killed while driving to the press conference. Someone in a rented SUV ran us off the road."

Steven held his arm up like he was holding Preston back from taking a swing at the man.

"The SUV was rented by Whittaker Enterprises," Steven said. Bob's face paled. "I understand that the car was for you."

Preston couldn't read Bob's expression. Had he not known about the attack, or did he just have a good poker face?

"I—I had no idea the accident was so serious, Preston. I apologize. My comments were out of line." Bob shifted his gaze to Steven. "I did ask Margot to rent a car for the day. Mine was in the shop and I needed a loaner. But when I headed to the garage, the car was gone. I verified that it was delivered, but I checked everywhere and couldn't find it. I eventually gave up and reported it stolen."

He rummaged through a stack of papers on his desk and pulled out a pink sheet. "Here's the police report for the missing vehicle. It looks like it was stolen from the parking lot."

Steven inspected the paper. "Did you tell the car rental place about the theft?"

"The police indicated that I could send them a copy of the report, but I haven't gotten to it. Figured I would let the insurance adjuster fight that battle. We pay enough in premiums so they can handle it."

The fake leather squeaked when Steven shifted in the chair. "Tell us about the night Walt and Ethan took the boat out. Apparently, you were supposed to be with them. We have confirmation that you organized the fishing charter."

Bob hung his head. "I already told the police this when they questioned me earlier. Walt and I were going to go out for some night fishing. But at the last minute, I got sick and suggested that Walt take Ethan instead, since we'd already paid for the trip. Believe me, I've been distraught over how close I came to being on that boat."

The man only thought about himself. What about the fact that Preston's brother and father had died on the boat? Was Bob capable of murder?

Preston tried to determine if Steven was buying the man's remorse, but the detective kept a straight face. "You understand how this looks, don't you, Mr. Zimmerman? You've publicly expressed your disdain for Preston, and now we find out the boat trip was your idea, but you conveniently got sick and missed it. And the car that tried to kill Preston happens to have your name on the rental contract. That's one too many coincidences."

"I've got alibis for everything. Call my wife and she can give you the details of how I was puking my guts out the night of the boat accident."

"It wasn't an accident."

"W-what do you mean? I was told there was an electrical fire on board."

"Evidence is pointing to a bomb on the boat. Designed to kill everyone on it."

"B-b-but I was supposed to be on that boat. Why would anyone want to kill me?"

"Someone wants control of the company," Preston said, "and seems to be taking out key players one after another. I've been the target several times."

Bob's eyes widened. "You can't possibly think that I want control of Whittaker Enterprises so badly that I'd kill your father and Ethan. That's not possible. I loved Walt like a brother." Tears rimmed the man's cold eyes, a flicker of sincerity flashing for the briefest moment.

Preston's dad had started the company in his family's

garage with Bob. How could Preston think Bob would resort to murder?

Preston sighed. "I honestly don't know what to believe."

"Preston, please—"

"Bob, just don't."

The man settled back with a low sigh, his face pale and hands curled into fists to hide the tremor Preston had already seen.

Steven stood, signifying the end of the conversation. "We'll be in touch if we have further questions."

They left Bob's office and reconvened with Laila and Juliette in Preston's office after Laila swept it for listening devices.

"Do you believe Bob?" Steven asked Preston.

"It's hard to imagine him killing my father and brother. He and my dad were old college buddies. But I'm finding too many coincidences for comfort. Then again, I suppose someone could be framing him."

"Maybe," Laila said. They fell silent, then Laila looked up. "I think Derek is up to something. Could he be framing Bob to avoid suspicion?"

"It's possible," Preston said, running his hands through his hair. "I certainly wouldn't put it past him."

"He may have been the one to let the gunman into the estate the night of the shooting. And someone poisoned Sebastian's drink. Derek and Bob were both at the party that night."

"Have you considered that maybe your sister is behind this?" Juliette had been reserved up until this point, so all eyes swiveled to her when she spoke to Preston. "Her fingerprints were on the glass that poisoned Sebastian. I've been stalking her social media pages, and she seems to like having the attention focused on her. Not to mention that she's trashing Preston all over the internet. Some pretty nasty stuff. But maybe she's out to get her husband that promotion by any means necessary."

A shiver raced through Preston. Could Katrina be so evil? Dramatic, sure. But was she capable of cold-blooded murder? He recalled last night how broken up his sister had been over his near-death situation. Emotions like that were hard to fake, but then again, Katrina had a theatrical side.

"Anything is possible," he said, "but despite her social media image, I don't doubt her love for my father and brother. Plus, she'd need help. She can't do anything by herself."

"I think it's time to dig into the real lives of Derek and Katrina and not just their social media pages," Steven said, making a note in his notepad. "Let's see what they're hiding."

"What about Veronica Whittaker?" Laila said. "She didn't realize her husband had cut her out of the estate. Could it be that she tried to kill him for the money, not realizing she wouldn't see a dime?"

Preston's stomach roiled at the thought of Veronica being involved. He still hadn't told Laila the full story of his meeting with his sister-in-law. "I'd think Veronica has more motive than Katrina. She's a viper and will strike when you least expect it if you cross her. But murder? That's taking things to a whole new level. I just don't know."

The suspect list kept growing, and they didn't have any evidence to support their theories. But they'd find it. They had to, before someone else died.

12

FRIDAY, 2:15 A.M.

The day had dragged on without any progress in narrowing down their list of suspects. Laila had kept busy trailing Preston while he ducked in and out of meetings. After enduring another awkward family dinner, they'd decided to call it an early night.

She'd passed out the minute her head hit the pillow, since her body hadn't fully recovered from her adventures the day before. But her mind refused to quit, and she woke up at 2:15 a.m. Duke whined in his sleep while Preston slept like a rock on the couch. At least he didn't snore, unlike the dog.

Who was behind these attacks? She kept adding names to the suspect list, not crossing names off. Preston's notoriety meant he'd encountered a lot of people, but who could be behind this kind of betrayal?

The threats seemed to have escalated, which made her wonder if the killers were operating on some type of timetable. It had taken guts to run Preston off the road in broad daylight, with onlookers and traffic cameras watching their every move. Of course, news of the attack had gone viral when word got out that Preston was involved.

The criminals seemed sharp, so if Bob was behind the assault, why would he leave a paper trail? A cell phone camera had caught the SUV's license plate on video, which traced back to Whittaker Enterprises. It was all too easy, as if someone wanted the police to jump on the Bob connection.

But one question lingered in the corner of her mind and caused her heart to stumble. Would Preston want to see her again once this assignment ended and the danger subsided?

The question she should be asking herself was, why did she care whether or not they connected after this job? It wasn't like she spent time visiting other former clients. When had Preston moved from client to something more?

Sleep eluded her. Rather than toss and turn, she decided to take a walk around the estate. And if she happened to find herself in Walt Whittaker's private, locked office, she'd chalk it up to getting lost in the giant maze of rooms and secret passageways.

She put on her shoes, grabbed a small bag she never left home without, and headed out the door, leaving Preston still sleeping soundly.

With the layout of the place permanently etched into her memory, she could probably navigate her way in the dark, but she grabbed a flashlight just in case.

Walt's office was on the main floor, next to the study where they'd met with Quinn and Steven. The family hadn't been in the office after the police swept the room for any evidence of foul play. Preston's mother was in no shape to go through Walt's things, and his sister refused to do anything that remotely resembled work. Preston hadn't had the time, and no one in the family could seem to produce a key.

The office didn't have access from the secret passageway, so she'd have to sneak through the great room to the back hallway.

Moonlight flickered across the marble floor, creating shadows that played with Laila's mind. She rested her hand on the butt of her gun and willed herself to calm down. Her breath rattled in her ears but seemed to be the only sound in the stillness of the house. Each footfall hit the stairs without so much as a creak, and she navigated toward the back of the house.

Laila pulled a small lockpick tool kit from her bag and finagled the lock. A satisfying *click* signaled her success.

"What do you think you're doing?" A voice tore through the silence.

She jumped, barely containing the shriek crawling up the back of her throat.

Preston.

She whipped her head around to find him standing in the hallway with a goofy grin on his face.

Busted.

"I just...I mean..." What could she say? He'd caught her red-handed with a lockpick tool in her hand after 2:00 a.m. in front of his dad's private office.

"Well, since you're already in, let's take a look."

She pushed through the door.

Preston's harsh gasp echoed hers. The room had been ransacked. Papers were strewn about, the monitor had been flipped over, and desk drawers hung open.

"I don't think the police did this," he said. "Looks like someone came in after them."

Laila nodded. "Someone's looking for something."

White powder dusted the desk and bookcase where the police had lifted fingerprints. But the room was a disaster. She perused the books on the bookshelf. What if there was a secret passageway to this office? According to the blueprint she'd memorized, this room had no other access points.

Laila dropped to her knees and looked around the floor. The carpet fibers appeared to be flatter on one side of the area rug than the other. Keeping that in mind, she stood and examined the books on the bookcase. It seemed so clichéd, but what if there was a secret door? In this creepy old mansion full of secrets, anything was possible.

She pulled out various books, stacking them on the desk, feeling less like a spy and more like a character in *Scooby Doo.*

And then she spotted it.

A button hidden behind one of the books at the base of the shelf where it would be easily overlooked by the police. Would the button open the door or burn the place down? She shrugged. Only one way to find out.

She pressed it.

Click. A lock disengaged, and the bookcase swung open a crack.

She looked at Preston. "Um, I think I discovered your dad's secret office." She ducked through the opening, Preston hot on her heels.

This was Walt's real office, the one that wasn't listed on the map of the estate.

The ten-by-ten room resembled a time capsule of Walt's last days. His cup of coffee sat ice cold on a leather coaster next to his keyboard, and papers were stacked on one side of the desk.

"Don't touch anything," she said. "The police will want to do a search. We'll just take a quick peek." A laptop hummed to life when she poked the mouse with her lockpick tool. Of course, it asked for a password, so she took pictures with her phone to document how they'd found things. The laptop would be a gold mine of information, giving them a much-needed break in the case.

She snapped more pictures, careful not to touch anything. Filing cabinets lined one wall, and Preston pulled a drawer open with his shirt covering his hand.

Laila weighed the consequences of breaking and entering. The police would need to search the room for any evidence that might help in the murder investigations. For now, she wanted to poke around and see if anything seemed out of place. If something had been left out in the open, well, then it was fair game.

Although, if she wanted to get technical about it, this office now belonged to Preston, so...she wasn't really breaking and entering. Right?

Walt's desk held the usual assortment of office supplies. Pens, paper clips, and a stapler were stationed around the workspace. A few receipts were stacked neatly next to the computer monitor. The corner of a piece of paper stuck out from under the mat that lined the desktop. She pulled her long sleeve over her hand and tugged the paper free. It was a photo, like an old school yearbook picture. It looked like Ethan, around ten years old. The dark hair and dark eyes resembled the pictures she'd seen of Preston's brother.

She lifted the mat a little more. Two more grade school photos caught her eye, both with that old-school, pale-blue background. One picture looked like Preston around the same age as the photo of Ethan.

But why a third picture? It resembled Preston, but why keep two photos of Preston and only one of Ethan?

She scrutinized the three pictures side by side, and something didn't add up.

In the third picture, Preston's hair would have been too light. And she didn't recall him wearing glasses. She flipped it over and found a handwritten name. *Seth.* The only reason Mr. Whittaker would keep a picture of Seth would be if—

She opened her mouth to call to Preston so he could see the pictures, but the creak of footsteps stole her voice.

They weren't alone.

Preston stared wide-eyed at her, confirming he'd heard the noise. She put her finger over her lips and shoved the three pictures into her pocket. She twirled a finger in the air and pointed at the door, signaling to Preston that they needed to move back into the main office. The bookcase made a faint click as it slid back into place, but at the same time, a key jangled from the hallway. The knob twisted. Instincts kicked into overdrive, and she rushed the shadowy figure entering the room. She grabbed his arm, spun him around, and had him pinned against the wall before he could let out more than a grunt.

"What's going on?" he finally yelled.

"Derek?" Preston asked.

Derek? She released him and moved back.

Derek spun to face them. "What in the world are you two doing here?"

"We should ask you the same question," Preston replied. "And how did you get a key? I didn't think anyone had one to Dad's office."

"I may have had a copy made a while ago." The man shrugged. "For emergencies like this."

"What emergency brings you here in the middle of the night?" Laila asked.

"I—If you must know, I set up an alert on my phone that would let me know if someone accessed Walt's office."

"Why?"

"In case of a break-in. I don't want someone stealing company secrets." He glared at Preston, apparently not thinking Laila had been the one to pull off the breaking and entering.

Did Derek know about the secret room? Why was the man interested in monitoring Walt's office?

Was there anyone in this family that didn't have a motive for murder?

Heat rose in Preston's face, and he bit back the verbal tirade aimed at his brother-in-law. What was Derek up to?

"Why are you monitoring this room? And you have a key when Mom told me she couldn't find a key. What game are you playing, Derek? Are you behind my father's and brother's deaths?"

Derek jerked. "What? Are you kidding me? Walt treated me like a son, especially after you abandoned the family. What would I possibly gain from his death?"

"The head position in the company, for starters."

Derek let out a mocking laugh. "Right. Because I just do what Bob and Katrina tell me to do." His face grew serious. "I made more money with Walt alive than I will with him dead."

Preston stood there, too stunned to say anything. The good news was that it seemed that Derek didn't know about the secret room, otherwise his dad's laptop would have disappeared a while ago.

"So, what information did Walt have on his laptop that you're so desperate to get back, Derek? You might be playing Katrina and Bob, but I think you're scrambling to cover your tracks." Laila's accusation sliced through the air, silencing both Preston and Derek.

"What?" Derek muttered.

Preston echoed the sentiment. How had she connected the dots that fast?

"You're the only one with a key to the office, and it's trashed. The police didn't find it this way. What are you looking for?"

"Walt's laptop is missing. If it falls into the wrong hands, valuable corporate secrets will get out. Like I said, I'm just trying to protect the company."

Derek only protected his self-interests. Laila stared the man down. "Well, I guess we'll find out the truth when we turn the laptop over to the police. If you're innocent, then I guess I'll apologize."

Derek's face paled, followed by a flush of anger. "You found the laptop? Where is it? I can handle things from here. It's corporate property."

"Which means it belongs to me," Preston said. "What did you do, Derek?"

"Look, you can't give the police the laptop."

"Of course I can."

A long groan slipped from Derek, and he pressed his palms to his eyes.

"What's going on, Derek?" Preston asked.

"If you turn over the laptop, I'm a dead man." Derek kept his self-assured mask in place but shifted from one foot to the other. What was he hiding?

"What do you mean? Why are you a dead man?"

Derek stuffed his hands into his pockets and shrugged. "Let's just say there's information on Walt's laptop that you don't want made public. Wouldn't want your investors to get wind of any impropriety now, would we?"

Great. Just what the Whittakers needed. Another scandal in the making. The headlines careened through Preston's mind.

"Impropriety? Just spill it, Derek. I'm sure we can handle it, whatever it is. But I have to know about it to help you."

Laila stared daggers into Derek. "Don't worry. We'll let the police figure it all out. I've already called them."

As if on cue, the doorbell rang. Derek growled and shot Laila a challenging look.

A defensiveness rose in Preston that surprised him. "Leave Laila out of this and let me help you," Preston pleaded. "We can wake up one of our overpriced attorneys, but you have to let me know what we're facing. What did you do?"

A sneer flashed across Derek's face. "While you were off gallivanting who knows where, I found a way to make some serious cash. Do you think it's easy being married to your sister? That woman spends every dime I have."

He looked around the room as if to see who else might be overhearing the conversation. "I've been selling information to a competitor. They've offered me a job, bigger than the one Bob promised me. I'm looking for Walt's laptop to erase the evidence of the tracker software I placed on it."

"You've been selling out my family? What about my sister?"

Derek's shoulders slumped and his cockiness dissipated. "I love my wife, but I needed some money that she couldn't spend. A guy needs to make his own way in life at some point, right? I can't rely on your family's money forever. I figured it was harmless and that Walt would never find out. It wasn't big intel that could take down the company. I just monitored a few of his emails. But I didn't kill anyone. I swear I had nothing to do with their deaths."

Laila put a hand on Preston's chest to stop him from punching his moneygrubbing brother-in-law in the teeth.

Voices in the hallway halted their conversation. Backup

had arrived, and Preston loved that Laila had friends on the police force.

Sure enough, both Quinn and Steven rounded the corner with Julian. Quinn barked orders to lock down the house and sent everyone back to their rooms while the police went to work in both offices. Derek scowled and stormed away.

Regardless of whether his brother-in-law was involved in his father's murder, the pain of betrayal drove daggers into Preston's heart. How could the man be so selfish as to sell his wife and family out for a payday?

Quinn scrutinized Preston and Laila. "Seems like we might as well move in with you two for as much time as we've spent at the estate. Can't you two stay out of trouble? Or at least uncover crucial evidence at a reasonable hour?"

He sighed and turned to Laila. "I guess we need to take your statement, *Mrs. Whittaker*."

Preston bit his lip to keep from snickering. Quinn would never let Laila live this fake marriage down.

Steven pulled out his notepad, and Laila showed them the secret door. "You'll want to question Derek," she whispered. "He had been hunting for the computer because he's been stealing corporate secrets. He planted some sort of tracking program on Walt's laptop."

"Do you think he could be our killer?" Quinn and Steven asked in unison, and all eyes turned to Preston.

"I don't trust him, but I don't believe he has anything to gain by killing my dad and brother. He said he has a better job offer, so if he wanted out of the company, there'd be no reason to kill for it. I think he's shady, but I don't see a motive for murder."

Steven put away his notebook. "Quinn and I will have our forensic team look over the laptop, and then we'll question

Derek. Maybe you two should see if you can catch a few hours of sleep."

"Yeah, while you've completely ruined my night," muttered Quinn with a wink to Laila. She ignored his jab and headed back to the room. Preston followed.

When the door closed and they were alone, Preston pounced. "How did you know that Derek was dirty? When did you figure that out?" Had she held back information? He trusted her, but a flash of guilt clouded her eyes.

Laila moved to the couch and sat down. "I've been at one too many crime scenes and added up all the clues. I assumed he had to be the person that trashed the office. Why else would he monitor the room? He was looking for something, so I took a shot that he wanted the laptop. Derek is a lowlife crook, but unless Walt had threatened to expose him, I don't think he's our killer. Steven and Quinn will probably find that tracker on your dad's computer, just like he said. He could go to jail for corporate espionage."

"I can't believe Derek would sell out my dad like that. Or my sister." Preston sank onto the couch next to her. A flicker of unease flashed across her face, as if she had some bad news to deliver. "What's wrong?" he asked.

"I found something else." Laila hesitated, and evidence of a raging internal debate sparked through her brown eyes. "I didn't even tell the police yet because I wanted you to be the first to see it. I was about to show you when Derek interrupted."

She pulled something from her pocket. "I'll get these to Quinn. He'll blow a gasket that I removed evidence, but I didn't have time to think about it before Derek showed up. I found these pictures under the keyboard mat in your dad's secret office."

She laid three pictures on the couch cushion between them. Preston recognized his picture. And then Ethan's. A jolt of warmth shot through his body at the fact that his dad had kept their childhood pictures in his office. The man hadn't been known for his sentimental side and had rarely showed public affection toward his children.

But there was something out of place with the third picture. It wasn't a shot he remembered, and it wasn't himself or Ethan in the picture.

"Who's in this picture?" Preston asked. Laila flipped the yellowing paper over by its edges, and the handwritten name said it all.

Seth.

"Is it possible that Seth is your half brother?"

Preston struggled to find words. Of all the low and despicable things his father had done, he'd never thought of his dad as a cheater. But he'd always known his parents' relationship was rocky. Maybe because of infidelity?

"If he had a secret love child, then they've kept it hidden all these years. Maybe we need to have another talk with Margot. Wait, you don't think that Margot has something to do with my dad's death?"

"I have no idea, but she just got bumped up the suspect list. A jilted lover makes a good motive for murder."

"But why now? Seth's doing great, and I'm sure my dad took care of them financially. That family has never lacked anything."

Laila shrugged. "Maybe she thinks she should get more?"

A thousand different emotions sucker punched Preston in the gut. He dragged in a breath. His dad was gone, leaving behind a mess. His sister's husband was a no-good crook. And someone wanted him dead.

But no matter what happened from this point forward, he'd never get to see his dad and brother again. The years had escaped them. If only he'd made an attempt to reconcile with his father. The thought of missed opportunities suffocated him. "I just wish I'd talked to my dad," he finally said. "I left and never looked back. And now I have this ache to talk with him. One last time. I never got to say goodbye."

Laila wrapped her hand over his. "I'm so sorry, Preston. I can't imagine the toll this has taken on you. To lose both your brother and father so suddenly. It's going to take time for you to properly grieve."

He and Laila had a connection that he couldn't quite explain. It was like she could look right through him and see his heart.

"I didn't lose my father to death, but I lost him a long time ago," Laila said, never taking her hand from his. "I was twelve when he announced that he'd had an affair and another child. I have a half sister who is only two years younger than me." She paused. "I suppose that's why it was so easy for me to jump to the conclusion that Seth might be your half brother."

"That's awful." He couldn't imagine what his own father's affair would do to his mother. Had she known about his infidelity? "I'm sorry that happened to you."

"He came home and announced that he wanted to live with his other family. For years, I refused to let him go, making sure he saw me and all that I accomplished. But eventually I had to take care of my brother and mother, who couldn't recover from the loss. We came to the United States, and I hardly talk to him."

"So you know a thing or two about trying to earn a parent's approval. But it goes back to what you said earlier. You aimed for perfection. I gave up."

She nodded. "I remember that he would attend my karate tournaments occasionally. One match in particular, I didn't do well, and I'll never forget my father leaving before the end of the tournament. It was like he only wanted to be there when I was winning." She paused. "I was only good enough if I was winning, but not worth supporting if I had a bad day."

Who would do something so cruel to his own child? But then, his father had betrayed the people he supposedly cared about.

Laila's vulnerability touched him. She didn't share intimate details of her life with just anyone, making it hard to resist her. Understanding shone in her eyes as she reflected on her own past. An invisible rope tied around his heart and pulled him toward this woman.

Preston brushed her hair back away from her face and then froze. The movement had come from reflex, almost like someone had switched him on auto pilot. "I'm sorry," he said in response to the intimate gesture. He'd almost kissed her the last time they had sat in the bedroom like this and talked. Now the electricity that surged between them was practically visible.

A knock at the door startled them both. He let out a sigh as Laila moved to find out who was at the door. Maybe they needed an interruption, because...wow.

Laila opened the door to Julian. His pale face communicated trouble without him having to say a word.

Preston jumped up and rushed to Julian. "Is my mom okay?"

The elderly man shook his head. "Sorry to bother you. It's about Derek. Katrina found him in their room, unresponsive. They just called for an ambulance."

Laila looked at Preston, her eyes wide. The situation reeked of foul play. Could this be another attack? When would this all end?

13

FRIDAY, 6:00 A.M.

Laila shrugged off the blanket of exhaustion wrapped around her and raced across the house with Preston to the wing where Derek and Katrina lived. She chided herself for her emotional free fall with Preston. Their situations were similar, and his grief hit too close to home for her.

Yes, they had a connection, but she had a job to do and needed to focus on keeping Preston safe.

When they got to the room, the paramedics were wheeling a lifeless Derek out on a stretcher.

"What happened, Kat?" Preston asked his sister, his tenderness melting Laila's heart. She studied Katrina. When the makeup came off, she was quite stunning with her natural beauty.

"He— I couldn't wake him up." Tears flowed and Preston wrapped his sister in a protective bear hug.

Steven held up a bag with a bottle of scotch in it. "We think that after we sent Derek out of the office, he started drinking.

175

According to Katrina, someone had sent a bottle of scotch to the house for Preston, and Derek helped himself to it."

Katrina took a step back from her brother and wiped her eyes with her sleeve. "Someone sent the bottle to you, but Derek figured you wouldn't mind if he kept it, since it's his favorite and you don't drink anymore. I swear I thought he'd asked you. He must have drunk it right before coming back to bed. I woke up and he was unconscious." More sobs escaped her throat.

"Did you save the box the package came in?" Steven asked.

Katrina sniffed. "It's probably around here somewhere." She went to look for the packaging.

"I'll bet someone tampered with the bottle," Steven said. "We'll send it for testing."

"That used to be my favorite drink, back in the day. If someone was trying to poison me, it's someone who knows me well."

"Derek was top on the suspect list," Laila said, keeping her voice low. "He wouldn't poison himself. Unless he had a partner that turned on him, he might not be our culprit."

"It's six a.m. and we've got two crime scenes to contain," Steven said. "I'd better get back to it. I'm going to track down Katrina."

He left and Preston looked at Laila. "I'm going to check on my mother."

"Of course," Laila said. "I'll go with you."

Turned out Sophia's sleeping pills worked wonders, and she'd slept through the commotion.

Laila flinched when she thought of Preston's impending conversation with his mother about Walt's infidelity. Did she know her husband had cheated on her? Did she know the truth about Seth's parentage?

Once they confirmed Sophia was sleeping, they headed toward the kitchen for some much-needed coffee.

Preston slumped at the table, hands wrapped around the cup. Laila sat down next to him. "What do you think about taking the day off today? After all that happened last night, maybe it's not a good idea to head to the office."

Preston shrugged. "I'm so tired, and I do have my laptop, so I can get some work done. I hate hiding out, but you're right. I'm in no shape to head to the office. But I do want to talk to Margot. If I have another brother, my family deserves the truth."

His eyes held a sorrow that tore Laila in two. She wished she could help ease his pain. "I wonder if she'd meet us here at the estate."

"I'll text her and ask. Part of me wonders if Seth knows. If so, he's never let on. But before I talk to him, I need to ask Margot."

Preston texted Margot. A ding indicated a response. "She'll be here at nine. I told her I wanted to go over the schedule."

Laila nodded. She wanted to say something, but the coffee hadn't jump-started her brain just yet.

Her thoughts swirled. Had she almost kissed Preston? She'd thrown all her professionalism out the window while danger drove them closer together. They'd already kissed under the pretense of marriage, but she'd almost caved and kissed him for real.

Veronica swept through the kitchen, and Preston immediately stood. "I'm just going to take my coffee to go," he said. "I'm going back upstairs. See you in a bit."

Laila could see the tension in Preston's shoulders as he passed Veronica. His sister-in-law smiled, and he just kept walking. Laila made a mental note to ask him about his obvious disdain for Veronica. Was it more than just the issue with Ethan cutting her out of the will?

"Do you want some coffee?" Laila asked Veronica with forced politeness.

"Sure, sounds good." The sun hadn't even risen yet and the woman was already in full makeup and dressed to perfection. Laila looked down at her sweats and long-sleeved T-shirt. A grin escaped her lips before she could stop it. She had no desire to impress Preston's former girlfriend.

Laila poured a cup of coffee and handed it to Veronica. "Crazy night, huh?"

Veronica sat at the table and took a sip of the coffee. Laila sank into the seat across from her.

"I feel awful about Derek," Veronica said. "How is he doing?"

"Katrina texted Preston from the hospital. He's not out of the woods yet but is stable and should make a full recovery."

Veronica nodded. "I wish they'd catch the culprit. I fear for Preston's life."

Laila couldn't tell if there was a sincere bone in Veronica's body, but this morning the woman didn't appear to have any ulterior motives in talking with Laila. Maybe Laila could get some information out of Preston's sister-in-law. "I know what you mean, but who do you think could be evil enough to do something like this? I'm concerned about Preston's safety. Any ideas on who could be behind these attacks?"

Veronica sipped her coffee as if pondering her response. "Well, Bob has been out to get the family for years. I wouldn't put it past the man."

Bob's name kept moving up the suspect list. But did Veronica possess any inside knowledge on who might be the killer? Or was she the one setting the man up?

"I have to ask," Veronica said, "how did you land Preston? I mean, many women have tried. Including myself." She gave a sheepish grin. "That's way in the past, but how did you get him to settle down? He's so devoted to you."

Laila took a deep breath. Was Veronica baiting her? "I was in the right place at the right time, I guess. We just connected from the moment we met." Which was the truth. She and Preston shared a deep connection and similar values, despite having just met.

"Watching you two makes me miss Ethan. Although I don't think we ever had what you two have. If you want my advice, you'd better hold on to him."

Veronica took her coffee and left before Laila could utter a word. What was that about? It almost sounded like a challenge more than sage wisdom.

Laila stared at her surroundings and willed herself to wake up. This had to be the least used room in the house, since it wasn't designed for entertaining. The small table where she sat nestled into a nook opposite the commercial-sized kitchen.

She glanced at the time on her phone. Maybe she should stop fighting sleep and take a nap.

Laila stood to leave, but Sophia stumbled into the kitchen, looking hung over. Tears stained her rosy cheeks. When she saw Laila, she paused and pressed fingers to her swollen eyes.

"Sophia. I think you could use some coffee."

A small smile trembled on Sophia's lips before she nodded. "Definitely."

Laila helped her to the table and got her some coffee. She set the steaming mug in front of her. "I assume you heard the news about Derek."

Sophia nodded. "It's just so awful. It's this curse that's on our family."

Laila covered the fragile woman's hands with her own.

While Sophia spent big bucks to maintain a youthful appearance, her hands reflected her true age.

"I'm just so glad Preston found true love. You cherish him, and when he's with you, somehow I know he's safe. You look out for him."

"I think we take turns saving each other." Warning bells rang in Laila's ears, and she wanted to take the words back. She couldn't forge a mother-daughter relationship with Sophia, because it would end. She needed to tread lightly.

Thoughts of her own mother assaulted Laila. The drunken confessions of love as Laila helped her mom to bed. The days where her mom stayed in bed when the depression overtook her. She blinked away the memories, but the similarities between her own past and Sophia's present haunted her. Someone needed to take care of Sophia, no matter how pretentious and Botox-injected she became.

"I see the way he looks at you. You mean the world to him. I'm just glad Preston found someone like I found my Walt."

Laila's heart squeezed at the mention of *her Walt*. What if they discovered the truth about Seth? Had Sophia suspected Walt's infidelity? "Why don't you get some more rest, Sophia? It's going to be a busy day."

"Rest. Yes, that would be lovely."

Laila walked Sophia back to her bedroom with her coffee. Preston had an uncomfortable conversation with his mother looming on the horizon. How would Sophia take the news that her husband hadn't been as faithful as she may have believed?

Preston and Laila waited in the library for Margot. He wanted to make sure they picked a room that wouldn't allow anyone to eavesdrop for this conversation. But to be on the safe side, Laila had swept the area for listening devices.

Julian announced Margot's arrival, and the woman stopped short when she entered the room and saw Laila. "Hello." The question in Margot's one-word greeting spoke volumes.

Preston motioned for the woman to sit. "Thank you for meeting with us."

"Us?"

"I've decided to put Laila's numerous skills to work. She's agreed to be my social coordinator and manage my calendar. She'll keep you updated on everything." He took Laila's hand and smiled into her eyes. Eyes that widened a fraction at his tender look. "And, I suppose, I may have been looking for a reason to keep her close by. I miss her when she's not with me."

Laila's cheeks pinkened. She cleared her throat and squeezed his hand. Hard. Preston fought a laugh.

Margot sat across from them and pulled out her iPad. "So, did you decide on the birthday party for Bella tonight? I know your mom would love for you to attend. The families have always been close."

Preston nodded. "We plan on going but might not stay long. It's been a rough week." He filled her in on the previous night's events, leaving out a few key details like finding the laptop. Laila flashed him a smile, which lifted some of the weight off him from the impending heavy conversation. "We did find something in Dad's office, though. I'm hoping you can explain it to us." He handed her the three photographs. "Why would my dad keep a photo of Seth?"

The color drained from Margot's face, and she stared at the

picture. "I—I don't know. He always had a soft spot for Seth, being raised by a single mother."

"Margot." Preston worked to keep his voice calm. "He looks like Ethan and me at that age. I'm not sure how no one's noticed before, but it's clear to me that he's my brother." The words were half statement and half bluff.

Silence filled the room, and Margot remained still as a statue. The ticking of the grandfather clock counted off each passing second. Preston held his breath, waiting for Margot's reaction.

She finally let out a sob and covered her face with her hands.

"Your father didn't want anyone to discover the truth," she said, her words muffled by her palms. She dropped her hands. "He didn't want anyone to know about the affair, the baby, any of it. He loved you and Ethan, and it would have destroyed your mother. We agreed to keep it a secret. He promised to take care of us, and I believed he would. Walt was a good man—"

"A good man who cheated on my mother," Preston muttered.

Margot shuddered but lifted her chin. "Back then, they were headed for divorce, but he had a change of heart and wanted to give his marriage another try. He broke it off with me before I found out I was pregnant. I contemplated not telling him, but I needed to keep my job if I was to support a baby."

"Does Seth know?" Preston asked.

Margot shook her head, tears creating rivers down her makeup. "I don't think he's put the pieces together. If he has, he's never told me. I promised your dad I'd keep it quiet. Despite the affair and your dad choosing your mother over me, I believed in him and his vision for the company. Nothing happened between us after he ended it with me. We kept it strictly professional."

Other than his dad probably paying the woman off.

"So, you two worked side by side for all these years, keeping Seth a secret from everyone? Didn't it occur to either of you that you were robbing Seth of the opportunity to be a part of his family?"

Margot scoffed. "I saw the way you, Ethan, and your sister turned out. I refused to let Seth squander his life away. I wanted him to have a normal life, not one in the public spotlight."

"I think Preston turned out just fine," Laila said, and Preston's heart thumped at her defense.

It occurred to him that Margot wasn't the innocent victim she claimed to be. She could have left and found another job. Instead, she'd attached herself to a married man and ridden his success to the top.

"I'm glad to see he's changed his ways since his reckless youth." Margot smoothed an invisible wrinkle from her skirt.

Could this woman be psychotic enough to kill his father out of revenge for past rejection? Was this some sort of jilted lover's quarrel? But why keep coming after Preston if that were the case?

"I want to tell Seth," Preston said. "I think he has the right to know."

Margot's eyes darkened. "I don't know if that's a good idea. Seth thinks his father died before he was born. Walt's gone. What good can come from dredging up the past now?"

Preston ran a hand through his hair. "I want a relationship with my brother. I lost my chance with Ethan. Maybe I can start over fresh with Seth." He tried to keep his anger in check, but he refused to miss out on being a part of Seth's life. They'd always hung out as kids, but this was different.

He had another brother.

Margot let out a long sigh, then stared him down. "No.

Word will get out immediately, and I won't have your father's name tarnished now that he's gone. The more people that find out, the sooner the story will wind up as headline news. It's the very thing I've tried to shield Seth from. He doesn't need to live his life under public scrutiny."

Preston steeled his nerves. "If you don't tell him, I will. He deserves to know about his family. He could have had a relationship with my dad."

Margot scoffed. "Your father didn't want anything to ruin his precious image. What kind of relationship do you think Seth would have had? The kind you and your dad shared? Your father favored Ethan. Everyone knows that."

Her disdain-laced words shot daggers through his heart. Maybe Seth would be better off not thinking he was second best like Preston had all of his life.

But Seth had been surrounded by family and never known the truth. "I'd like to get to know my brother. Why don't you let Seth decide what's best for him?"

Margot's whole body stiffened, but she regained her composure. She dabbed at her tear-rimmed eyes. "Fine. I'll tell him since I know you will. But don't blame me when the media finds out. How will your mother feel, reading about her husband's infidelity in the news? This is going to affect your whole family."

Preston bit back his irritation. If Margot had cared about his family's reputation, she wouldn't have had an affair with his father.

"Does my mom know?"

Margot shrugged. "Your father liked to keep secrets. I don't know what she knows. She never said anything to me about it if she did find out."

She stood, apparently deciding to be done with the conversation. "Just give me some time to talk to him before you say anything. But if you'll excuse me, I need to get back to the office and take care of a few things."

Margot rushed out of the room.

"Are you really going to work with the woman who had an affair with your dad and kept your half brother a secret all of these years?" Laila asked.

"I hadn't thought about that. She's been my dad's assistant forever, and she keeps the office running. But you're right, I can't trust her."

He ran a hand through his hair. "I need to tell my mom at some point. Before others find out. I don't even want to think about it."

"That's not going to be an easy conversation."

Preston sighed. "What I really want is to run away again. I just don't want to deal with all of this today. What if we blow off all responsibilities and do something fun?" Maybe just the two of them? He'd give anything to spend the day with Laila but didn't want to push things with her. After all, what kind of relationship could they have once her job was done? They lived in different worlds.

For now, he'd have to soak up as much time with her as possible.

Laila checked her phone. "Oh no. I forgot to cancel my class this afternoon."

"What class? You teach?"

"It's a self-defense class at a community center near my house. It's Krav Maga."

"Okay. Let's go." What could be a better way to get to know Laila than on her own turf? He'd been dying to see her outside of her bodyguard and fake wife roles. Something that would show him the real woman beneath the layers of identities.

"Do you have amnesia? Have you forgotten that you're

being targeted by a killer? Not to mention your paparazzi stalkers. We can't go anywhere without planning for your safety."

"We'll probably throw off anyone tracking us by not going to the office today. It'll be like old times for me—when I used to ditch the reporters."

He watched her ponder the idea, wishing he could read her mind. Either she was laying out the security hazards for the trip or she was just dead tired. She blinked and her long lashes fluttered, causing his pulse to spike. Good grief, he was in trouble.

"If Charlie can go with us, I'll be less concerned. But it's still a risk."

Preston did a fist pump in the air and Laila laughed. "Fine. You win. We can make it work if you're sure you're up for this. I can teach the class, and you can play some basketball with the guys. Charlie always picks up games there. But only if you get some rest. We've been up all night."

"Yes, Mom."

She punched his arm.

"A long nap does sound good to me."

She sent a text. Seconds later, she looked up. "Charlie's good with the plan."

A day with Laila. What could possibly go wrong?

"We need to move the timetable up. I can't wait any longer."

The voice on the other end of the phone grumbled. "We just ran the man down in broad daylight. Pushed his car into the river. What more do you want us to do? I'm not going to jail for you. Sooner or later, we're going to be caught. We need to skip town. Now."

Was this guy serious? How dare he make excuses and try to run. Maybe he needed to be the next to die. "You and your brother will do what I say. You're on my payroll, remember? The last thing you want to do is cross me."

"And the last thing you want to do is get your hands dirty or have any evidence pointing toward you."

The plan had been spiraling out of control since the second Preston Whittaker strolled into his father's funeral. Pacing helped tame the rising panic. "The job isn't done until Preston is six feet under. You don't get the rest of the money until that man is dead and buried. I'll double your fee. Just kill the man already. Your brother needs to follow him today, and you two need to do whatever it takes to end his life."

14

FRIDAY, 11:30 A.M.

Preston and Laila both managed to find a few hours to rest before sneaking out of the house and down to the garage where Charlie had the car waiting. A quick nap and Preston was ready to go.

They ducked down in the back seat, but the paparazzi must have found bigger stories, as the crowds gathering around the perimeter had dwindled each day to a few stragglers. Charlie managed to evade those, and soon they were on the road, headed to the community center.

Flashbacks of their near-fatal experience taunted Preston. Would his mind dredge up the memories every time he got in a car?

When Charlie turned into the parking lot, Preston noted the place was packed with people getting a jump start on their weekend. The center offered classes, a pool, and a gymnasium for basketball and other sports.

Charlie threw a gym bag over his shoulder. "You don't have

to hang out in the self-defense class. I don't think I've ever seen a man in that class. I've got some guys lined up for basketball if you're interested."

"Don't listen to him. Everyone's welcome," Laila said. "It's not just for women."

Did he dare make a fool of himself in front of a bunch of Laila's friends for a chance to catch her in her element? "Hmm, sounds tempting, Charlie, but I think I'd like to brush up my self-defense moves. I need all the help I can get." He made a lame karate chop in the air, and Laila cringed.

Preston recognized a few of Laila's friends as they entered the complex, Lizzie being one of them. She ran up and gave Charlie a kiss—and the man didn't seem to mind one bit.

When Preston got into the workout room, he spotted Juliette and Christina from the Elite Guardians. Juliette introduced him to Alana Flores and Noelle Burton, two women who worked with the Guardians.

A woman approached Laila and gave her a big hug.

"Preston, this is Katie Matthews. We take turns teaching this class. I haven't seen her for a while since she's been out on maternity leave." Katie shot Preston a don't-mess-with-my-friend-Laila look. These Elite Guardians took protection to a whole new level.

When the class started, he tried to stake out his spot at the back of the room, but Laila grabbed his arm and pulled him to the front. "I'll be your partner when we pair up for some moves."

He shook his head and laughed. "Looks like I don't have much of a choice, do I?" At least he didn't see any cameras. Probably wouldn't be good to be on the six o'clock news for looking like a fool.

"Don't worry. I'll go easy on you."

A few more people filled in the space, and Laila kicked off

the hour-long session. They started with some warm-ups, tiring him out before the actual instruction officially began. Laila made it look easy, her motions smooth and flawless. When was the last time he'd hit the gym?

A quick glance around the room told Preston that they'd been working on the mechanics of a few punches for a while. He tried to find his groove during the warm-up and watched Laila, but he heard a few snickers behind him.

Of course he'd be the sideshow.

He looked over his shoulder, and Juliette shot him a thumbs-up with a smile. "Nice moves, Whitt," she called out, which garnered a few snickers. He shook his head and laughed.

"Looks like Preston just got volunteered to help me with a demonstration," Laila announced.

If only he'd taken Charlie up on the offer for basketball. He surrendered and marched to the center of the class.

"Today's lesson is how to get out of a choke hold."

Oh boy. This had the potential to head south real fast. She'd have him on the ground in no time. He was a rookie compared to her skills.

Laila slid next to him.

"Go easy on me," he whispered.

She smiled and addressed the class. "If you're attacked from behind, it only takes about six seconds for your attacker to render you unconscious. Preston, pretend to attack me from behind with your arm around my neck."

He followed her instructions and wrapped his arm around her throat, loose enough that she could still talk. "You might not ever see your assailant if he comes at you from behind. This is a common way attackers grab someone and drag them away to an isolated area."

She grabbed at Preston's arm in an attempt to free herself, but he held firm. "Now, your first reaction is going to be to try and pull his arm away from your throat. But as you can see, his arm won't budge when it's locked in tight like this."

Laila moved one leg forward. "Okay, Preston. Time to crank up the pressure a bit." He hesitated but complied. Faster than a lightning strike, Laila maneuvered herself back, ducking and twisting out of his grip.

A few people clapped. "Now I'll walk through this move in slow motion." She repositioned herself in Preston's grip again. "I move my front leg out, placing my back leg between us. I move away from the arm he's choking me with, twist, and duck." After a few more demonstrations of the technique, the group broke up in pairs to work on the move, one person being the attacker and the other attempting to break free.

"How are you going to practice a choke hold on me?" he whispered. "I've got at least ten inches on you."

He shouldn't have asked.

Before he realized what was happening, she kicked his legs out from under him and had her arms tightly wound around his neck before he'd fallen to his knees. "Now let's see what you've got," she said.

Her strength blew him away. He'd assumed because of her size that he'd dominate her and get out of the choke, but her crushing grip indicated otherwise. Gasping for breath and tamping down the panic, he recalled her steps on how to move away from her arm, twist, and break free, which was a lot harder to do from the ground. He managed to twist and felt the pressure release. He rolled away from her. She offered a hand to help him stand.

Applause erupted amidst a few catcalls. He'd been so laser focused on getting out of the choke hold that he hadn't noticed the women in the room gathered around to watch his performance. "Not bad for your first try," Laila said.

The class worked through a few more maneuvers that Laila

showcased, then they practiced as a group. Sweat dripped down Preston's back by the time the class ended. What a workout.

After the class dispersed, a few of Laila's friends decided to catch the tail end of the basketball game. "You want to join them?" she asked.

"Sure, why not?" He followed her to the gym and slipped inside.

The screech of sneakers on the floor brought Preston back to his days in Magellan Falls, when he used to play pickup games with some friends. Back when he'd had the freedom to be himself and didn't have to worry about it making headline news.

They grabbed spots on the bleachers to watch the game. Laila chatted with Juliette, and he enjoyed the sound of their carefree laughter. Being around Laila and her coworkers evoked a sense of peace he hadn't experienced since returning. He relished living a low-key life. But that wasn't the role he'd been dealt.

An elbow in the ribs brought him back to earth. "What are you thinking about?" Laila asked.

He shrugged. "Just wondering how many opportunities I'll have in the future to be myself. To not have to perform. It's been a nice afternoon."

"Well, you kind of put on a show being the only man in a *women's* self-defense class."

"Hey, you said everyone was welcome. You tricked me."

Her smile sent shock waves rippling through him. "Guilty."

The basketball game ended, and Charlie headed over to the bleachers. "We're playing another round. Want in, Whitt?"

"Sure."

Charlie introduced Preston to a few of his friends, and

Preston shook hands with Grey Parker. "I've met Christina. Congratulations."

The man beamed at the mention of his fiancée. Despite being in a wheelchair, Grey had dominated the court for the time Preston had been watching. With any luck, they'd be on the same team.

"So, you're here with Laila?" Grey asked.

He nodded but didn't elaborate. How did he explain his relationship with Laila? Her friends wouldn't believe they were married. But before his mind formulated any kind of response, Charlie jumped in and changed the subject. "Grey met his fiancée when Christina was his bodyguard." With Charlie's quick elbow jab to his side, Preston picked up on Charlie's not-so-subtle hint.

Grey laughed. "Yeah, I guess that worked out in my favor. But technically, Christina was my dog's bodyguard. Don't remind her of that though."

"Oh yeah, that's right." Charlie and Grey laughed.

Preston smiled at their camaraderie. "All I can say at this time is *no comment.*"

They moved to the center of the court to start the game, but Preston's mind was far from the gym.

What would it be like to have all of this with someone like Laila? He longed for community with friends and laughter. An afternoon where they could relax and enjoy themselves without cameras vying for his attention.

Because he definitely could get used to this kind of life, especially if it meant Laila was by his side.

Laila watched the guys play basketball. The second Preston was out of earshot, Christina, Lizzie, and Juliette flanked her.

"What's going on with you and Preston?" Christina couldn't contain her enthusiasm. "He's totally got stars in his eyes for you."

"It's professional. I'm his bodyguard. That's it."

The three laughed. "I might not know you very well," Juliette said, "but that man is smitten. He hung out with a bunch of women today just to be with you. That's bold."

Laila shook her head. "I just need to keep him alive, which is my job, remember? That place where we all work?"

"Your job is to pretend to be married to a very good-looking, extremely wealthy man," Lizzie said. "Of course he's going to fall for you. Who wouldn't? Especially after seeing you in action."

She watched Preston shoot the ball. His natural athleticism shone on the court. But she needed to keep her head in a totally different game. A game of life and death. Her burgeoning personal feelings had to take a back seat.

But what happened when the assignment ended and she wasn't Laila Whittaker any longer? A pang of sadness gave her pause. How had this intense chemistry ignited in such a short time span? She'd just met him, and yet the connection between them ran deep.

"Earth to Laila," Lizzie said. "I'm thinking Preston might not be the only one who's smitten."

"What? I mean, I've gotten to know him, but come on. I'm not relationship material, and he's got a lot on his plate. Not to mention the fact that we live in two different worlds and his is very public."

Christina placed a hand on Laila's arm. "But look at me. I'd walled myself off from the possibilities of love. And I found Grey when I least expected it. All I'm saying is, don't dismiss something special because of fear."

Special would be one way to describe the connection she

felt to Preston. He seemed to understand her on a level that most people didn't get.

The basketball game ended. Laila parted ways with her coworkers and headed to the locker room to change and grab her gym bag. When she emerged, Preston and Charlie had showered and were ready to go. Everyone else had already taken off.

All of Laila's senses kicked into overdrive the moment the three of them stepped out the exit of the building. A chill swept over her, and it wasn't from the cold air. Warning bells blared in her mind, signaling that someone was watching them.

She looked at Charlie, unease threading through his face. He sensed it too. "Would you wait here with Preston?" Laila nodded to the car. "I'm going to take a look around first."

She stuck her hand in her gym bag and pulled out a mirror with a telescopic wand attached.

Preston's eyes widened. "Do you really think they followed us here?"

Laila shrugged. "These attackers are relentless and seem to have inside information. I wouldn't put it past them to tamper with the car. After all, they ran us off the road in the middle of the day with witnesses all around. They're bold."

She approached the car, unable to shake the thick cloak of uneasiness. It was as if unseen eyes were boring holes into her. She glanced at the woods across the street from the gym but didn't see anything suspicious. Stopping a few feet from the car, she dropped to the ground, slid the mirror underneath, and maneuvered it so she could get a good look. At the click of a button, white LED lights chased away the shadows, illuminating the space beneath the car.

Her body tensed at the sight of wires hanging down from a small rectangular box attached under the passenger's side door. Glad she'd trusted her instincts.

"Found something," she yelled to Charlie and Preston.

Charlie moved Preston back toward the building, his phone pressed to his ear, calling for reinforcements. She could hear him barking orders from her position on the ground.

There weren't any lights glowing on the device. Was it a tripwire, set to go off if they opened the passenger door?

She was about to retract the mirror and get away from the vehicle when she heard a faint beep. A red light glowed in the mirror.

Someone had used a remote to set a timer. Seeing the number ten followed by a nine sent Laila sprinting back toward Charlie and Preston.

"Run!" She caught up with them under the awning of the entranceway when the earth rocked beneath her feet.

They hit the ground, Charlie and Laila on top of Preston. A deafening blast rang through her ears followed by a chain reaction of several car alarms activating. Flames turned their car into a hollowed-out metal skeleton, scorching the cars on either side of it with the power of the blast. Heat singed her arms from her position on the ground.

Preston groaned, and she realized his arms were wrapped around her just as tightly as she was holding him. She disentangled herself from his grip and rolled to the side. "Preston, are you okay?"

He sat up and looked at her, his eyes wide. "You...you could have been killed."

"Or you could have been killed." Laila stood. "These criminals are getting bolder. This needs to end." Adrenaline pumped through her veins. The killer had watched her approach the car and then set off the bomb. Which meant he had to be close.

She found her gym bag that she'd dropped on the sidewalk earlier and rummaged through it. Her hands hit the cool metal of her binoculars, and she used them to scan the area through the haze of smoke. At the edge of the woods, a glint of metal sparkled through the lenses, causing her heart to stop.

Her eyes connected with another set of binoculars held by a man dressed in camo-covered tactical gear with a rifle slung over his shoulder. She pulled down the binoculars and blinked. Another look confirmed it wasn't a mirage. This time she saw the man's back as he bolted through the trees.

"Charlie, stay with Preston."

"Wait! What are you doing? What do you see?"

"Someone's watching," she said, her words getting lost in the cacophony of sirens and car alarms still blaring.

Her brain unfolded her options as she ran. This could be their sniper, who had probably waited for the perfect opportunity to remotely detonate the bomb. He had to have known they'd check the car out before opening the door.

But what if he stopped running and decided to shoot? She'd seen his expert sniper skills on more than one occasion.

She paused at the edge of the four-lane highway and used her binoculars to get her sights on the enemy. A rustling in some bushes drew her attention. The man continued with his escape plan. Which meant he wasn't likely to take the time to set up camp to take a shot at her. A chance she'd have to take.

Traffic was unusually thick because of an accident, and vehicles crawled along the highway. Her adrenaline pumped hard, and she dashed between the cars. A few drivers gave her some startled looks, but she pressed on. She hurdled the concrete median and maneuvered across the rest of the lanes.

Nothing was going to stop her from tracking this guy down. It might be their biggest lead yet. There were at least two perpetrators. Was the second one also hanging around?

Her pace slowed when she morphed into stealth mode at the edge of the woods. Moving from tree to tree, she dropped the binoculars in favor of her gun.

A twig snapped just ahead of her, and she followed the sound. The foliage grew denser. Footsteps pounded, heading away from her. "Oh no you don't. You're not getting away this time."

She picked up speed. Dodging leafy branches and tree trunks, she caught sight of a black-and-green blur fifty yards from her. The gap between them closed.

He turned, fired a gun in her direction, and kept running. The shot went wild.

At the crack of the bullet hitting the tree next to her, she dropped, rolled, and jumped back up.

The time he'd taken to shoot had cost him. Laila launched herself from a few feet away, landing on the man's back and wrapping her arms around his neck in a choke hold. He fell to his knees, gasping for breath. Only when she felt the man go limp did she release the tension from his throat.

Catching her breath, she checked the guy's pulse, which thumped a steady rhythm under her fingertips. Her leg muscles screamed from the exertion, but it felt great because she'd caught the guy red-handed. They were one step closer to catching their culprit if they could get this man to talk and turn on his partner.

She riffled through the man's belongings. A pair of binoculars dangled from his neck, and he had a cell phone and Beretta M9 in his possession, plus the rifle. Could this guy be former Army? The M9 was a lot of firepower for an average citizen. The cell phone must have been how he'd detonated the bomb remotely.

She checked his back pocket and scored some zip ties—interesting. Using his own restraints against him, she bound his hands and feet. This guy wasn't going anywhere except to jail.

Police sirens echoed in the distance. She whipped out her phone and called Steven.

He picked up on the first ring. "Where are you?"

"I'm in the woods across from the gym. Caught our suspect watching us, and he was up to no good."

"I'm almost there. Stay put."

Distant sirens grew louder. The call disconnected and the gravel on the side of the highway crunched with an approaching vehicle. She ducked behind a tree in case it wasn't the good guys approaching. Her nerves settled when she saw Steven and Quinn trekking through the woods. "I'm back here," she called out. Preston and Charlie must have caught a ride, because they were right behind the police officers.

The second Preston spotted her through the trees, he charged toward her with his fists clenched at his side. "What were you thinking?" His voice bounced off the trees.

"I was chasing down our only lead. We needed to catch this guy in the act."

He got within an inch of her face. "You could have been killed. You ran across a highway. I watched you take off running, and you just didn't stop." He gestured to the man on the ground. "The guy was armed. Did you even stop to consider that you could have been killed?"

The intensity in Preston's eyes gave her the chills. "He was watching from the woods and set the bomb off with a remote detonator. The whole thing was well orchestrated, and he bolted when I spotted him. I took a chance."

"But you could have been killed," Preston repeated, choking on the word *killed*. He cleared his throat. "What if you'd misread the situation? What if you were wrong?"

"You could have been blown up," she said, biting back the urge to shout. Why didn't he understand she'd done this to keep him safe? She took a deep breath. "I went with my instincts. We needed this break. This guy"—she rolled him with her foot and he groaned—"can give us the answers to put away this threat for good. I'm doing my job."

"How can you do your job if you're dead? You ran straight into danger without thinking of the consequences."

Without thinking? Every single move she made was calculated and centered around protecting him. She scowled and crossed her arms. "I'm here to protect you. I don't have to explain my actions to you."

"Well, I'm not going to stand around and watch my wife die."

Wife? She looked at him as the word soaked through her. When had the lines between personal and professional become so blurred?

She opened her mouth to reply, but no words came. Preston gaped at her. They stared at each other until Quinn and Steven interrupted their standoff.

"If you two are done with your little lover's quarrel, do either of you recognize this guy?" Quinn revived Laila's quarry and dragged the man to his feet.

Preston shook his head. "I've never seen him before." The perpetrator gave a snarl, and Quinn moved the man toward the police car.

Steven pulled out his old-school pen and flip notebook. "Preston, I'll need to get your statement, starting with the car bomb. Let's head back to the cruiser."

Preston glanced at Laila, a frown still pressed to his face. "Sounds good." He spun and followed Steven.

Charlie put a hand on Laila's shoulder and pulled her aside. "He's come to care about you. I'm sure that had to hurt, watching you run across the highway like you were invincible. Might want to ease back some of that stubborn *I'm indestructible* personality of yours."

"I'm not stubborn," she said. But sadly, her sharp tone

proved his point. She schooled her voice. "If I hadn't run down that guy, we wouldn't have caught him. How long can we keep jumping at shadows, hiding out waiting for the bad guys to strike? We need to catch these criminals so Preston can get his life back."

"I know. You got lucky. This time. But you should have waited for backup. What happens if one day your instincts are wrong or you misread a situation? You're so used to being a team of one that it's going to backfire someday. And you may very well drive Preston away for good." He looked into her eyes. "And I don't think you want that."

"What are you talking about? Once this assignment ends, so does my relationship with Preston. I...I..."

Why was she flustered? Heat spread across her neck toward her face.

"I thought so," Charlie said with a wink and walked away, leaving Laila alone, her thoughts churning like the winds in a hurricane.

No, it wasn't possible. She wasn't falling for Preston. Her mind shouted reason after reason why they couldn't be together.

Now if she could only convince her heart to fall in line.

15

He'd almost lost her.

The moment they'd returned to the estate, Preston had retreated to the bedroom with the excuse of getting ready for the party. In reality, he needed some time alone to process his discovery.

He cared for her. A lot—as evidenced by his blunder in throwing out the word *wife*. Where had that come from?

When he closed his eyes, all he could picture was Laila running down the gunman. She'd darted across a four-lane highway without giving it a second thought. After almost being blown up by a car bomb. Once she'd ducked into the woods and he couldn't see her, he'd assumed the worst. The sound of a gunshot had ripped him to shreds. He ground his teeth thinking about it, and a knot formed in the pit of his stomach.

It had taken almost losing her to realize what he wanted. He wanted Laila by his side—and not in some imaginary role.

She could have been killed, and he didn't want to live without her.

Once the case was solved and she left, there'd be a hole in his heart that nothing else could fill. She made him a better man. But how could he deal with her death-defying behavior and reckless abandonment of her own safety? She'd go back to her life as a bodyguard, which demanded certain risks from her.

Risks she was obviously willing to take.

He paced the bedroom and replaced the terrifying images of her dying with a different image. One from the night before. Her honesty had melted his heart when she'd let her guard down, and it had taken every ounce of his strength not to kiss her. But then today, the tough-as-nails Laila was back in action, and he couldn't wrap his mind around the contrast.

Who was the real Laila? The one from this afternoon or the vulnerable woman from the night before?

She acted invincible, but what if she couldn't outrun the next bullet aimed at her?

Their professional relationship had evolved into something...but what? They'd just met, and he'd sworn off women up until Laila had waltzed into his life and taken over.

Temporarily. That was his biggest issue.

Their relationship was fast and intense but had a defined expiration date. It wasn't meant to last. Nothing about their situation screamed long-term, despite his longing for more.

He kicked Duke off the couch and sat down. The dog huffed and moved to the bed, snoring again moments later.

What was he supposed to do once Laila left? Ask her on a date? With camera crews trailing every move they made? Would she even want to see him again?

Even if her future included him, what would it be like? Would she ever shed her bodyguard exterior and let the real Laila out? Despite the assortment of roles she'd played, he'd caught glimpses of her true self piercing through her protective layer.

Could he continue a relationship with her if he had to worry about her dying every time he wasn't near her? He'd never been involved with someone so self-reliant, so... What was the word he was looking for?

Dangerous.

She put her life on the line in the role of protector. But who was watching her back? Would he even have a place in her world? It wasn't like she needed him for anything. All the money in the world didn't interest a woman like Laila.

And that's why he liked her. A lot.

But he needed to end it. He'd never subject anyone to public scrutiny the way he'd grown up. It was his burden to carry, and that meant sheltering Laila from a life of dodging the press and dealing with his superficial family. Money might make them comfortable, but what kind of life could he give Laila? Hiding from paparazzi and having her every move broadcast was the opposite of having a life. It was a prison, and it was his sentence to bear. Not hers.

A knock at the door jarred his thoughts. It opened and Laila stuck her head in. "I'm just checking on you. You kind of retreated once we got back."

He shrugged. "I thought I'd get ready for the party. I think the stress of the week is finally taking its toll."

He stared at his biggest stressor, the woman who'd nearly died trying to provide for his safety. His emotions warred within him. Part of him wanted to yell at her again for being so reckless, but the other part screamed to kiss her senseless.

Laila sat down on the couch next to him and his pulse spiked. What was this woman doing to him?

"Are you still mad at me? You've been cranky since we got home."

"Are you kidding me? Laila, you could have been killed. You dove across a highway, chasing a confirmed killer that might have had a gun and taken you out."

"Look, Charlie already reamed me out about not waiting for backup. I don't need this from you. I was doing my job. I assessed the scene and saw an opportunity to catch this guy. I don't expect you to understand."

"But what if you were wrong? Why didn't you wait for backup? You think you're indestructible, but I'm not going to stand by and watch you face a situation you can't get out of."

"Not to worry, Preston. I always take care of myself. Not to mention I was hired to do a job, so I'm doing it." She glared at him, then made a beeline for the window, her usual lookout perch.

Maybe this was for the best. Once the danger subsided, they'd go their separate ways. It was better to end things before becoming emotionally entwined.

If only he could tear his eyes from her. This woman had the perfect balance of fierceness and beauty. His hammering pulse told him it might be too late to walk away.

Her eyes caught his and, like a magnet, drew him close. He stood, anchoring his feet to the floor to keep from rushing to her side. While they were only a few feet apart, it might as well have been the length of the Grand Canyon with all the obstacles they faced.

"We lead very different lives." His voice rasped like he'd just run a marathon. *Get it together, man.* He cleared his throat. "The police will catch this guy and you'll be rid of me."

She watched him. The setting sun flickered through the window, giving her hair a warm glow. Even in the shadows, he recognized the passion burning behind her eyes.

Wait. Was it possible she had these intense feelings for him too?

"Sounds like a winning plan," she said, but her voice was low and flirty. And then she took a step toward him. The gap between them shrank, but the voltage of the electrical current that raced between them ratcheted up.

His resistance cracked and he inched a few steps closer. He tried to keep his voice firm and even, but it came out as a whisper. "You are the most dangerous woman I've ever met. It would never work out between us."

"So, we agree?" And again, she moved closer.

His heart thumped with each step she took. He didn't know what was happening, but he didn't hate it.

"We'll both go our separate ways once you're no longer my client."

Automatic reflex kicked in, and his thumb traced her jawline. Her fingers traced circles up his bicep.

"Are you always this bossy?" he whispered.

"Are you always so stubborn—" Her words were cut off when his lips met hers.

Fireworks ignited, turning him lightheaded and breathless. His hands tousled her hair. She wrapped her arms around his neck and pulled him into a deeper kiss.

He was a goner.

A fire kindled in him that he'd long ago doused. The taste of her lips left him begging for more. Their fake relationship had solidified into something oh so real. He trailed kisses down her neck.

"I— I don't know what we're doing," she murmured.

He responded with another kiss. They could worry about the future tomorrow. Because right now, all he cared about was the feel of her silky hair between his fingers and the softness of her lips.

Now that he had Laila in his arms, he never wanted her to

leave. But he stopped to catch his breath and rested his forehead on hers.

"This is moving way too fast," she whispered with an intensity flashing through her eyes that gave him chills. "I mean, we hardly know each other. And we're not really married. And—" His lips silenced her, and they sank into another kiss that sent shock waves racing up and down his spine.

Her cell phone chime broke them apart.

She snagged the phone from her pocket, her bodyguard face back in place—except for the high color in her cheeks. "It's Steven. Let me answer it." She walked to the other side of the room to take the call.

His arms ached without her in them. So much for ending things.

He resumed his spot on the couch, catching bits and pieces of Laila's conversation. But his mind was still wrapped around kissing Laila.

She ended her call and returned to sit down next to him, noticeably too far away.

"What did Steven say? Did the guy talk?" But frankly, the only thing he could think about was the touch of her lips, the taste still with him. Probably he should care more about what Steven had found.

"They discovered some interesting stuff when they ran his fingerprints. His name is Corey Porter. He's a former Army sergeant, and he said that someone paid him to plant the bomb. It didn't take him long to throw his partner under the bus."

Preston failed to hold back a gasp. "Is he the man that killed my dad and Ethan?"

"It's possible. But it does lead us one step closer to finding the culprit. The police are going to continue questioning him, and let's just hope he talks."

"It would be great for this to be all over. I'd say so that life

207

can get back to normal, but I don't know what *normal* looks like anymore."

"It means you won't have to look over your shoulder all the time. And justice will be served to the people behind your father's and brother's murders."

But it means not seeing Laila again.

The thought came unbidden, a piece of truth rising to the surface of his soul. He liked being with this complex woman, unearthing the pieces of her heart that she never made public. Their arrangement had given him a lot of one-on-one time with her that normally wouldn't happen in a new relationship. The awkward first-date syndrome had been fast-tracked from the instant they'd met.

"I guess if the case is solved, you can go back to your life."

"What? And give up all of this?" She gestured her hands around the room. "A girl could get used to living in a place like this."

He laughed. "Right. Living with my mother and sister? You won't miss that for a second."

"But I'll definitely miss you."

He watched her cheeks turn a pretty shade of pink. Was she simply flirting, or did her words hold a deeper meaning?

Did she think they had any kind of future together? His heart pounded double time at the thought, because if there was even a sliver of chance they could make this work, he'd take it.

He leaned in for another kiss, but her cell phone buzzed with a text. She picked it up quickly. Almost too quickly, as if she was relieved by the interruption.

"Thanks to a fast-tracked warrant, the police have already dug into Corey's financial records. A large sum of money had been deposited into his bank account—a transaction made a few hours after your father's and brother's deaths. The police were able to follow the money trail back to an account owned by Bob Zimmerman. The police are headed to take Bob into custody."

The text message interruption provided a necessary excuse for Laila to make a graceful exit. "I should get ready for the party. Remind me again, is this a friend of your mother's?"

Preston grimaced at the mention of the party. "It's my mother's friend Bella Cora. I don't know her well, but they've been friends for years. It's her annual birthday bash, and it's become quite the event over the years."

Laila nodded and rushed to the bathroom. She shut the door, leaned her back against it, and stared at her reflection in the mirror.

She'd kissed Preston. She hadn't expected to lose the battle between her head and her heart quite so easily. Preston's concern over her safety had sparked something foreign in her, something she didn't quite understand. One look at him standing there with concern filling his eyes and her resolve had melted. All she'd intended to do was comfort him. Yet despite everything within her warning her to run, she'd found herself locked in his arms, drawn to him by some inexplicable force.

And for the first time in her life, she felt safe trusting another person.

She smacked her palm on her forehead. What was she thinking? Like she and Preston had a future. The lines between professional and personal were now a blurry mess. The false intimacy created by the fake marriage toyed with her emotions.

Then another conclusion surfaced. She'd developed feelings for the man that she couldn't shake off so easily. Pangs of loneliness nipped at her heels. If only Preston's future could include her. Memories of their kisses had communicated silent promises that a relationship was possible. But the man had a billion-dollar company to lead. When this was over, she'd go back to her empty apartment and most likely throw herself into her job again. It was inevitable that they'd go their separate ways and life would ruin any chance of a relationship into the ground.

She took a shower, wrapped herself up in a super-soft bathrobe, and fixed her hair and makeup. She opened the bathroom door a crack, and a note fluttered to the floor. Preston had left to find Charlie. At least she had the room to herself to change.

The ice-blue chiffon-and-lace, floor-length dress hung on the closet door. Another classy pick by Christina, dropped off earlier at the house. As Laila slipped into the dress, her fingers lingered over the silky material. On the outside she looked every bit the part of the wife of an ultra-wealthy man. But on the inside, she knew this wasn't the role she'd get to play forever. Her relationship with Preston had an expiration date.

She descended the stairs and stopped short at the sight of Preston. Her faux husband could fill out a tux. Not to mention his signature lopsided grin and the look in his eyes that set her cheeks on fire.

When Preston looked at her, everything else faded into the background. His protective and possessive gaze sent chills up her spine. She was supposed to be watching his back, but in this moment, something sparked inside her. A feeling she barely recognized.

Freedom. For the first time in a long time, she could just be herself.

"You look stunning," he whispered in her ear as he escorted her to the car. Laila chided herself. *This is not a date. I repeat, this is not a date. This is a job.*

While Bob might be the mastermind behind all of Preston's

troubles, she couldn't let her guard down for even a second. She had texted Steven, and they hadn't located Bob, so he might show up at the party.

Charlie dropped them off at the entrance to the estate. Another mansion for Laila to contend with, but Charlie had already scoped out the area earlier and reviewed the guest list.

They walked in, arm in arm. Too bad Preston hadn't taken his eyes off her since they'd left the house. Her heart thumped a rapid beat. So much for getting her head in the game.

They walked into a ballroom that looked like it belonged in a pricey hotel, complete with a stunning chandelier twinkling in the center of the room.

Laila reminded herself not to gawk. "This place is incredible."

Despite the size of the place, people filled every space, even spilling outside to the pool area with drinks in hand, making security logistics Laila's worst nightmare.

She was about to make a beeline for Charlie to do her usual scan of threats when Preston said, "Let's dance." He whisked her to the center of the room and slid his hands around her waist. The live swing band pumped out a sultry tune, and they swayed to the melody. If only it could have been just the two of them instead of this house packed with people, because the moment was perfect.

If only it were real.

"Preston," she murmured. "We can't do this. Reality is that there's still a killer on the loose. Besides, you belong here, in this world. I'm not a part of it—"

His finger covered her lips. "Let's not talk about it now. For tonight, we keep living the fairy tale. The one where we're married and the only ones stalking us are the paparazzi wanting a picture. Tonight, it's just you and me. Even if it all falls apart tomorrow."

And so they danced. But she kept one eye out for danger. She refused to allow her emotions to be swept away any farther than they had been.

A few familiar faces dotted the edge of the dance floor as Preston spun her around. Margot hung to one side, chatting with guests. Katrina stood at the edge of the dance floor, alone, brows pulled tight and lips curled down. Her hard eyes showed her true colors as she watched Preston's every move as if waiting for him to do something outlandish so she could capture it for her live stream. What was the woman up to now? Derek wasn't attending, but at least he was out of the hospital and recovering from his near-death experience with the poison. Sophia lingered at the opposite end of the room by the bar, engaged in a lively conversation with a drink in her hand, fitting right into the party scene.

Veronica lurked in the shadows. A wicked smile crossed her lips when Laila spotted her.

What was that about?

The musicians took a break, and Preston pulled her to a stop but kept her hand in his. "I guess we should make the rounds before we duck out early."

"Sure."

He led Laila toward where his mother stood. "Let me introduce you to Bella Cora."

A memory shot through Laila's mind.

The night she'd followed Jesse Cora to that hotel.

Bella Cora? Why hadn't she connected the dots earlier? Bella. As in Anabelle Cora, who'd hired Elite Guardians to follow her wayward husband. She held back a groan. Had Jesse's rendezvous really been about orchestrating a party?

Before they reached Anabelle, a voice from behind her confirmed all suspicions. She turned around to face both Jesse Cora and Celia, the party-planning mistress.

Preston and Charlie had asked her what would happen in the future if she was wrong and misjudged a situation. Apparently, her snap judgments were about to cost her greatly.

"You!" Jesse yelled, drawing all eyes on her. "You dare to show up to this party after what you put us through?"

Katrina and Veronica made a beeline for the drama.

"Jesse, what's wrong? How do you know Laila?" Katrina asked, acting with the concern of a best friend.

"Oh, she's some bodyguard my wife hired. Anabelle thought someone was stalking me. But she definitely wasn't on the invitation list."

He crossed his arms and glared at Laila. Charlie moved in close, his hand under his tux jacket. Laila shook her head at him. and he stilled, but he left his hand where it was.

Katrina pounced. "A *bodyguard*?" She glared at Preston. "Is she even your wife?"

Jesse snickered. The buzz of the room died to a low hum. All eyes were glued to the scene unfolding like a bad reality-show fight. Several phones snapped pictures and videos.

Great. This was about to blow up on the eleven o'clock news.

Katrina moved closer, almost nose to nose with Laila. "No one cares if your wedding was a sham. Preston's been hooking up with Veronica. It was only a matter of time before he kicked you to the curb. Real wedding or not."

16

FRIDAY, 7:15 P.M.

Laila curled her fingers into a fist. Katrina was yet again smearing her brother's name in public. But more than that, Laila needed to divert the attention away from the fake marriage. "He's not cheating with Veronica."

Katrina pulled something out of her sparkly designer handbag and thrust a piece of paper into Laila's hand. She looked at the color photo of Preston and Veronica kissing in the study. She gaped at Preston.

"I can explain—" he started to say, but Laila held up a hand. No truth ever came out of the phrase *I can explain.*

Solomon had spouted off a bunch of excuses to talk his way out of things. Her father had given a litany of reasons to justify his conscience when he abandoned his family.

Heat seared through her. Lies. All of it. Everyone lied. Preston was no different. How had she been such a fool? She should have seen this coming.

Preston pulled her away from the crowd. "Veronica came on to me. You know how she can be. But nothing happened."

"I *don't* know her. And apparently, I don't know you."

Preston flinched, but his eyes narrowed. "You honestly think I would cheat on you? I thought you trusted me."

"Don't worry, Preston," she whispered. "It's not cheating when it was never real to begin with."

Katrina and the crowd inched their way toward them. "Did he tell you about his money? He probably sold himself as this broke mountain guy, but you realize he's a millionaire, right? Outside of the family fortune."

What was Katrina talking about? "You told me you didn't take any of your family's money when you left."

"That's true, but I happened to start my own furniture business that took off."

The Berringer rocking chair on his mom's lanai. That was his design? The pieces began falling into place. How had she not seen this connection?

A conversation replayed in her mind. Preston had felt responsible for Chelsea Berringer's death, and he'd wanted to find a way to remember her name.

"See?" Katrina said, louder than necessary. "He doesn't need the family money." She pointed at Preston. "Why don't you go back to where you came from? All you've done is bring trouble to the family since the day you showed up." She stormed off with her usual dramatic flair. Cell phone cameras caught every juicy second of Katrina's show.

Katrina's words hit their mark, because Preston deserved so much better than this. Yet he'd never told Laila about the money.

Preston looked from his retreating sister to Laila. "I need some air." He headed for the door to the patio in the backyard. She followed, but he held out his hand. "Just let me be alone for once. I've got plenty of other security guards to trail me around."

She wanted to follow, but her lead feet held firmly in place while her heart splintered into a thousand fragments.

Had he really betrayed her? Just like everyone else?

Or was it possible she'd read the situation wrong and jumped to conclusions? Just like in the case of Anabelle Cora and her husband's alleged cheating?

Whispers and fits of laughter rustled through the room, all directed at Laila. One by one, everyone backed away, shaking their heads. More bursts of mocking rang out, led by ringleader Jesse Cora. But they left her standing there.

Alone.

She'd been outed, the truth released into the wild for public entertainment. *Preston hired a bodyguard to pretend to be his wife.*

Her plan had backfired, and Preston's reputation was decimated. And they still didn't have the killer behind bars. How had things derailed like a head-on freight train collision?

She needed to find Preston. Her job wasn't over until he was safe. She spun on her four-inch heels and ran right into Charlie.

"Where is Preston?" he asked.

"He headed outside. I saw the security team follow, but I was about to go find him."

"We should keep a close eye on him. He's not safe until the culprit is behind bars."

Laila nodded and pulled Charlie to the side of the room. The party guests' stares lingered, but she didn't want to be overheard. "Did you know about the money?"

His eyes squinted. "How did you not know? I gave you all the files on a flash drive."

The flash drive that she'd shoved into her pocket before

their dip in the river. Laila groaned. "That drive is fish food. It was in my pocket when we sank. I never looked at the files."

Charlie shook his head. "It's all there. Preston's financials, his business, his charity. The guy's been making millions and secretly giving it away through some charitable foundation. He started an organization called Chelsea's Hope."

The fog cleared in Laila's mind. Preston strove to keep Chelsea Berringer's memory alive. He probably sank every penny he'd ever made from his rocking chairs into helping the community. She ran a hand through her hair.

"But what about the picture?" she whispered, her voice infused with zero confidence. How could she be so far off base? "The one of him and Veronica?"

"I didn't see it, but anything can be staged nowadays." Charlie scanned the room, then looked at Laila. "I've spent time with the guy. I can't imagine that he's into the likes of Veronica. Not anymore."

Her head throbbed in time to the fast-paced tune the band pumped out. A profound sense of loss threatened to overtake her, stomping out the little joy she'd recently allowed herself. Had she just ruined any sliver of a shot she had, real or imaginary, with Preston?

Certainty hit her like a bolt of lightning. Her own instincts might have let her down, but she could trust Preston.

Of course there was no fling with Veronica. It was all a setup.

"I need to find him." She pushed past Charlie and saw Quinn and Steven heading their way. The party had kicked into full swing again, and no one seemed to be alarmed by the police presence.

"We have a warrant for Bob's arrest." Quinn didn't bother with any pleasantries. It was always business with him. "The DA is convinced there's enough evidence to hold him for twenty-four hours. Our officers lost track of him, but we think he showed up at the party."

All the signs pointed to Bob. The boat contract had been registered in his name. The car that'd run them over had been conveniently stolen from Bob. Then a criminal had blown up their vehicle in a parking lot and they'd found money in his account, all linked to Preston's new business partner. The pieces fit.

If Bob was the killer and he was at the party, then Preston was in imminent danger.

She grabbed Charlie's arm. "We've got to get Preston out of here."

How could she automatically assume he'd cheated? Preston could almost laugh. They weren't even in a real relationship.

But his feelings were real. Not a fake one in the bunch.

Preston sat on the stone wall that separated the patio from the garden area. He'd wandered a little farther away from the house than he probably should have, but it felt good to breathe in the crisp night air. At least his security guards hovered at a comfortable distance. He was sick of being watched, having his every movement tracked. He understood it and was grateful for the people willing to do it, but he would admit he was tired of the necessity for it.

If only he could time travel, he'd go back to his small-town anonymity. Before his father had died.

Before he'd met Laila.

He'd been back less than a week and already managed to tank his career and reputation—and the possibility of a relationship with Laila. Veronica must have planted a camera in the study before their meeting. What a snake. What was her end game? Blackmail? Or was she just plain mean?

How could Laila believe the smear campaign against him? Their relationship was phony, but that kiss still sent shock waves rippling through him. He couldn't deny his attraction—and not just on a physical level. His interest went much deeper. While everyone else presumed he was destined for disaster, Laila had defended him numerous times. But had that just been part of her cover story? She'd fooled a lot of people, pretending to be his wife.

Had he been fooled by her too?

A memory sprang up from the night Laila had shared some of her past betrayals. Her fiancé had done a number on her. Of course she'd fallen apart at the thought of Preston lying to her. But they both had lingering hurts from the past, and that she had assumed the worst in him stung like a million hornet stings.

What was he going to do now? He needed to face the possibility that things were over between him and Laila. Better to find out before he risked any more of his heart. Did she only see the bad side of him, like everyone else?

"Preston?" His heart jumped out of his chest as a shadowy figure stepped into the walkway.

"Bob?" Had the police questioned Bob and let him go? Did this mean Bob was in the clear and wasn't responsible for the murder of Preston's father and brother?

"I'm so glad I found you. We need to talk."

Preston gave his security detail a side-eye look. One of the two men nodded back and moved in closer. "What's there to discuss?"

Bob shoved his hands into his coat pockets. "I know we've had our differences, and I heard about that scene in the ballroom just a few minutes ago. There's no shame in realizing that you weren't meant for all this. Please consider letting me buy out your shares of the company. I'll pay more than they're worth. Your mother will be taken care of, and you don't have to work ever again. That's not a bad deal. You'll have money, but more importantly, you'll have freedom. You can disappear, and this time you won't have to return."

Bob's idea burrowed into Preston's mind. There wasn't any shame in taking the easy way out, and who cared what anyone thought of him if he skipped town? He'd be gone and wouldn't have to deal with the aftermath of the party.

Something pricked his heart. An emotion he wasn't used to. What was it?

Pride.

He wanted to do right by his family. The company needed better leadership, and he could bring about that change. Memories of Laila's encouraging words came back to him, straightening his spine. At one point, she'd believed in him. But what about now?

He shook his head. "Bob, thank you for your generous offer, but I'm here to stay. We'll have to figure out a way to work together, because I'm not going anywhere."

A scream rent the silence of the garden. "Preston!"

Laila! Was she in trouble? He turned to see if he could spot her. Bob put a hand on Preston's shoulder. "Please, reconsider."

A gunshot rang out. Pain tore through him, and both he and Bob toppled to the ground.

17

The sound of the gunshot stopped Laila's heart. She'd just turned the corner from the house to the garden area when she caught the glint of a gun muzzle sticking out of the bushes that were stacked along the wrought iron fence.

Her scream had risen over the thumping party music, but the warning had come a split second too late. She'd watched Preston and Bob hit the ground.

She ditched the bricked pathway in favor of the shorter route through the lawn. Her heels dug into the grass, so she kicked off the shoes and sprinted in her bare feet. Out of breath, she reached the blood-soaked men on the ground. Bob lay on top of Preston. Neither of them moved.

Please, God, let them be alive.

Steven rushed to her side. Quinn bypassed them and raced toward the location of the shooter. Screams from a few party guests who had meandered outside added to the chaos.

Had one bullet gone through both men?

A groan from under Bob lifted the thousand-pound rock from Laila's neck. "Preston!"

Steven checked Bob for a pulse and shook his head. Bob was dead.

"Help me lift Bob off Preston."

Bile rose in her throat. The bullet had shattered the back of Bob's head, and the gore shook her to the core. But had the bullet also hit Preston? They rolled and shifted Bob onto the ground next to Preston. She couldn't tell if the blood that covered Preston was his own or Bob's.

"Preston? Are you injured?" Tears blurred her vision, and she blinked to hold them back.

He groaned and tried to sit up. "I...I don't think so. The bullet grazed my shoulder. It burns, but I'm okay."

A few minutes later, sirens blared and flashing lights flickered across the garden. The paramedics strode in and rushed to aid Preston. The crew loaded him onto a gurney. Guests milled about, faces washed with the glow of their phones taking pictures and live tweeting the action.

"Are you his wife?" a paramedic asked. "You can ride in the ambulance with him if you want."

She nodded, but Preston spoke up. "She's not my wife."

The words slapped Laila in the face. Of course she wasn't his wife. How could she have let this fantasy run wild? Her stomach twisted in a knot, and she pressed a hand to her mouth. Preston owed her nothing, but that old wound in her heart started to tear open. Why had she expected him to stand by her side when everyone else in her life had walked away?

"No," she whispered as she backed away. "I'm not his wife."

Quinn returned and barked orders at two officers to escort the ambulance to the hospital and keep watch over Preston.

Laila forced a smile at the paramedic. "I'll follow and meet him at the hospital."

They took Preston away, and she just barely restrained herself from lunging after him. How had things gone so horribly wrong? She'd failed to protect Preston. She never should have let things get so personal between them. Maybe they'd catch a break and locate the shooter, but she wasn't holding her breath.

Steven placed a hand on her shoulder to still her. A pair of spiky heels dangled from his fingertips.

"My shoes. Thanks." She'd lost her mind and her shoes.

"Don't beat yourself up over this," Steven said. "You saved his life. Again. If you hadn't yelled his name, I think Preston would have been toast. He turned and Bob stepped into the bullet's trajectory."

A chill sent goosebumps up and down her arms that had nothing to do with the falling temperatures. The image of Bob lying on the ground would haunt her for a long time. She pushed the thoughts aside. "Preston trusted me to do my job and I failed. What if he dies?"

"It looks like the bullet scraped his shoulder. He'll be fine. It could have been a lot worse."

She opened her mouth to respond, but the words stuck in her throat.

What if he never wants to see me again?

Laila patted the side of her dress up and down before remembering she didn't have any pockets. She needed something to stop her hands from trembling. "I don't know what to do, Steven. Just tell me what to do to make this right."

He grabbed both of her hands, which stopped them from trembling. Why was she unraveling? "Just breathe. I think we should get you to the hospital. You'll see that Preston is okay, and you two can hash out your feelings later. Once we catch a killer."

She started to protest but knew it was a lost cause. There was no use denying her feelings for Preston. But the romantic fantasy had almost gotten him killed. In the real world, a murderer still lurked in the shadows, and she'd let her guard down.

Steven dropped her hands, and she held on to his arm for balance as she wrestled her shoes back on. They both walked down the stone pathway to the house.

"Who could have done this?" she whispered to Steven, looking around to make sure they couldn't be overheard. Guests had dispersed once the drama died down, but news crews clamored at the fence line for the best positioning.

"I don't know, but our list of suspects keeps dwindling. Bob is dead, Derek poisoned. Quinn and I are going to interview our man in custody to see if he'll give up the name of his partner." Steven steered them away from a pack of reporters who shouted questions from the edge of the property and took her out a side gate to where Charlie had the car ready and waiting.

Laila collapsed into the back seat and groaned. "Just say it. I feel a lecture coming on."

Charlie shrugged. "No judgment from me."

"But I should have been with him, protected him. Instead, I got too personal and it clouded my perspective." She pounded her fist into the soft seat, wishing it were a punching bag at the gym.

Charlie met her eyes in the mirror for a split second. "Or maybe you've suppressed your heart for so long that it's coming out and you can't control it. Give yourself some grace."

Fatigue settled into her bones and zapped her last remnant of energy. "It's over," she whispered. "I accused him of cheating. Thought he wasn't trustworthy. I misread the situation, just like you said. What am I supposed to do now?"

Charlie looked straight ahead, focusing on the road. "Maybe it's time to let other people help you. You weren't meant to do this alone."

Preston's words flashed through her mind, and she bit back a smile. *Maybe it's time you put down the spoon.* Maybe she did need to lay down her weapons and let someone else fight for her.

Clarity parted the fog in her brain. She'd been fighting her battles on her own strength. She refused to count on others and had shut out God a long time ago.

The best words to describe her current predicament were *tired* and *alone*.

She closed her eyes and rested her head on the back of the seat. Clearly, she was capable of misreading things. And she only had a finite amount of strength. It was time to start trusting in someone outside of herself. Her weapons weren't serving her well. If Preston was right, she needed God to fight on her behalf when she couldn't. *God, please fix this mess. Help Preston to get through this. Oh, and find the killer too.*

They pulled into the parking lot, and she and Charlie raced to the waiting room. A few people had beaten them there. Preston's mom and sister huddled in one corner.

Katrina stood, posturing like a lion ready to take down a gazelle. "You're not welcome here. Some bodyguard you are. He's been shot." She over-enunciated every word while holding her phone to livestream the confrontation.

Laila walked away. The paramedic had indicated that it wasn't severe, and Laila refused to be pulled into Katrina's drama. She nodded to Charlie. "I'm going to get a cup of coffee."

He nodded in return, silently communicating that he'd

keep an eye on the waiting room for any signs of trouble. After all, he hadn't blown his cover in an epic public display.

On her way to the cafeteria, someone called her name. She turned to see Margot running down the hallway toward her, her tear-stained cheeks catching Laila off guard. "What happened?" Laila asked.

"Oh, thank goodness I found you. Something terrible has happened. Seth is missing."

Laila pulled the woman into a small waiting area for some privacy, but this wing of the hospital seemed like a ghost town. "Missing? What do you mean?" She ushered the woman to a plastic chair, and they sat down.

"I told him about his real father, all of it. He got so mad he stormed off. I haven't been able to get ahold of him and I'm worried. What if the killer went after him? What if someone knows he's a Whittaker?"

Laila froze. What if the killer learned there was another potential heir and targeted Seth?

"I haven't called the police yet," Margot said. "I mean, I might be overreacting. It's possible he just needed some breathing space and he's not been...kidnapped." The last word came out choked and garbled.

"Where do you think he might go, if he wanted to get some space?" Laila's stomach tightened into a knot. Something was definitely setting off her spy senses.

Was Seth in trouble? Or was his own mother somehow involved? She slid her phone out of her pocket to text Charlie her location.

Margot wailed. "Please help me find my son. My car is parked right outside. We could go to his house and then his friends' houses. What if he's in trouble?"

Laila wasn't going anywhere with the woman, but she could help locate her missing son. "Let me get the chauffeur to pull up the car, and then we can trace Seth's last known whereabouts."

Before her fingers hit the buttons to text Charlie with another update, a mist of spray hit her in the face. Her vision blurred and tears poured from her burning eyes. The room spun, and she slumped out of the chair and onto the floor. Her muscles tightened and spasmed, and her vocal cords released only a faint squeak.

A man in a nurse's uniform entered with a gurney. "Get her onto the table and cover her," Margot commanded. "We'll take her out through the morgue."

Laila wanted to protest, but her consciousness slipped away.

The doctor finished stitching up the three-inch gash in Preston's shoulder and left the room. The bullet had scratched him after slicing through Bob's skull, an image that was indelibly etched into his brain forever.

How many more times would he narrowly miss falling into this killer's death grip?

Exhaustion forced him to sink into the bed once the nurse exited. They'd given him some painkillers, but nothing that should knock him out. Which meant the recent losses played on an endless loop through his mind.

His brother and father.

Magellan Falls and his anonymity.

Laila.

The last thought shot pain through him like a lightning bolt, worse than the physical throbbing in his shoulder.

Could he lose something he'd never had to begin with?

The grief on her face when he'd uttered the words *she's not my wife* piled on more guilt. Even if the relationship had been fake, his words may have destroyed his chance at a real one.

Maybe it just wasn't meant to be. He'd lost hope years ago of ever having a real relationship. This was the exact reason he'd stopped dating.

Preston Whittaker always found a way to show his bad side to the world.

A knock at the door startled him. "Come in."

His mother entered and hurried to his side. "Preston, darling. How are you feeling? I was so worried." Tears stained his mother's heavily rouged cheeks. She'd been drinking at the party, but she seemed sober, a side of her he hadn't seen in a long time.

"I've been better. The bullet just grazed me." But not Bob. Even though Preston had despised the man, Bob hadn't deserved to be murdered at the hands of this cold-blooded killer. Especially if the killer had been aiming at Preston.

"It's such a shame, everything that's happened. I just wish you'd made up with your father before you left. He thought about you every day you were gone."

"I doubt that." Instant regret punched him in the gut for speaking badly of his father to his grieving mother. "Sorry, Mom."

She shook her head. "You know, he was always proud of you. He always had a spot for you at Whittaker Enterprises. You weren't meant to leave but to split the role of CEO with Ethan. He had it all planned out."

He looked into his mother's pale-blue eyes, which shone clear and coherent.

"He told me I'd never be good enough to run the company."

"Nonsense," his mother replied. "He had a quick temper, and you knew how to push his buttons. You were just so different from him that he didn't know how to handle you. He thought if he pushed you, you'd try harder. But the opposite happened. He pushed you away."

Could this be true? He'd spent most of his life believing that his dad considered him second best. And he'd assumed others thought the same way.

"I can see you don't believe me." His mother interrupted his thoughts. "But he had hopes that all three of his sons would join him in running the company. He never meant for you to leave."

Preston's mind spun. Had his father thought of him as more than a troublemaker? He'd given his dad plenty of grief and stress, but had his dad looked past Preston's adolescent mistakes and antics to see the man he could become?

Then his mother's words hit him like a tidal wave. *Three sons.*

Had she misspoken and meant three kids? Or did she know about Seth?

He cleared his throat. "Mom, when you said three sons, did you mean Katrina? Or..."

She held up her hand, silencing him. "I know about Seth. I'd always had my suspicions. How could I not when the child was the spitting image of you and Ethan? Eventually your father confessed what he'd done. I just stayed quiet to keep it out of the media."

Preston's mind refused to form words. Images of the family he'd always longed for materialized before him. Could he recoup the loss of life and years to form a stronger relationship with his mother? What about his sister and his newly discovered brother?

"Maybe this time around we can be a real family." He hadn't meant to say the words out loud, but they hung in the room like a thick fog.

She grabbed his hand. "Please stay. Don't leave again. I can't lose you. Or your wife."

Hmm. Apparently, his mom wasn't as lucid as he'd thought. She had received a front row seat to the whole public showdown at the party.

"I'm so sorry about Laila. I never meant to—"

His mother waved a hand and shot him a dismissive look. "Nonsense. Of course she's your wife. So you had a public spat? Who hasn't? She makes you a better man. I know love when I see it. Her smile lights up a room when you walk into it, and she's got your back when no one else does. She's got it bad for you, and you two are good for each other. Don't let her get away. Fight for love."

"But what if it's over?"

She winked. "Then you do whatever it takes to win her back."

A nurse entered to check on Preston. His mom kissed his forehead. "I'll visit you later. For now, get some rest."

The nurse scrutinized a few of the monitors. "Things look good, Mr. Whittaker. We'll discharge you in a few hours."

He sighed and nodded, his soul settling with his mother's words. His father had been proud of him. Tears welled in his eyes. If only he'd taken a chance to make amends with his father. But there was one thing he could do now. Honor his father's legacy by running Whittaker Enterprises. In a way that honored his family and God.

Because God didn't see him as second best.

A memory surfaced—one that seemed lifetimes ago but was only a few weeks old. He'd been in church in Magellan Falls, and the pastor's sermon had been about grace. *Your life is more than just a laundry list of mistakes and failures,* Pastor Thomas had said.

At the time, Preston had dismissed the message. Because

how could that apply to his messed-up life? Every stupid mistake he'd ever made lingered online forever, and people went out of their way to remind him of his shortcomings. He could work until he was dead and never repay his debt for past mistakes. Like Chelsea's death. When he'd become a Christian, God had made him a new man. A forgiven man. But if Preston truly believed that, why had he held onto the past for so long? He was trying to repay a debt that no amount of time, effort, or money could resolve.

His advice to Laila rang in his ears. He was still using his own limited arsenal of weapons. Showing up to fight the enemy and flinging himself into battle like he even had a chance of winning.

In the silence of the room, he whispered, "God, I need to be released from the past that has a choke hold on my life. This battle is unwinnable on my own efforts. It's time for a new strategy—one where You fight for me."

A weight lifted off his shoulders, a burden he'd carried around since Chelsea had died. Peace settled around him.

He'd thought escaping to Magellan Falls would give him freedom, but all he'd done was drag his old baggage to a new location. Now he knew that his past didn't have to define his future, and he couldn't wait to share the news with Laila. Because if God could do this for him, He could do the same for her. She needed to let go of her self-reliance and let God break down the walls of her heart.

But he'd ditched her at the party—left her to deal with the fallout from their public spectacle while he walked away. No wonder she fought her battles alone, when the people in her life abandoned her the second things got tough. Like her father walking out of her karate tournament because she was losing.

He didn't want her to be alone any longer.

His mother's endorsement of their relationship tugged on his heart. *She makes you a better man.*

With Laila, the pieces of his life that always seemed so fragmented somehow fit together. His desire to run away lessened the more time he spent with her.

They came from two different worlds, yet somehow, they belonged together. Maybe this was just another battle God had to fight. And Laila was worth fighting for.

He swung his legs over the edge of his bed. Time to get out of here and find her. Confess to her how wrong he'd been. A knock on the hospital room door spiked his pulse. "Come in," he called, praying it was Laila stopping by for a visit.

Seth entered the room. "Is this a bad time?"

Preston wasn't ready for a heart-to-heart conversation with his brother at this moment, but maybe now was the perfect time. He waved Seth in with his good arm and sat back in the bed. "No. I'm ready to leave this place, but they haven't officially checked me out yet. Have a seat."

Seth took the chair that his mother had just vacated.

Did he know the truth about his father? Seth met Preston's gaze. "When I heard that you'd been shot, I couldn't wait any longer. I need to know the truth. Are we brothers?"

18

The crunch of tires on gravel brought Laila to her senses. She tried to stretch out, but duct tape around her hands and feet immobilized her. Her head throbbed in time with her thumping heart.

She forced her mind to relax in order to assess the situation. Someone had stuffed her in some sort of wooden box and was on the move. She attempted to recall the last few hazy memories before she'd succumbed to unconsciousness.

Margot had drugged her. A big guy had come in disguised as a nurse. They'd managed to get her out of the hospital undetected. Fuzzy voices hid in the recesses of her memory bank. Something about the morgue.

The first thing they would have done was ditch her phone, so she didn't bother looking for it. She tried to kick the lid of the crate, but they must have secured it with some type of lock. Not that she had much power in her legs with the duct tape, but it didn't budge an inch. The box was lined with some sort of silky material.

Wait. The morgue?

They'd put her in a coffin.

"Help! Please help me!"

Her cries for help were muted by the roar of an engine. No one would hear her now that she was in a vehicle. She hit the top of the box with her bound hands, knowing it wouldn't do any good but feeling like she had to do something.

Her breath came in gasps, and the walls of the coffin seemed to shrink. She was going to die in this casket. They'd stick her right in the ground where no one would find her.

Breathe. Just breathe.

She closed her eyes and let her years of training take over. She'd gone through many scenarios just like this when she'd trained for Mossad. The first thing was to stay calm and slow her breathing to conserve oxygen.

The effects of the drug had sapped most of her energy, and just moving her arms made her want to sleep. She'd have a tough time fighting her way out of this without a weapon, not to mention a clear head.

Voices caught her attention. A man and a woman. She strained to make out words, but the engine drowned out the ability to overhear the conversation.

The vehicle picked up speed, as if on a highway. They could be taking her anywhere, and the drugs had her disoriented.

Margot had been on Laila's suspect list, but she'd been so focused on Bob, she'd failed to see what was right in front of her. Maybe she should stick to bodyguarding and not investigating. At least she had her combat skills. But first, she'd have to catch them off guard.

Her brainpower began to return after the drug-induced haze subsided.

She shifted her arms so she could work the duct tape with her teeth. The taste of glue sent her gag reflex into overdrive, but she kept at it. If she could free her hands, she'd have a fighting chance of survival.

The car slowed, and Laila noted that the terrain had changed. The gravel seemed looser, and the car bounced in what felt like potholes.

Every muscle in her body tensed when the movement stopped. If they opened the coffin, she needed to be in position to jump out. She attacked the duct tape harder, shredding it with her teeth, but they'd wound several layers around her hands.

A beep pierced the silence, and a tailgate creaked open. Apparently, her prison box had wheels, and they maneuvered it out of the back of the vehicle. They must have stolen the transport equipment from the morgue. Had they hijacked an ambulance too?

Her casket jostled and then hit the ground with a *thunk*. Something metallic clicked and a motor hummed.

She groaned at her own personal horror show. What if they tried to bury her alive? Waves of nausea washed over her at the thought.

The lid of the box swung open, and Laila squinted as a bright light blinded her.

"Good. You managed to not get your hands free," the female voice said.

Margot.

The shadowy outline of a person hovered above the coffin's edges. "I just wanted to give you some oxygen so you have a chance to survive this ordeal," Margot said. "Tonight is your opportunity to see if Preston has really fallen in love with his fake bride. I'll admit, you two put on a great show. But I'm betting on love. Some things just can't be faked, you know."

Laila squinted, trying to get a sense of direction. If she flung herself over the edge of the box, how far could she get with her arms and legs immobilized?

"Why, Margot?" she asked. "You could have blackmailed Walt into giving you whatever you wanted. Why kill everyone?"

"Because Seth deserves his rightful place in that company. The other two Whittaker sons needed to get out of the way. Permanently."

"You poisoned Bob to get Ethan to take his place and then pointed the blame to Bob?"

"Well, look who's smart and pretty. Preston sure knows how to pick 'em."

"What's your end game?"

The woman let out a maddening laugh that sent shivers racing up and down Laila's spine. "I'm going to force Preston to trade his life for yours."

"But you'll never let me go. You can't. I know too much."

"True. But don't worry. I have his grave not too far from yours so you can spend eternity together. How *Romeo and Juliet* the whole thing is."

Margot took a picture with her phone before slamming the lid back into place. A click of a padlock sealed Laila's fate.

Then they lowered her into a grave.

"Is it true? Is Walt Whittaker my real father?" Seth's face went whiter than the hospital sheets.

Preston nodded. "I just recently discovered the truth. Did your mom tell you?"

"Yes, earlier today. I still don't understand everything. Like why she hid the truth all these years. I had family all around me and never knew it."

Margot had robbed them both of a relationship. "I'm sorry we both found out so late in life."

Seth shrugged. "I can't believe we hung out together as kids and I never knew you were my older brother. I just wish I could get that time back."

Preston looked at Seth, his younger brother, who'd followed him around all those years. "I always liked having you around when we were younger. In a way, you were a little brother to me. It just wasn't official."

Seth nodded. "You always defended me, even when no one else did. And you let a socially awkward kid who had no dad tag along. You've always cared about others. Even if you partied a lot." He rolled his eyes and Preston laughed.

"Yeah, I'm glad those days are behind me."

Seth hung his head. "I just don't know why my mom kept secrets from me."

Preston knotted the bedsheets into a ball with his fist. Seth and Preston had missed out on a relationship because of other people's lies and scandals. This was why he'd come back—to change his family's legacy. And it would start with his new brother.

A knock at the door jarred his thoughts. Charlie opened the door a crack and stuck his head in. "Sorry to bother you, Preston." He nodded to Seth. "I'm actually glad I found you both."

Charlie stood at the foot of the bed and ran a hand through his hair. "I can't find Laila. She went to get some coffee earlier but texted me that she ran into Margot. I haven't been able to find them. Laila's phone is off. I was just heading to security to pull the footage from the area, but I saw Seth head in here." He stopped moving and turned to Seth. "Do you know where your mom is?"

Seth's eyes widened. "Mom texted me earlier that she went home from the party and wasn't feeling well. I didn't realize she'd come to the hospital. I can text her and see if she's with Laila."

Seth pulled out his phone, and Charlie did the same. "I'm calling Steven. Something's not right with this situation."

Laila consumed Preston's every thought. Where could she be? What if someone had tried to get to Preston by taking Laila? He shuddered and prayed that Laila was okay. Because he couldn't live if something happened to her.

Another knock at the door and Steven entered. Charlie pulled the phone away from his ear. "Well, that was fast."

"I just returned from questioning our suspect," Steven said, approaching the edge of the bed. "We now have a lead. Corey Porter is our man in custody, and he admitted to being hired to plant the bomb on the boat. He's the low man on the totem pole, claiming to not know who hired him. But he told us who his partner is. His brother, Lucas Porter. He's an ex-Marine and our sniper."

Preston gasped. "We need to find Lucas. And Laila."

Steven spun and turned to Charlie. "What? Where's Laila?"

Charlie looked at Seth, who shook his head. "I can't get ahold of my mom. She's not answering her phone."

Charlie's face paled. "Laila texted me and said that she was with Margot at the hospital. But now we can't find either of them."

The quiet hospital room erupted into chaos. Steven barked orders into his phone while simultaneously shouting instructions to the officers that had streamed into the room. Charlie stood in the corner and furiously pounded out text messages, and Seth paced by the window while trying to get his mother to answer the phone. A nurse stuck her head in the door to give a stern reprimand about the noise, but all Preston wanted to do was break out of this hospital prison and search for Laila.

Where was she? They needed a plan so they could start searching. Now. Because he had a bad feeling in the pit of his stomach that Laila was in trouble. He shoved images of her being captured and tortured out of his mind.

Seth moved back to Preston's bedside. "I think I've met Lucas Porter before," he announced, and the room fell silent. All eyes were glued to Seth.

"What do you mean?" Steven roared, the volume of his voice paying no heed to the nurse's noise warning. "Where did you meet him?"

Seth raised a trembling hand to his lips. "My mom started seeing a man a few months ago. I met him when I showed up to her house unannounced one night. She introduced him as Lucas Porter. I hope he's not a bad guy, for my mom's sake."

Puzzle pieces connected in Preston's mind, and the final picture rocked him to the core. Margot had access to a lot of information. Had Lucas Porter used Margot for information? Or worse, was Margot involved with his father's and brother's deaths?

Impossible.

Preston's mouth hung open, unable to form words as he tried to wrap his mind around the situation.

Charlie and Steven shared a look. Steven pulled up a picture on his phone. "Is this the man you saw at her house?"

Seth's eyes widened and he nodded.

The room started to spin, and Preston gripped the bedrails. "Where is Laila, Seth?"

"I—I have no idea. I'm sure there's a logical explanation for all of this. If I could just get ahold of my mom, I'm sure she can explain this—"

Steven cut Seth off. "I'm going to send some officers to her house. Seth, don't go anywhere. I'll need some more details from you." Steven blasted out of the room like a rocket, the phone still pressed to his ear. The remaining officers in the room trailed him out.

"I'm going to find Olivia and fill her in," Charlie said and followed in Steven's wake.

The pale color of Seth's face had been replaced by a new shade of green.

"Sit down, Seth. You don't look so good."

Seth complied and scrubbed his face in his hands. "Why would my mom have anything to do with this?"

"I don't know what's going on, but the only thing I know is that I need to find Laila. Will you help me?"

Laila needed him, and he'd move heaven and earth to find her.

"Of course," Seth said. "I'll give the police all the information I can about Lucas, but I only met him that one time."

The buzzing phone pulsed on the side table. Preston unlocked it. A text from an unknown number flashed on the screen.

If you love your "wife" you'll come alone. Tell no one or Laila dies. We are monitoring your phone. An Uber will pull up at the east side door in three minutes to pick you up. If you're not there, she dies.

Preston's heart jackhammered, but before he could say anything, the phone vibrated in his hand and he almost dropped it. Another message.

A picture.

A weight crushed his lungs.

Laila.

She was bound and lying in some type of box. Or was that a casket?

He dropped the phone on the bed. Seth picked it up and gasped.

"They're going to kill her," Preston muttered. "I have to go. There's not time to formulate another plan. If I can find her, at least she has a chance of escaping." The odds of the kidnappers letting Laila go were slim. But Preston would die trying to make sure she lived.

He swung his legs over the edge of the bed, and Seth put a hand out to stop him. "You can't go alone. You don't know who has her and what they'll do to you. We've got to tell the police."

"You stay here. Tell Charlie or Steven where I am." Preston picked up the phone again. "There's no way they'll let me keep a phone, so give this to Steven and maybe they can track the number that sent the text."

The image of Laila tied up and lying in a box shot fire through his veins. He looked at Seth. "I have to go." He may have just sealed his own death, but if he didn't go, he risked losing Laila forever.

Preston eased himself into his clothes. Pain radiated through his shoulder, but he'd walk through fire to save the woman he loved.

And later, he'd need to unpack his subconscious declaration of love.

Seth took the phone and nodded. "I'll get this to Steven."

Preston steeled his nerves and stuck his head out the door. He nodded to the guard on duty.

"I need to use the restroom. This one isn't working. I'm just heading down the hall."

The guard squinted as if trying to decide if it was a good idea to let Preston leave the room, but the man consented with a nod.

Preston walked down the hall and paused at the bathroom, but then ducked into the stairwell next to the restroom. With any luck, the guard wouldn't question which door Preston had used.

He made his way to the first floor and walked out the door to the exit. How he'd managed to escape everyone's notice, he had no idea. The paparazzi were probably stalking the front exit. These bad guys thought of everything.

An Uber was parked off to the side. Preston approached and the driver, a man, pointed his gun toward the back seat. "Get in," he rumbled.

19

The walls of the casket vibrated, and Laila felt her portable prison cell sink. The hydraulic lift sputtered, bringing her one step closer to death with every mechanical clank.

She pounded on the top with her bound hands, but the lid held fast. It wasn't made of cheap particle board that would crumble. This wood was strong and had no give, but she wouldn't rest until the last molecule of oxygen was consumed. Given the strength of her prison walls, this kidnapping had been well coordinated. They'd counted on Laila showing up to the hospital after the attack on Preston.

She screamed and kicked the lid as hard as she could with the tape around her feet, but exhaustion overtook her. Tears and sweat ran down her face. Every breath inhaled hot and sticky air, and her lungs burned from the exertion. She chided herself for squandering precious resources like energy and oxygen. How long would she last in the box without air? A few hours?

Terror threatened to rip her to shreds. The only light she had was the faint glow of her watch.

For a moment, everything went quiet. All she could hear was her own labored breaths.

Then dirt pelted the casket. The sound reverberated through the confined space with each shovelful dropped on her grave. She sucked in a breath, and hot, stale air stung her dry throat, sending her gag reflex into overdrive.

Think, Laila. Think.

She had to do something, or she'd go crazy. Using her teeth, she again attacked the tape on her hands with a fury. The binds frayed, giving her enough leverage to break her hands free. But the dirt that covered the lid made it immovable. Not to mention the padlock.

Silence filled her coffin, and all she could hear was the thumping of her own heartbeat in her ears. She must be completely underground now. Since yelling for help would use up her oxygen faster, she resorted to a different plan. Removing her belt, she used the metal prong to tap out a Morse code SOS to anyone who might be in the vicinity. The rhythmic tapping calmed her mind and occupied her hands. Maybe someone would hear her knocks from the grave. But so close to midnight, the cemetery would be deserted.

Margot had to have an end game. She'd probably sent that picture to Preston to lure him to the graveyard. But Laila hoped he was smart and stayed away.

No sense in both of them dying.

Dizziness hit her in waves. What she wouldn't give for a drink of cold water. Salty tears stung her eyes.

Last time she'd faced death, her mind had gone numb, but this time the flashbacks of her life mounted one by one in an endless replay, synchronizing to the taps of her belt buckle. She prayed someone would hear the three short taps, then three long taps followed by three more short taps that spelled out S-O-S.

Tap-tap-tap. Her father leaving the karate tournament early because his daughter was losing. Her mother drinking herself into oblivion, forcing Laila to pick up the pieces of their shattered life on her own.

Tap. Tap. Tap. Her fiancé, who'd ripped her heart out by selling classified information that compromised her mission.

Tap-tap-tap. Preston, with his gut-wrenching and very public departure at the party, leaving her in the middle of that ballroom, alone.

In the flood of memories, one theme ran constant. During her most painful moments, she'd shouldered the burden alone. So it was only fitting that she'd die in this box alone. She shook her head, pain radiating through her stiff neck. Her body craved fresh air.

Everything she did was always in her own strength. She took charge because she thought she had to. If she didn't, things would fall apart. Her family would unravel. Missions would fail. But no amount of toughness would get her out of this mess. No amount of willpower or training had prepared her to escape being buried alive.

She coughed, her throat dry and itchy.

And now she'd never get to tell Preston how she really felt about him. To explore a relationship with an incredible man. Forget the money and fame. She'd spent her whole life believing that people couldn't change. That everyone lied. All she'd focused on was the negative.

But Preston had managed to defy the odds. He'd taken stock of his own life and course corrected. Maybe she could do the same.

If she lived.

Tap-tap-tap. No way was she going down like this. She

wanted a future, one that she could share with others. Especially Preston.

Tap. Tap. Tap. God would fight this battle for her. Because it would take a miracle for someone to find her. She just needed to lay down all of her weapons. She closed her eyes and forged a new image. One in which she didn't have to be the lone warrior.

A vision of a fire emerged, and she pictured herself throwing all her weapons into the flames. She added stones from the wall she'd built around her heart to keep people out. She threw the years of ignored anger and her self-reliant attitude into the heart of the inferno. Laila chucked her Chinese throwing stars into the blaze, for good measure.

And as she walked away, flames engulfed the discarded remnants of her life, reducing the stack to ashes.

Tap-tap-tap. She took a deep breath, and instead of the stale air, she tasted freedom for the first time, because God saw her. And that was enough. She no longer had to do everything on her own, because whether she lived or died, she wasn't alone. It wasn't her battle anymore.

Tap-tap-tap.

Preston prayed like he'd never prayed before. He recognized the driver as Lucas Porter from the picture Steven had on his phone. The big man waved a wand across him, checking for weapons. "I have nothing on me. I even left my phone behind."

The man grunted.

They rode in silence. Preston sat in the back seat of the car with no phone, no weapons, and only a thin remnant of hope of getting himself and Laila out of this alive.

Who was behind all of this? Had Margot been played by

this maniac, or did she have an agenda of her own? He shuddered. Could Margot be so vindictive about the affair that she'd kill his father and brother? But why? His dad would have given Margot anything to buy her silence. Why turn to killing? Vengeance was a powerful motive, and she'd been living in the Whittaker shadow for a long time. But could she have resorted to murder?

The SUV pulled into a cemetery. Darkness cast shadows on the headstones, giving him a premonition of his own death.

Or Laila's.

The icy silence grated on every last nerve. This man had taken Laila and now had Preston under his control. He pulled the car into a space and motioned for Preston to get out.

With a gun at his back prodding him forward, Preston trudged across the pathway that wove around the cemetery. Complete darkness plus the uneven concrete caused him to stumble a few times. He'd lost hope of anyone finding him in the deserted cemetery at midnight. There wasn't a soul in sight.

His shoulder throbbed with each step he took, serving as a painful reminder of his failures. His last words to Laila scrolled through his mind. *She's not my wife.* And she wasn't. But he'd known those words would land like daggers to her heart.

What if he never got a second chance with her? What had they done to the woman he loved?

"Stop right there." A woman's voice echoed off the headstones in the cemetery, shattering the silence.

Margot.

She moved from behind a tree, a Cheshire cat-like grin spread wide across her face.

"Where is she?" he yelled. "What did you do with Laila?"

The gun slid up his back and pressed into the base of his neck. The cold metal sent a shiver down his spine.

"Look around you, Preston." Margot walked closer to him. "You're not the one calling the shots here."

"Why? Why would you kill my dad and Ethan?"

"I did it for Seth. The son your father refused to acknowledge."

"Coward." He spat the word with all the venom stored up inside him. "You hid behind some hired guns and let them do your dirty work. And for what? So your son could be crowned king for a day? You know that if I'd known I had a brother, I would have gladly turned Whittaker Enterprises over to him. He's a Whittaker, after all, and deserves to have every penny my father ever made. Now he'll wind up without a father or a mother once I'm through with you."

She circled him. "You delusional, spoiled rich kid. You're not one to share the limelight. No. Seth deserves all of it. The estate, the company, the money. Everything your family took from him. He gets it all."

"Which he can enjoy while watching his mother sit on death row for her crimes."

The slap came hard and fast. Preston's cheek stung from the impact. "I might be a criminal, but Seth is innocent. Without you or me in the picture, he'll still be an heir." She shrugged and paced.

Was she starting to crack?

"Where is she?" he whispered.

"Your fake wife? The bodyguard? I'll admit, I know every-thing that's happening with your family, and yet I never saw that one coming." Margot cackled.

He watched her become unglued right in front of him. How had she hidden this craziness from everyone for so long?

Margot stopped moving and spun to face him. She held up a cell phone.

What had this maniac done with Laila?

"Here's the deal, Whitt. Your 'wife' is buried." She waved her hands in a sweeping motion around her. "She's in one of these burial plots. In this hundred-acre cemetery. She has about thirty minutes of oxygen left before she suffocates underground, and no one will ever find her." The pacing picked back up. "But I'll make a deal. Or more like a trade. Your life for hers."

The hired gun nudged Preston forward. He stumbled out of surprise and almost fell into the open grave in front of him. And then the realization hit him like a freight train.

His own grave.

"We are going to bury you, Preston. In exchange, I'll text the location of Laila to that chauffeur—I know he's really a cop or something. But I'll send the text, and he can rush to find her. But they'll never find you."

"Get in the hole," the gruff voice rumbled from behind him.

"Your choice, Preston."

"Why don't you just shoot me?" Preston asked, stalling for time. Maybe if he kept Margot talking, Charlie might be able to trace the message and find him.

"Yeah, why don't we shoot him and be done with him?" Lucas grunted. "Who cares if he's dead once he's in the ground?"

Margot growled. "You're on my payroll, you'll do as I say. I want him to suffer. A bullet in the head isn't good enough for Preston Whittaker. I want him to have time to think about everything I've taken from him before I steal his last breath." She turned and stared at Preston. "Because everything you have belongs to my son. All of those opportunities you wasted should have been given to Seth. Now my son can take his rightful place as CEO of Whittaker Enterprises. And you'll die with nothing."

This woman was mad. How had he not seen this evil side to

her? Instinct told him to stall. He sent up a silent prayer that somehow Seth had managed to get help. "How do I know you'll send the location?"

She typed on her phone and flipped it so he could see. It looked like a string of numbers. GPS coordinates? "Unlike the Whittakers, I honor my word. Here's the text. Get in the coffin and I'll press send. Then you can suffer, just like your father and brother did."

He took a breath and schooled his voice, willing himself not to do something stupid. "You set the whole thing up. You got Dad and Bob to charter the boat, then poisoned Bob so he couldn't go. You knew Dad would take Ethan."

"I was the one who suggested he take Ethan." Her nonchalant attitude made Preston's stomach churn.

He lunged at her, not caring that a man had a gun to his head. A meaty arm yanked him around the throat before he could grab the phone out of Margot's hand. He hit the ground, gasping for air. The man's boot connected with his side and sent him sprawling closer to the edge of the hole.

"One last chance, Preston. It's either you or Laila. If you want to save her, get into the grave."

Even if Seth got the phone to Steven, how long would it take to track the message and find him? Was there even enough information on his phone to find his location?

He loved Laila. If Margot would be true to her word and send the text to Charlie, maybe the police could find them both. If not, at least Laila would be rescued.

Deep down in his heart, he knew he'd trade his life for hers. If his life ended for her to be safe, he'd do it.

He scrambled to the edge of the hole and swung his legs down over the side. Standing in the coffin that had been lowered into the ground a few feet, he looked up at Margot.

"I want to see you send the text."

Margot stared down at him, a sneer plastered across her face. "You're not in a position to give orders anymore."

"I know you're going to take off with your hitman boyfriend and never be seen again. At least let Laila live."

"Oh, don't you worry. I plan to stick around long enough to see my son take his rightful place at Whittaker Enterprises."

"Not if I have something to do with it," a voice said from the darkness.

20

Preston's heart stopped. Seth stepped out from behind a tree. Did this mean help was coming?

Margot's face turned beet red in the light of Lucas Porter's flashlight. "Seth! Everything I've done is for you. You deserve the house and money. You've always been so responsible. The Whittakers are bad people. You're better than them, and we're going to take everything they have."

Preston heard Seth suck in a breath. His brother stepped out of the shadows and lowered himself into the grave, directly in front of Preston. "What happened to you, Mom?" Seth looked up from the grave to meet his mother's eyes. "You killed my father and Ethan, my brother. You need to get help. I'm not going to let you kill Preston."

Margot's hitman ordered Seth to turn over his cell phone.

Seth tossed it toward the man, and Preston lost all hope of a rescue when Lucas smashed it under his thick boot. "Let's kill them both and be done with it," the man grumbled as he trained his gun on Seth.

"No!" Margot screamed at Lucas. "Just let me talk to Seth, and he'll see this is all for his benefit."

Lucas glared at Margot. "We need to get out of here. The police are on to us."

Preston whispered to Seth, "I hope you brought backup."

Seth gave an imperceptible nod. "I left a note for Steven and then followed you. But I called 9-1-1 just before I got out of the car."

If the police arrived, this whole thing would be over, and he could rescue Laila. They just had to stall a bit more.

"You two, no talking." Lucas leveled his gun at Seth's head. "He knows too much. They both have to die."

"No! Not my son," Margot yelled and threw herself at Lucas. He shoved Margot to the ground and pointed his gun at her.

Seth jumped out of the grave and raced toward his mother. "No, don't shoot her!"

Lucas pivoted and pointed the gun at Seth, and Seth froze.

"Police! Get down on the ground."

Lucas lowered his weapon. The darkness lit up with floodlights and police flashers from the patrol cars that swooped in. SWAT officers rushed in, guns blazing.

The police had Lucas Porter facedown in the dirt and in cuffs before Preston could blink at the quick-lighting change. Steven and Charlie came out from behind the trees.

Preston exhaled. "Nice timing."

"Oh, don't thank me," Steven said. "We saw Seth take off. I had a feeling he'd lead us to his mother somehow, so we followed." Steven offered a hand to Preston and helped him out of the grave.

The second Preston's feet were on solid ground, he made a

beeline for Margot. "Her phone!" he yelled to one of the officers. "It should have an unsent message."

The officer grabbed it and pressed Margot's finger to the home button. She glared at the man, but the screen lit. The officer passed it to Steven.

"Laila's buried somewhere in the cemetery. Margot said she'd send a message to Charlie with the coordinates."

Steven studied the phone and frowned. "It's just a bunch of numbers. Hey, can we get a map of the cemetery over here? Maybe it's a plot number."

Officers scrambled to find a groundskeeper, but Preston refused to wait any longer. "I'm going to search for a recently dug grave. If she was just buried, then the dirt should look different." What else could he do?

The cemetery sprawled in every direction. In the dark, his mission seemed impossible. He bolted down the concrete path that wove through sections of the headstones, screaming Laila's name. Steven fell in behind Preston, shining a light on the area.

"Seth stayed behind to talk to his mom," Steven said. "Maybe he can get a location out of her since her text held no clues. She was never going to send the true information."

Flashlights bounced off the grave markers. Preston raced through the graves looking for any signs of disturbed earth.

There! One area had a mound of fresh dirt packed on top of a grave. "Over here. There's fresh dirt on this grave," Preston called out. Steven lit the area with his flashlight, and Preston's legs wobbled. He hit the ground and started to dig with his hands. This had to be the right place. An officer arrived with shovels, and both Steven and Preston started digging.

"Laila!" Preston called but heard nothing. *Please, God, let her be alive.*

Preston dug with every ounce of strength he had, flinging dirt all around him. What if they found Laila but she'd already run out of air? He shivered. Were they just digging up a body at this point?

He pushed all negative thoughts aside. She had to be alive. This was a rescue mission. They were going to find her.

And then he heard it. Faint rhythmic tapping came from somewhere in the dirt.

"Quiet, everyone. Do you hear something?"

Tap-tap-tap. Steady beats. Short, then spaced out.

"It's Morse code," Steven said. "It's an SOS. We've found her and she's alive."

Laila's head pounded. She'd been breathing in and out the same air in the two-by-seven box for close to thirty minutes. The faint glow from her watch illuminated her grave enough for her to watch each second of her life tick by.

She forced herself to keep hammering out her SOS message. The delusions had set in a while ago, but she could have sworn that someone had called her name. Was it possible Preston had found her? Her concern grew for him when she thought of Margot on the loose. Was he at the cemetery?

Wait. Was she hearing things again or were those voices?

Her SOS turned from a tap to a bang. She tried to scream for help, but it came out a croak. And then she heard it. The distinct sound of earth shifting above her.

"Laila!"

"I'm here!" She wasn't sure if anyone could hear her, but she heard them. Digging and talking. Music to her ears.

A tear ran down her cheek.

Thunk. The blade of a shovel hit the wood of the coffin.

"Don't worry, Laila. We'll get you out." Tears fell at the sound of Preston's voice.

The lid cracked a bit as someone stuck a crowbar under it. Light streamed in. With a loud crack, the wood splintered, the lock shattered, and hands lifted Laila out. Strong arms enveloped her and pulled her up into the crisp night air.

Air! She sucked in a deep breath and squinted in the light. Her first sight once her eyes adjusted was Preston's dirt-stained face. She wrapped her arms around his neck.

Preston carried her to a patch of grass, and they both collapsed. But Preston never released his hold on her. Someone handed her a bottle of water, and she gulped it down. An officer cut the tape from her feet.

"It's all over," Preston muttered against her ear so he could be heard over the ruckus around them. "They caught Margot. I'm never letting you out of my sight again."

She sank against his chest, feeling the steady rhythm of his heartbeat against her cheek. "You...you came," she said between labored breaths.

He caught her face in his hands. "I'll always come for you. I love you, Laila."

She swiped at a tear, but it mixed with the dirt on her hand and formed mud. Preston brushed back a wisp of hair stuck to her forehead.

"Preston, I...I trust you. And I love you. I'm sorry I doubted you—"

His finger pressed against her lips, silencing the regret and hurt from the past. "No explanation needed. It's time we both leave the past behind. We have the rest of our lives to get it right."

His lips covered hers before she could say anything else. A kiss that conveyed a promise. He'd always come for her. He'd never walk away from her and would fight by her side.

The sound of someone's throat clearing jarred them back to the present. "If you two lovebirds are done," Charlie said with a mock-impatient tap of his foot, "the paramedics would like to check Laila out. But don't let me interrupt."

Laila bit her lip and offered Charlie a contrite look.

Media vans dotted the horizon with camera lights and tele-photo lenses jockeying for the best position. Preston nodded to Charlie. "Let's get out of here."

They scurried to the ambulance and rode back to the hospi-tal. Preston refused to let go of Laila's hand the entire ride.

They were greeted by chaos at the hospital. Reporters lined the front with lights blazing and cameras rolling.

Once they were ushered inside by the paramedics, they met a waiting room filled with Laila's friends and coworkers. She attempted to give everyone hugs but settled for a wave when the doctors whisked her back to check her out.

She sprawled out in the hospital bed, and her outstretched arms didn't hit the sides of a wooden box. Her lungs filled with fresh air, and she didn't care that it smelled like antiseptic in the hospital room. They were going to discharge her later in the morning once her oxygen levels returned to normal.

A knock at the door startled her. "Come in."

Preston, Steven, and Charlie entered. "We only have a minute. The nurse was nice enough to look the other way so we could sneak in for a moment."

She laughed. It was so good to see them.

Preston sat on the chair next to her bed and grabbed her hand. "How are you feeling?"

"Way better than an hour ago."

"I'm just glad this whole ordeal is over," Charlie said. "You gave me quite a scare. But now life can quiet down a bit."

"When has the life of a bodyguard ever been quiet?" Laila said. But a sadness washed over her. Life would return to normal, but that meant that her time with Preston would be reduced to whatever moments they could finagle in between two busy schedules. She'd take new assignments. He'd have to pencil her in on his crammed calendar.

Her newfound peace started to erode. Did they have what it took to make a relationship work?

Steven filled Laila in on a few things that had gone down when she was trapped underground. When he got to the part about how Preston had willingly crawled into a grave so Margot would give up Laila's location, her heart stopped.

Preston had put his life on the line for the chance to rescue hers. And suddenly, despite knowing him for a short amount of time, she couldn't imagine a life without Preston in it. He was the glue that helped repair the fragmented pieces of her heart. And her life seemed empty without him in it.

She didn't care about how hard it was—she'd figure out a way to make it work.

Steven cleared his throat, a signal that they needed to finish business before things took an emotional detour. "Let me just take your statements so I can get out of your way," he said with a wink.

They answered questions, and after he'd jotted down a few notes, he and Charlie issued their goodbyes. Laila checked her dirt-encrusted watch, which read 3:45 a.m.

Preston ran a hand through her hair. "I'll let you get some rest." He leaned down and kissed her forehead, but she refused to let go of his hand.

"Stay," she whispered.

"Of course."

They sat in silence for a long while. The feel of his touch chipped away at the lingering memories of the horror she'd just endured.

"I don't ever want to let you go," she whispered. "I can't believe you were willing to let Margot bury you if it meant freeing me. Why would you go to such lengths? I mean, you had no idea if I was dead or alive. Or that she'd keep her word."

He caressed her cheek. "I couldn't imagine if anything happened to you. I'd take a thousand chances if it meant you'd live."

"Wait, I'm the bodyguard here. Shouldn't I be saying those types of things?"

He laughed, and she soaked up the sound.

"How are you really holding up?" she asked.

"I can't wrap my head around any of it. Margot's path of destruction decimated so many lives. But I'm determined to move forward. I won't let the past define my future. God showed me that while I'm far from perfect, I don't have to make up for my past mistakes. He's got that debt covered."

She looked at Preston and saw that peace had begun to melt some of the grief from the past few days. While the culprit had been caught, she knew that God was healing wounds in him that ran much deeper. And God was doing the same thing for her.

Laila flashed back to her time in the coffin. "I've got to admit, God showed up for me too. I thought I was going to die in that grave. I had nothing—no way to get out, no weapons, no air. Nothing I could do would change the situation. The only one I could rely on was God. And He sent you to find me."

Preston ran a hand through her hair. "It makes me wonder if we should stop fighting this attraction and just let God work out the details. Because I can't imagine life without you by my side. I mean, who's going to keep my sister in line? I need you, Laila."

A giggle escaped her lips, but then she sobered at the thought of leaving him. "Right. I haven't thought about what I'll do when they discharge me from the hospital now that everyone knows I'm not really your wife. I guess I'll head home. No need for us to be married anymore."

Tears pricked her eyes at the thought of not seeing him every day. Would they make time for each other once he wasn't her client?

Preston sighed. "It won't be the same without you. I'll miss having you around. I guess we'll go back to normal life. Well, me with all the money and fame, and you with all of your ninja moves and a collection of Chinese throwing stars."

They both laughed. "I'm going to miss this," Laila whispered.

"It's not over, Laila. This is just the beginning." And he leaned in with a kiss that left her breathless.

21

ONE WEEK LATER

FRIDAY, 7:00 AM

The week flashed by quicker than a bolt of lightning. Between media interviews, police questionings, and emergency board meetings, Preston had barely had time to breathe.

It was early Friday morning, and he'd finally caught a break. He sat in his dad's chair. Correction, *his* chair. With a coffee in one hand and a pen in the other, he jotted notes for his upcoming press conference. Now that Bob was gone, the company needed to regroup, and there were a few announcements to make public.

The busyness helped him to not think about Laila. She'd checked out of the hospital, and he'd failed to find a moment to connect with her. Not the way he wanted to start a relationship with her.

He couldn't blame her for dropping off the map, what with the media trying to score interviews with her. But was this a sign of how things would be from now on? Empty promises that

LYNETTE EASON & KELLY UNDERWOOD

they'd spend time together until life demanded too much from both of them?

His first meeting was with his brother, Seth, who showed up right on time.

"How are you dealing with everything?" Preston asked. "I'm sure it can't be easy."

Seth fell into the chair across from Preston, the dark circles under his eyes revealing the heavy toll the last few days had taken on him. He'd lost his mother and the opportunity to have a relationship with his father, changing the trajectory of his life forever. "I just can't believe I didn't see how unstable my mom had become. I wish I'd figured it out earlier, but at least she can't hurt anyone else."

Preston looked at his brother and saw a flicker of his father's face looking back at him. How had they not seen the resemblance before? "It's over now," Preston said. "And we can help each other slog through the interview requests and the paparazzi circus."

"So, are you sticking around? Please tell me you aren't considering leaving again."

"I'm all in and not going anywhere. I opted to keep my house in Magellan Falls, for times I can't handle city life. I plan on visiting whenever I can. But as far as the furniture business, I had a couple of friends who were helping me. They agreed to take over and keep it going. My full-time focus is going to be on Whittaker Enterprises."

Seth shifted in his seat. "I hope you'll consider keeping me on, but I understand if you want me to leave after what my mom did. She's the reason your...*our* father and brother are gone."

"Nonsense. You aren't your mother, and you're not responsible for the choices she made. You belong here."

"Thanks, Preston." Seth's voice cracked, betraying the

struggle that warred within the young man at his mother's betrayal. He cleared his throat. "Please understand that I don't want anything from you, money-wise or anything else. Your friendship has always been the only thing that ever mattered to me. I want to go back to the way things were, not some trumped up expectation as to how things are supposed to be."

Preston sat back in his chair, staring at his brother. "But that's just it. Nothing will ever be normal again, for either of us. We have no choice but to move forward. I'm in over my head, but with your degree and knowledge of this company, I was hoping you'd agree to join me and fill Ethan's role. You're more than qualified, and I want us to run Whittaker Enterprises. Equally."

Seth's eyes brightened. "I—I don't know what to say. That's an amazing offer, especially in light of what my mom did. I don't feel qualified—"

"Neither do I, Seth."

Seth smiled. "Well then, how much time do I have to mull it over?"

Preston looked at his watch. "About thirty minutes." He flipped his notepad around for Seth to read through his press conference notes.

"You were so sure I'd say yes that you've already got the announcement ready for the press conference?"

"Too presumptuous?"

Seth laughed. "Well, if I'm going to be your new chief operating officer, I guess I'll have to learn to deal with your impulsive decision-making style."

The heaviness of the last few weeks had begun to fade, and Preston couldn't think of anyone he'd rather work with than Seth. "Well, let's make it official then."

If only Margot had been truthful from the beginning, his

dad and Ethan would be here, and Seth would have been a part of the family all along.

Someone knocked on the open door, giving them a welcome distraction from the onslaught of emotions. Preston looked up and smiled at Steven. "Come on in." He offered Steven a seat next to Seth.

"I wanted to stop by and update you on the latest news," Steven said. "Apparently, once Corey Porter realized his brother had been apprehended, he gave a full confession before Lucas could rat him out. Margot tried to claim it was Lucas's idea that he forced on her, but Corey has proof of the transactions. Margot paid Lucas and Corey to plant the bomb on the boat."

Preston looked at Seth, who shook his head in stunned silence. How had Margot hidden her evil ways in plain sight of everyone? On the surface, everyone had known her as a loyal and dedicated employee, but her deceit had run deep.

Steven continued. "Since Margot was your father's and Bob's trusted assistant, she had access to Bob's account and transferred money around to make it look like Bob paid the brothers. She told Bob it was a bank error that she was getting corrected, so he didn't think anything of the weird transactions. Then she poisoned Bob's lunch so he'd bail on the boat trip, then convinced your dad to take Ethan."

Preston shuddered at the evil that had attacked his family and nearly ended his life.

"After burning down Sebastian's cabin, they decided to target the reporter to spook you into running. But Margot was behind the whole thing. She let Lucas into the estate, where he tried to shoot Laila in the garden. Corey told us she poisoned Sebastian and the bottle of scotch was meant for you. She manipulated everyone and abused her access to the family. No one really suspected her because of her status in the company, and her background check was clean as a whistle."

Preston refused to let negative emotions reign. He'd always carry the hurt and betrayal, but he wouldn't let this define the rest of his life. "I'm just glad that my father's and brother's killers have been brought to justice," Preston said. "And that Sebastian and Derek will make full recoveries."

"Well, I hate to say it," Steven said with a hint of smile, "but I hope our paths don't cross anytime soon. Unless, of course, you and Laila want to have dinner with Haley and me some night?"

Preston willed his face not to flush at the mention of Laila. "I think that would be the only way I want to see you in the future, Steven. I hope to have a few days where my life isn't an endless string of crime scenes."

Steven headed back to the police station, and Preston and Seth worked on a few more notes for the press conference. They headed down to the main lobby, where the makeshift stage had been set up. After flashbacks of traveling to the last press conference, Preston made the media come to him.

Lights flashed. The room erupted in a cacophony of voices and camera snaps. Questions assaulted them from all around. Preston and Seth maneuvered their way to a microphone stand and stood together in front of the crowd.

"Thank you all for attending," Preston said, and the noise dimmed to a dull murmur. "I know there's been a lot of activity these past few weeks, and I appreciate everyone's prayers and support for my family. We especially want to give condolences to Bob Zimmerman's family.

"One important announcement I'd like to make is that Seth Harrington, my brother, has recently accepted the role of chief operating officer. He and I will be working together at Whittaker Enterprises to make the company stronger than ever."

Cheers erupted, as did the stream of never-ending questions from reporters. But the questions had a common theme.

Laila.

He couldn't dodge the topic forever, but the world wanted to know all about the mysterious wife that had turned out to be a bodyguard.

After two near-death experiences, Olivia had forced Laila to take a week off. Laila sat on her couch in yoga pants, eating ice cream straight from the carton. At 10:00 a.m.

She was glued to the TV as Preston held his first press conference. Her pulse spiked because, no matter the setting, he was way too good-looking. Thus far, she'd managed to dodge reporters and requests for interviews, but it hadn't been easy. Between the announcement of Walt Whittaker's secret love child and Preston's wife-turned-bodyguard, the world was clamoring for any inside information. So she'd hidden out at her apartment.

She whooped and cheered at the news that Seth would take on a lead role in the company, even though she was alone in her apartment. Preston needed someone by his side that he could trust, and Seth would be a great asset. He had that same natural-born-leader Whittaker gene. Both men would shake things up at Whittaker Enterprises, but their impact on the business and local communities would be limitless.

She'd been tempted to call Preston several times during the week but had chickened out. He had a lot on his plate, and she could see the stress in his eyes even through the television screen.

The reporters assaulted Preston with questions, and they all wanted details about his relationship status. Now that news had hit the streets that his marriage was a sham, women would line up again for a chance with Preston. Who was she kidding? She might as well relegate herself to the back of the pack. How had she dared dream that she could have any kind of relationship with Preston Whittaker?

Laila sat on the edge of her couch, eyes glued to the television, while waiting for him to address the questions that sealed her future with him. "It's true, Laila isn't my wife. She's a bodyguard who was hired to go undercover and protect me from a killer."

"What's your relationship status now?" a reporter asked.

"I thought I might start by asking her out on a date and seeing how far that gets me."

Laughter erupted among the reporters, and Laila let out a breath. With the fast and furious speed of their relationship, she'd hoped for some time to get to know him without the pressure to find a killer. And it looked like he was interested too. He'd actually mentioned asking her out on a date. The press ate it up, of course, but was he serious?

After the press conference ended, she spent the rest of the morning binge-watching Netflix before cleaning up her apartment. Laila didn't handle boredom well, and a week off from work was more torture than relaxation.

She looked forward to her standing Friday afternoon self-defense class. It would be good to get back into a routine until her next assignment came along. But it wouldn't be the same without Preston's guest appearance like last time.

Laila arrived at class thirty minutes early to set up, but also because she needed to get out of the house. Her thoughts were miles away from teaching self-defense. Daydreams played out various scenarios, analyzing if she and Preston had any kind of future together. How could they build a bridge to connect two very different lives? She wasn't going to trade her day job in to become some trophy wife. And she couldn't fathom the thought of not working with Olivia, Katie, Christina, Lizzie, and Juliette. They'd become her surrogate family, and after facing death twice, she'd never trade the camaraderie and friendships she'd only recently discovered. Now she'd treasure them even more.

What would her life look like with Preston in it? He'd be running a billion-dollar company, living at the Whittaker Estate, all while trying to catch his breath from being constantly hounded by the media. Would he have time for her?

It wasn't as if they could just go on a date without it being headline news. And she wasn't too keen on all the notoriety, especially in her line of work, where she tried to go unnoticed. But despite the obstacles, she longed to be with the man that had stolen her heart with his signature crooked smile and sarcastic comebacks.

She hoisted a punching bag into position. *Get it together, Laila.*

Since when did she get all moony over a man or starstruck over some celebrity? This wasn't high school, and Preston led his life in the public eye. There was just no way—

"I guess I'm the first one to class tonight," a man's voice said, snapping her back to reality. Her heart stopped at the familiar voice. She turned, and Preston stood in the doorway, a wide grin spread across his face.

She willed her feet to stay in place, because everything within her wanted to run to him, throw her arms around him, and kiss him. Instead, she just returned the smile.

"I figured you wouldn't be back after that last class."

He crossed the room and stood in front of her. "What can I say? I might have a thing for the smoking-hot brunette who knows how to choke a guy unconscious."

"Is that so? I hear she's kind of tough. Do you think you've got what it takes to keep up with her?"

He laughed. "I'm pretty sure I could spend the rest of my life trying, but she'd still run circles around me."

Several women filtered in for the class. Preston leaned in and lowered his voice. "What are you doing after class? Want to go out for pizza? I have a great place in mind. It's in New York, so we might need to take the helicopter to get there, but it's really good pizza."

Laila laughed. Warmth rose in her cheeks, and she shook her head. "You and your helicopters. But I'm in."

"Then it's a date," he said as he took his place with the rest of the class participants.

WHAT'S NEXT...

Laila, Preston, and the whole gang will return in
Christmas in the Crosshairs: An Elite Guardians Anthology
Coming December 2023

Have you read *Driving Force*, Book 1 in the Elite Guardians
Collection? Turn the page for a sneak peek...

SNEAK PEEK

DRIVING FORCE

SIBERIA, RUSSIA

DECEMBER 29, 10:29 A.M.

Today was going to be a breeze—a thirty degrees below zero in the frozen tundra of Siberia breeze.

Captain Grey Parker bounced his knee in time with the blades of the tilt-rotor aircraft as they sliced through the Arctic sky. He leaned his head back against the side of the airplane and picked at the skin near his thumbnail while he rehearsed the mission in his head.

An extraction with three hostiles and one friendly was a simple in and out job for the Special Ops Air Commando unit he led. Always the first to deploy into hostile areas, they cleared the path for other operatives by disarming explosives and neutralizing enemies. Yes, this mission was a sure thing.

So why did the hair on the back of his neck stand on end?

He sensed eyes watching him from across the aircraft. Eyes

that belonged to his friend, First Lieutenant Marshall Wallace. They stared at each other for an uncomfortable minute, each refusing to look away.

Wally broke, his perfect white teeth glinting behind a broad smile. He ran a hand over his thick beard and thrust his chin toward Grey. "Boss looks more relaxed than all of us. How's that when he's got the most dangerous job?"

The Belgian Malinois swayed his tail at the sound of his nickname. He lay on the bench beside Grey, right where he always was. Side by side, fighting together for the last four years. Boss was a sniffer dog cross trained in search and rescue. Countless times he'd saved their lives, finding an IED or tracking an enemy before he could ambush their squadron. Boss showed an eagerness to learn, so Grey started training him to detect chemical weapons a few months ago.

Grey patted the dog. "Are you kidding? He's got more bravery in one paw than all of us put together."

"That ain't sayin' much," replied Briggs, the youngest of the unit. "My niece is braver than Wally, and she's only eight!"

Wally threw an elbow to Briggs's ribs. The man dodged it and gave Wally a playful shove.

Laughter filled the aircraft, and the men took turns telling stories of past adventures. Wally brought up the time Briggs almost lost his eye when a bullet ricocheted off a rock near his head. With laughter ringing around them, Wally pointed a jesting finger at the baby-faced soldier.

Briggs snorted. "Hey, that eye patch was a chick magnet."

The tension was still there, all their nerves stretched tight, but the joking helped them deal with it.

The pilot radioed Grey to prepare for landing. "Time to rock n' roll," Grey said.

The tilt-rotor aircraft made a vertical landing in the Purinsky Nature Reserve, 150 miles north of Norilsk, Russia, on the edge of the Arctic Circle. They suited up in snow camouflage to combat the thirty-below temperatures.

Their orders were to recover Dr. Anton Kalashnik, a Russian American biochemist forced to work in a chemistry lab in Akademgorodok before he escaped to America. Russian operatives had abducted the doctor and brought him back to Russia where they held him for ransom. Drone surveillance identified a small cabin in sparse woods giving off four human heat signatures, one of which was believed to belong to the kidnapped scientist.

Grey buckled Boss into his tactical harness and patted his haunches. "Good boy. You ready to work?"

Boss wagged his tail at the word *work*.

The pilot lowered the ramp of the aircraft and a frigid wind permeated the cabin. Grey squeezed his helmet over his head and powered on the full-color night vision goggles turning the moonless night into a computerized version of daylight. He settled his rifle across his chest and loaded Boss onto the snowmobile.

"Let's move," Grey said.

Four men followed out of the plane and into the night. The dense snowfall muffled their sounds as they traveled. Six miles from the camp, Grey stopped near a cluster of spruce trees, a location he'd handpicked from drone surveillance. The massive evergreens grew in a wide semi-circle, protecting three sides.

"Simmons and O'Donnell, wait for my call. Briggs and Wally, you're with me. We'll approach on foot and request extraction once the target is secure."

He clicked his tongue, alerting Boss to watch for hand signals, and pointed forward with two fingers. Boss went to work. He wagged his tail and pulled on his leash gently, sniffing the ground as he moved forward. Once Grey cleared an area, he moved into a safe position while Wally and Briggs alternated moving into position in line with Grey. He led the team using this bounding overwatch technique, zigzagging through the snow while Boss searched for explosives.

Boss paused about two hundred yards from the extraction point and circled back, tail stiff. He slowed his pace and backtracked, sniffing and snorting in a concentrated area. His rear dropped to the ground. Grey rewarded him with a hardy pat and a chin scratch. He tagged the area with infrared paint visible through their NVG. No telling when the bomb was buried. Maybe today, or maybe ten years ago. Either way, they wouldn't be disarming it.

A hundred meters before the extraction point, Boss perked his ears and his body stiffened. Without hesitation, Grey halted and signaled danger. He dropped flat on the ground and low-crawled beneath the branches of a snow-covered conifer tree. The sharp pine fragrance made his nose twitch, but he resisted the urge to scratch.

Grey peeked over his shoulder. Good. Wally and Briggs were down, rifles in firing position.

Boss lay flat, paws outstretched. Grey drew him close and scooped snow into a mound by his face to hide his frozen breath. Grey scoured the trees for human outlines.

A crunch at his three o'clock. He swung his rifle toward the sound and saw a slight bulge between two trees. It looked wrong. Before he could squeeze his trigger, a crack of gunfire shattered the silence. A rifle dropped to the snow and a man sank to his knees clutching his throat. Blood seeped through his fingers and ran down his neck.

Gunfire erupted and a patch of snow exploded over Grey's head. More bullets sprayed the trees where he'd taken cover. Clumps of wet snow dropped onto his back. He caught a glint of light on an embankment at his one o'clock. A slight deviation in the terrain. He aimed for the protruding lump and squeezed the trigger. A red mist sprayed the snowy ridge.

The forest went still.

He slowed his breathing and studied the trees. *Two down, one to go.*

The remaining kidnapper might be inside with Dr. Kalashnik, but if it were Grey, he would take the high ground and wait for his target to approach the building. He searched the horizon for anomalies. Nothing.

He signaled for Wally and Briggs to move. No telling where this guy was hiding. Grey slithered toward the cabin, careful to avoid brushing the low-hanging branches. Boss crawled alongside, expertly mimicking Grey's movements, alert and continuing to sniff for a mark. Grey reached the edge of the clearing in front of the building and paused.

He pressed his eye against the scope and studied the trees for a hint of a target.

Come on. Where are you hiding?

He glanced to his right. Wally had made his way to the first dead sniper and had a clear view of the cabin and forest beyond. Briggs flanked the building and covered Wally.

Find him, Wally. Pull the trigger.

His chest seized as a single gunshot echoed through the forest. Movement in the trees, followed by the sound of rustling branches. A body slumped over. The impact from Wally's bullet had almost knocked the kidnapper off the well-concealed tree stand. How'd Wally even see that guy?

Wally whistled and lifted his head from behind his rifle to salute Grey. It was good to see Wally in his element. He'd changed over the last few months, after the accident, but today he seemed on his game.

Grey gave him a thumbs up. He spoke low through his coms. "Sly one, up in the tree like that."

Briggs chuckled. "I hate to break it to you, but Wally's never going to shut up about this."

"Yeah, except he'll tell the guys how he took out all three snipers with a single bullet." Wally was the best storyteller, even if he embellished every tale. It was a coping mechanism for the necessity in taking a human life. None of them took pleasure in it, but the world was what it was. And unless things changed...

Wally turned serious. "The sound travels, you know."

"Good point," Grey said. They still had a job to do. "Let's move."

Boss pranced across the snow, sniffing the ground around the building. Briggs trailed behind, with Wally falling in beside Grey. They circled the cabin, alert to any threats.

They approached the front door and Grey radioed Simmons. "Bring the buggy. We're extracting the target."

"Affirmative. Moving in."

"Mines are marked. Keep an eye out."

"Roger."

Wally secured the door and Briggs covered the forest behind them. Grey signaled Boss to search. The dog sniffed his way up the uneven steps and around the small porch, lingering around the threshold. He whined and paced back and forth, nose to the crack in the door. Grey waited for him to sit but couldn't imagine they would set an explosive on the door. Far too risky for the scientist. A slight gust of wind could blow this rickety old cabin over. A bomb? It would obliterate the building and the asset the Russians had worked so hard to kidnap.

Boss stopped sniffing. He looked back at Grey, questioning.

"What is it, boy?"

He whimpered and flicked his tail, but Boss didn't sit. Grey asked him to search again, but the dog had the same reaction. A short whine and a flick of the tail. It wasn't making sense. Boss could detect nineteen thousand distinct scents down to the molecule thanks to the specialized training with the CIA in Chemical, Biological, Radiological, Nuclear, and high yield Explosives. If there was an explosive in this building, Boss would tell him.

Wally raised his eyebrows. "What are we waitin' for? There ain't no butler waiting to open that door for us."

Wally was right. They needed to get the job done and get home. "Briggs, guard the door. Simmons and O'Donnell are on the way." He lifted his chin to Wally, who nodded his readiness.

Grey flung the door open and jumped back. Wally rushed past with his rifle up, scanning for threats. "Clear!"

Grey entered the small cabin after Wally and stared down his rifle, examining the room. It was nothing more than a box with four walls and a roof. On a cot along the far wall, a wiry old man held shaky hands up, palms out. Wally hovered over him at the foot of the cot. The stench of sweat and urine penetrated Grey's ski mask. A kerosene lamp emitted a dim light on a table where the men had been playing cards. A small kerosene heater glowed with a dull amber flame in the opposite corner.

Grey positioned himself with his back to the wall opposite the cot. He tugged the face portion of his balaclava down and blinked as his eyes adjusted. "Dr. Anton Kalashnik?"

"Ye-yes?"

"I'm Captain Parker with the United States Air Force. We're here to rescue you. You can put your hands down."

The scientist wiped the sweat from his forehead with a trembling hand. "I am glad to see you," he said in a heavy Russian accent.

Distant buzzing from approaching snowmobiles permeated

the room and O'Donnell's voice came through Grey's coms. "Half a mile out."

"Copy that." Grey looked at Dr. Kalashnik. "Extraction team incoming. Sit tight."

Wally nodded and let his rifle rest at ease. He placed a hand on the doctor's shoulder. "The dog doesn't like you, man."

Grey glanced at Boss. The dog's fur was standing on end. Head lowered, eyes locked on Dr. Kalashnik.

"What is it, Boss?" Grey reached down and patted Boss on the side. The dog vibrated with a low growl and he bared his teeth.

Adrenaline shot through Grey's veins and every muscle in his body tensed. He looked to Wally, but he was busy sliding his gas mask over his face. His eyes darted from Wally to the doctor. The old man had his palms on the edge of the cot and was pushing himself up.

Grey took half a step forward. "Stop! Stay where you are—"

A blinding flash exploded from beneath the cot. The force slammed Grey against the flimsy cabin wall. The wood paneling splintered under the impact. A sharp pain surged through his back. His legs crumpled and he slid to the floor as a cloud of smoke filled the cabin.

His eyes watered and his lungs burned. The gas mask. He had to get his gas mask on before he breathed too much of whatever this was. Weighted hands fumbled at his side but refused to cooperate. He gave up and held his breath, forcing his eyes open to see through the smoke.

Relief washed over him. Wally was on his feet with his gas mask in place. Grey's eyes drifted shut. Voices and the sound of Boss snarling registered as distant noise. He tried to speak, but words wouldn't form. His body grew heavy, and his eyes wouldn't stay open.

A tugging at his shoulder. Snorting and wetness on his neck. Boss...

His world faded to black.

TWO YEARS LATER

COLUMBIA, SOUTH CAROLINA

THURSDAY, 3:45 P.M.

What she wouldn't give to feel the comfortable weight of her Magnum M24 long-range rifle pressed snug to her shoulder. Christina Sherman lay on the cold metal grate of the catwalk suspended in the rafters of the Federal Life basketball Arena. Tucked away like a nesting eagle, she scrutinized faces and body language discerning potential threats. No rifle this time. She was forced to patrol with a high-powered spotting scope. Too bad it was mounted on a heavy-duty tactical tripod instead of her rifle.

Her skin had flushed hot when Chief Webb denied her request to bring the M24. Didn't he know she was a former Army Special Ops sniper? Well, she wasn't about to point it out. He was in charge, and she knew how to follow orders. At least she carried her .45 caliber Smith and Wesson M&P tucked into the holster at the small of her back.

Why were so many people at a basketball game in the middle of the day on a weekday? Didn't these people have jobs or a school to attend? But then again, the weather was unseasonably cold for a February in Columbia, South Carolina. They'd probably jumped at the chance to do something inside.

The music and commotion from the spectators below floated up to the ceiling and settled around her. She'd nestled herself on the catwalk between a bank of lights overlooking the basketball court below where she could see all three thousand spectators. If anyone looked in her direction, they'd be blinded by the brightness. The blistering heat radiating from the halogen bulbs reminded her of the week she'd spent holed up in a sweltering shack in Musa Qala. Even without her rifle, this assignment was better than most of her sniper days. At least this place had air-conditioning—unlike Afghanistan.

The mic keyed up in her earpiece.

"Thirty seconds to team entry." It was the voice of Katie Matthews, a part owner of the Elite Guardians Agency, an organization that offered specialized protection to those who needed it most.

Christina had joined the Army to protect innocent civilians from evil, but after her retirement it was a struggle to find her place. She found herself in Greece attending bodyguard school where she'd met Olivia Savage, another owner of the Elite Guardians Agency. When Olivia called to offer a permanent position on the team as a bodyguard, Christina didn't have any other offers that intrigued her, so she accepted.

At least with this job, her skills in concealed surveillance and reconnaissance wouldn't go to waste. Staying back and protecting her clients from a distance was a dream job. Like tonight, from her position over the stadium, she studied every face for plausible threats. Yeah, she was in her wheelhouse, all right.

Her smartwatch said only ten minutes until their client, Governor Barry Winston, would kick off the Wounded Warrior Games Wheelchair Basketball season. During their briefing, his staff said the governor's appearance at the public event would send a powerful message to the sender of the threatening

281

letters—he would not be intimidated. In her opinion, it was an obvious political move designed to secure a nomination as a vice presidential candidate in the upcoming election.

The music picked up and Christina shifted her gaze to the wide opening where a group of men in specialized wheelchairs poured from the tunnel. The crowd erupted with cheers and applause. A man wearing a black and gold Team Army uniform sped up and down the court with an American flag. Several of the Team Air Force players wheeled along the fans in the floor seats, smacking outstretched hands. Christina noticed a few service dogs running beside their owners. One of them wore a custom Army jersey. How cute.

She pulled her eyes from the show below and began her strategic search of the audience, scanning section by section. A partial photographic memory came in handy for these assignments. Memorizing countless faces and their locations to keep track of anyone who looked suspicious. She'd already added two men to her mental spreadsheet and filed them under *Suspicious*. No need to call them in yet. That could wait until they found themselves in her *Threat* column.

The first suspect, a man in a blue hat, was sitting low at her 12 o'clock about mid-court. A long bushy beard and ball cap pulled low concealed most of his face and the Air Force T-shirt seemed a bit too tight over his bulging belly. His bulk was sandwiched between a teenage boy in need of a haircut and an excited grandmotherly woman decked out in Air Force gear. There was something odd about the man who sat ramrod straight, hands laced together in his lap, staring straight ahead. Even when Grandma sprang to her feet and cheered, Blue Hat Guy never moved.

Christina had no concerns about Grandma. The greatest danger the older woman presented was taking someone's eye out with the tiny flag she was brandishing. She was about to continue scanning the next row when Grandma pointed to the court and placed her hand on Blue Hat Guy's shoulder and looked into his eyes with something like love and pride, mixed with pity and regret. She ran her hand down his arm and squeezed his bicep. His focus never shifted.

Christina slid Blue Hat Guy into the *Safe* column.

"One minute until Winston is on the court," said Chief Webb, head of the South Carolina Law Enforcement Division.

Security for the governor fell under the jurisdiction of SLED. Chief Webb had requested additional support from the Columbia Police Department and the mayor had insisted he use the Elite Guardians as extra manpower—or, in this case, womanpower. He'd balked at the suggestion, but Katie and Christina took the assignment despite his complaints about using "so-called bodyguards" instead of trained law enforcement.

The radio in her ear keyed up, but no one spoke. Great.

She shook it off and continued inspecting the crowd. In the darkened section above the VIP box seats was the second man she'd marked *Suspicious*. The highest level of the four-tiered arena was technically closed, but SLED said veterans with PTSD might slip into the closed off areas to escape the crowd and noise.

Ah, there you are. Why are you sitting up there all alone?

A man so tall he appeared to be standing at first glance sat in the dim seating area. She pegged him to be at least six foot seven, and the way his shoulders blended into his neck said he was solid muscle. The shadows darkened his face, but she could tell his head was shaved close and he wore all black. She dialed in her scope and examined the image of a bulldog baring its teeth tattooed on his left forearm. It was a Russian mafia tattoo known to stand for hatred of government authority. This Bulldog guy could be harmless, but best to check him out.

"I've got eyes on a suspicious male sitting alone, upper level, section 223. Big and scary with a bulldog tattoo on his forearm. Need someone to check him out." The radio crackled, and Christina waited for a reply, but, again, no one responded.

Thundering applause erupted from the crowd, drawing her attention to Governor Winston's appearance at the East tunnel. Bleached teeth glimmered behind a picture-perfect smile, and not a single gray hair dared move. He walked onto the court, bestowing presidential waves upon his constituents, and maximizing the media attention.

Christina returned her attention to the suspicious man she called Bulldog and tried her radio again. "Anyone got eyes on my potential threat?"

The response came as static in her ear. Perfect. A nearby radio signal was overpowering their lower frequency channel. She might have better luck on the alternate. "Getting static up here in the rafters. Switching to secondary channel."

She identified herself on the new channel and waited for a response, but none came. Why couldn't she get an answer? She frowned. This is what they got for using SLED's radio communications instead of the military grade gear provided by the mayor. When Katie had recommended using their coms, Chief Webb dismissed the idea with a wave of his hand and said he wasn't about to change protocol after seven years of providing security detail for the governor.

Governor Winston made his way to center court, where each team of ten players and their coaches waited in formation. Team Army lined up on his right, and team Air Force on his left.

Winston stepped into the wide opening between the two teams and greeted the arena. "Good evening! We are here tonight to celebrate and support our wounded, ill, and injured military heroes." Winston paused, and the crowd filled the planned silence with cheers.

She checked the time. Everything was moving like clockwork. A six-minute speech, then the governor would call for the Air Force veteran with the dog for the presentation of an award. Winston's team orchestrated things so the veteran was in line farthest from Winston to maximize the photo ops when the man brought his dog to Winston for the award. The presentation of the award came after a short speech, then tip off.

Christina raised her scope and began her surveillance check from the beginning, sweeping across the crowd in her usual pattern, ticking off every marker by the nickname she'd given them. So far everyone was accounted for. She swept back up to Bulldog.

Wait.

Bulldog was gone.

It had been less than thirty seconds since she'd last checked on him, and now he was missing. The familiar icy touch of adrenaline crept through her veins.

She tried the radio. "My suspicious target is on the move. I've lost eyes, need backup. Possible threat."

The radio responded with the crackle of static.

Christina gripped her scope and scoured the sea of faces for the potential threat who'd vanished into thin air. The man she called Bulldog could have left his seat for the restroom or to get a snack, but a nagging suspicion deep in her gut meant he wasn't here to watch a basketball game.

This was a fine time for her radio to act up. Was this intentional interference? She prayed that her radio was transmitting even if she couldn't receive it. "Be on the lookout for a white male, approximately six-seven, dressed in all black, close-cut hair and a bulldog tattoo on his left forearm." If they heard her, they should be able to locate him. A man like that stuck out like a sore thumb.

The radio was silent. She verified her channel and the battery, but everything checked out. They needed eyes on the suspect and her coms were down. Perfect. She'd love to throw the thing against a wall and watch it burst into a thousand pieces. Of course, where she lay in the maze of rafters and suspension bridges, there wasn't a wall to absorb her frustration.

She rubbed a hand on the side of her pants. Sweat from her palm made the grip on the spotting scope feel like grasping butter. She fought the urge to swing it wildly back and forth, sweeping the crowd as fast as possible, but forced herself to follow her previous search pattern knowing it would yield better results.

"Where are you, where are you, where are you?" she whispered.

What if this Bulldog guy was a harmless veteran over-whelmed with PTSD who had decided to leave before the game started? Possible, but the idea didn't sit right. The way he dressed, his size, the prison tattoo—everything about him threw up red flags.

She clenched her teeth. There was no telling what he was up to. She had to find Bulldog. Now. Moving as fast as she dared, she skimmed the spectators one at a time looking for the big man. The crosshairs slipped past a pock-marked face and her heart stopped a beat. Was that him? She exhaled and slipped the scope a fraction of an inch at a time until it landed on its target.

Bingo.

Colossal shoulders and thick neck. It was him. Now she could see his face. A wide flat nose that looked as if it were pressed to a glass window and sunken dark eyes. The pock marks weren't the only scars covering his face. A long pink scar followed the curve of his cheekbone. And were those burn scars that accompanied it?

The man sat staring ahead while spectators took photos of Governor Winston and the players lined up. She lowered her scope and saw the same bulldog tattoo on his left forearm. His hands dug inside a black bag in his lap.

"No, no, no," she murmured. "This is all wrong."

Reporting over her coms at this point seemed futile, but she tried anyway. "Eyes on the threat in section 105, second row from the top. Possible concealed weapon."

She slipped her phone out of her pocket and risked taking her eyes off Bulldog long enough to text her team. A split second after she hit send, a message in red letters appeared under her text: *Not Delivered.*

Something was blocking the radio and cell signals, and she feared it had something to do with Bulldog. He could easily conceal a signal jammer in the bag on his lap.

Training said she should never leave her position, especially without backup. But what if she was the only person who had identified this man as a potential threat? Someone had to check him out. If she didn't act, then she risked not stopping a genuine threat. Leaving to investigate also meant losing her vantage point. He could slip away again unnoticed.

One thing she knew for certain—she couldn't lie here on the grate and do nothing. He could have a gun hidden in his bag. Or a bomb. She growled her frustration and smacked her hand on the metal floor.

A quick glance at the SLED agents closest to the target told her they weren't aware of Bulldog. Winston was still delivering his speech and he would only be in the open a few more minutes. Bulldog hadn't moved, but his hands still fumbled inside the bag in his lap.

Time to move.

She tapped out a message in Morse Code using her piece of junk radio.

On the move. Coms out. Suspect in section 105. Send backup.

She pulled herself into a low crouch to avoid being seen from below. If a spectator saw her moving around, they might blow her cover. Earlier today she'd viewed the catwalk from the seats below and had chosen her position with maximum concealment in mind. She'd mapped out every entrance and exit and knew the quickest route to take. Another benefit of her partial photographic memory.

She also knew exactly which access ladder would get her to the stairwell near section 105. Unfortunately, it was on the opposite side of the arena, which meant either taking the long way around, or risk being spotted making her way across the footbridge. The black tactical clothes would help her blend with the shadows, and she said a silent prayer that she could pass overhead without being seen.

Now or never, Christina.

CONNECT WITH SUNRISE

Thank you so much for reading *Defending Honor*. We hope you enjoyed the story. If you did, would you be willing to do us a favor and leave a review? It doesn't have to be long—just a few words to help other readers know what they're getting. (But no spoilers! We don't want to wreck the fun!) Thank you again for reading!

We'd love to hear from you—not only about this story, but about any characters or stories you'd like to read in the future. Contact us at www.sunrisepublishing.com/contact.

We also have a monthly update that contains sneak peeks, reviews, upcoming releases, and fun stuff for our reader friends. Sign up at www.sunrisepublishing.com.

ACKNOWLEDGMENTS

I'm not sure why writing the acknowledgements seems to be the hardest part of writing a novel! I'm overwhelmed and amazed for this opportunity to be part of the new Elite Guardians Collection and am blessed with a wonderful support system of family, friends, and coworkers who have never stopped believing in me.

Thanks to Lynette Eason for being a fabulous mentor and friend. Thank you for all of your encouragement. I'm honored to be part of this series.

Thanks to Susan May Warren and Lindsay Harrel for this vision to create a publishing company that takes a chance on new writers. You've poured so much knowledge and love into your authors and I'm beyond grateful for the opportunity you've given me. And thanks to Rel for keeping everything running so smoothly behind the scenes.

Thanks to my parents who have always believed in me and encouraged me to go after my dreams. Thanks to Greg and Dez for always coming to my rescue whenever I need anything. Special thanks to Dez for all her marketing skills that I've put to good use. Matt and Kristen, thanks for always cheering me on and for naming characters on occasion. Carrie—you were my first writing partner ever! You and Lisa have always been a strong source of encouragement for me (#Carrellisa). Eileen and Debbie—you have been my longtime friends and have ridden through so many ups and downs with me...and you still stick around! And Sandy, I can't thank you enough for your friendship and support (and for talking about fictional characters endlessly like they are real people).

Sami Abrams and Kate Angelo—I love our Elite Guardians team. I've enjoyed the countless hours spent writing, brainstorming, procrastinating, and researching together, not to mention the endless laughs!

Thanks to all of the Sunrise authors I've had the pleasure of getting to know. And a shoutout to Lisa Phillips for always being willing to lend advice and share your vast knowledge of everything from self-publishing to bear attacks. I still don't know how you do it all.

Finally, thanks to the God of the universe for making one girl's dreams come true. *"Never doubt God's mighty power to work in you and accomplish all this. He will achieve infinitely more than your greatest request, your most unbelievable dream, and exceed your wildest imagination!" Ephesians* 3:20 (TPT)

ABOUT THE AUTHORS

Lynette Eason is the best-selling, award-winning author of over 60 books including the Women of Justice series, the Deadly Reunions series, the Hidden Identity series, the Elite Guardians series, the Blue Justice series, and the currently releasing, Danger Never Sleeps series. She is the winner of three ACFW Carol Awards, the Selah Award, and the Inspirational Reader's Choice Award, among others. Her Elite Guardians series—featuring strong, successful female bodyguards—has captured readers' hearts and minds. Visit her at LynetteEason.com.

Kelly Underwood's favorite things are reading, writing, and drinking coffee. She was born in New Hampshire, but don't ask her about snow, because she's been a Florida girl since she was twelve. She writes book reviews for her blog bestinsuspense.com and is an active member of the Central Florida chapter of the American Christian Fiction Writers. She's a sucker for a good suspense novel, the kind you have to read cover-to-cover until the mystery is solved and the bad guys are in handcuffs. If you're looking for her, she's probably on her back patio with a Kindle in one hand and a cup of coffee in the other. Visit her at KellyUnderwoodAuthor.com.

Printed in Great Britain
by Amazon

19241204R00181